COLLUSION

EDEN WINTERS

ROCKY RIDGE BOOKS

Collusion © Eden Winters 2015

Cover art by LC Chase
Interior Layout by P.D. Singer

ISBN-13 978-1-62622-058-4

Published by:

Rocky Ridge Books
PO Box 6922
Broomfield, CO 80021
www.RockyRidgeBooks.com

Praise for the first two Bo and Lucky novels:

Diversion is one of the strongest gay romance novels I have read... It maintains a perfect balance between romantic comedy and hot sexual tension on the one hand and a solid, fascinating, complex plot about prescription drug smuggling on the other...

—Val, ARe Cafe

Forget sleep, I had to find out how this worked out. With a fast paced and tense external plot plus a relationship moving to a new level, *Collusion* kept me turning the page until I got to the end. *Diversion,* the first Bo and Lucky book, did the same thing to me, and this is a more than worthy followup.

—Cryselle, Reviews by Jessewave

So many things go on in [*Collusion*]. Some good (Bo and Lucky), some bad (Lucky in the children's cancer ward), but there's never a dull moment. Some smiley, happy ones (Lucky's confrontation with the neighbor from hell), some tear-jerking ones (the cancer ward), but you *need* to know what's going to happen. The story pulls you along to the ultimate, beautiful conclusion.

—Mrs. Condit Reviews

Diversion snuck up on me, which, given its title (and its author) is something I should have anticipated a bit more. Like Lucky, Eden Winters isn't afraid to go for the emotional jugular and she seems to nick mine pretty much every time.

—Lisa, The Novel Approach

Other titles by Eden Winters:

Diversion (Diversion #1)
Corruption (Diversion #3)
Manipulation (Diversion #4)
Redemption (Diversion #5)
Reunion (Diversion #6)
Suspicion (Diversion #7)

A Matter of When
The Angel of Thirteenth Street
Fallen Angel
Settling the Score
The Telling
The Wish
Duet
Naked Tails

Novellas and other shorts

Night Watch
The Match Before Christmas (Match #1)
Fanning the Flames (Match #2)
A Lie I Can Live With (Match #3)
Galen and the Forest Lord
Summer Boys
Tinsel and Frost
Highway Man
Almost Mine
The Pirate's Gamble

Many thanks to my own private support group: Pam, Feliz, Doug, Sarah, Chris, Z Allora, Jared, John A, and John R. I have no idea what I'd do without y'all. Thanks for helping me continue Bo and Lucky's story. Also, special thanks to Tam Ames for details about Canada, and the idea for Spirit Totems.

COLLUSION

EDEN WINTERS

AUTHOR FOREWORD

According to a November 2012 *New York Times* report, in 2011 the United States suffered the worst shortage of prescription drugs in thirty years, with 261 medications making the list. The reasons for the shortages varied from manufacturer equipment breakdowns to shortage of raw materials, causing medications normally readily available at reasonable prices to become impossible to obtain. Hardest hit were cancer drugs. For some patients, that meant delaying treatment, or using less effective therapies.

Both doctors and patients grew desperate.

CBS News reported in July of 2012 that seventy-nine US health care facilities were identified as purchasing illegal foreign imports during the crisis, drugs unapproved by the Food and Drug Administration. Some of those drugs were worthless, like a counterfeit of a brand name cancer drug found to contain no active ingredient.

Doctors and other health care professionals found themselves rationing medicines, openly discussing which patients should receive a portion of the limited supply, who could use other drugs, and who would be forced to postpone treatment. Pharmacy buyers scrambled to procure what they could. In this environment of need, opportunists abounded. Enter the gray market, not to be confused with the illegal black market.

Merriam-Webster describes a gray market as follows: *a market employing irregular but not illegal methods; especially: a market that legally circumvents authorized channels of distribution to sell goods at prices lower than those intended by the manufacturer.*

However, in the dire days of 2011, gray market buyers purchased shortage drugs for the sole purpose of reselling at a vast profit, to other wholesalers, or facilities such as hospitals and pharmacies. Their actions are not illegal as of this writing.

Through the gray market, counterfeit and misbranded drugs often enter the supply chain, prompting pharmacy buyers to shy away from a desperately needed drug for fear of harming patients.

Those who conducted business with the gray market did so at their peril. A vial of product sold by a manufacturer might cost seven dollars. After entering the gray market, the markup in some cases exceeded six hundred dollars, costing patients, insurance companies, and government programs, such as Medicaid, millions.

New legislation has been introduced, designed to stop the price gouging.

While the story you're about to read is a work of fiction, the drug shortage and gray market are not, and as of this writing, are both still going strong, though the situation has much improved.

CHAPTER ONE

"I got too fucking many names." The man once known as Lucky Lucklighter studied his employee ID badge. What the hell name did he go by this week? The laughably unsuitable "Marvin Barkenhagan" glared back at him. Who the fuck made up his name? At the sound of footsteps behind him, he brushed an imaginary bug off his badge.

"Hey, whatcha looking at there, Far-fig-Newton?" The guy the rest of the crew called Goose reached around Lucky to grab his time card from the rack and ram it into the clock. A loud *thunk* marked him as present and accounted for, right on time for the eleven to seven shift. Night shift sucked stump water.

Lucky scowled down at the joke of a name emblazoned on his badge. If he ever found the heartless son of a bitch who set him up with fake IDs he'd kick the shit out of the bastard.

"How's it going there, Barfin' Mutherfuckin?" Another coworker ambled up. A piece of tape with "Ferret" scrawled in marker hid his given name on his badge. *Goose, Ferret...Is this a distribution center or a damned zoo?*

"Hey! Go easy on Marvin, now." For one split second Lucky suddenly didn't mind Christy so much, the lone worker besides himself with an actual name and not a nickname. Besides, at five-foot-nothing, she also didn't tower over Lucky's five-foot-six-inch frame like the two six-foot-plus goons. She landed herself on Lucky's shit list with, "How the hell are you, Barks-at-the-moon?"

Okay, a beating wasn't near enough punishment. If Lucky found the person responsible for his latest stupid-assed alias, he'd stake the asshole out on an anthill...and pour on plenty of honey. Once the carnage started he'd toss in his current coworkers.

1

With one minute to spare, he jabbed his time card into the clock and tossed it back into one of the slots marked "Third Shift" by an official looking placard. A handwritten Post-it declared third "The Mushroom Shift—they keep us in the dark and feed us shit!" The writing matched Ferret's makeshift nametag.

Lucky slogged toward the warehouse to begin his eight hours of blue-collar torture, trailing behind his coworkers. As they crossed the concrete floor, Ferret nodded toward loading bay five, or in this case, unloading bay. They'd soon be schlepping pallets off the truck for dividing up, and later storing or reloading them on smaller carriers for the next leg of the trip to wherever the hell they'd end up.

"Whoo-hoo! Would you get a load of that? Wednesday night and right on time. Come to Papa, bay-bee!"

Ferret beelined for the trailer and grabbed a pair of wire cutters off the receiving desk. He made short work of snipping the thin metal seals from the door. Goose and Christy completed their pre-work equipment checks. Once done, the slip of a woman stepped back and let Goose take his seat behind the wheel of his forklift while Lucky checked out the trailer's paperwork. Seven pallets from Amerhill Pharmaceuticals. He shivered. Weeks spent working the docks of a similar place, Regency Pharma, less than a year ago, left him with absolutely too much knowledge of the inner workings of the pharmaceutical industry.

The trailer door screeched when Ferret raised it, and he stood rubbing his hands together, staring at pallets probably worth more in street value each than the late model dually truck he drove.

Although the bill of lading merely listed seven pallets with no description, and black plastic wrapped the goods to disguise distinguishing markings, according to the manifest, two weighed in at close to four hundred fifty pounds. Three weeks spent working at the distribution center, and previous time spent at a drug manufacturer, taught Lucky that four hundred fifty pounds pretty much guaranteed the good stuff. He'd also learned from his time at Regency that "the good stuff"

2

weighed a lot more than the not-so-good-stuff, and therefore nestled near the bottom of the pallet, in the perfect location to hide tampering.

Goose accepted the manifest from Lucky, who nodded and mumbled "One and seven," and loaded up the first pallet. He backed up and swung the load around, heading toward an empty storage rack. Unlike at Regency, controlled substances weren't kept in a locked cage, because the distribution center employees weren't supposed to give a rat's ass what the pallets held. They regularly received shipments of clothing, toys, appliances, pharmaceuticals, and even non-perishable grocery items. Lucky and "the animals" were betting on what this particular trailer contained, and cared very much.

Goose lowered the forks to nearly floor level and paused, pretending to study the paperwork. With the lift stalled at the right angle, the ceiling-mounted security cameras captured only a lone worker. Christy crawled out of hiding and wriggled beneath the forks. Lucky winced. No way in hell would he trust a moron like Goose not to drop the load on him. Thank God for the woman's size, or lack thereof. If not for her, for certain it'd be him scuttling around on the floor like a damned palmetto bug. And if Goose ever suspected Lucky's real identity, the company could kiss their thousand-days-no-lost-time-to-accidents-award goodbye. Someone might find Lucky's flattened remains years from now in the back of an abandoned trailer out in the yard.

Lucky and Ferret began unloading a truck in the next bay, carting out cases of cigarettes. From where he stood, Lucky spotted a red tennis shoe underneath the forklift. The third shift crew might not be smart or creative, but they made up for the lack with simple effectiveness. One by one Christy pushed brown bottles from under the pallet, dug out between the slats from the bottom boxes. Bingo! A dozen bottles wouldn't lighten the load enough to make a noticeable difference. With those pallets not scheduled for reshipment for a week, by the time the end customer got them and inventoried their order, there'd be too many fingers in the pie to easily lay blame. No one would notice until a hospital needed to ease someone's pain and opened the case to find the bottom pried open and several bottles of codeine missing.

The forklift began moving again and Christy disappeared, scrambling between conveniently placed boxes on a nearby rack to hide her bounty.

Next Goose unloaded a pallet of absolutely no interest to the crew, probably containing antacids or headache remedies, and promptly placed the inventory on a rack.

When they reached the last pallet, Goose and Christy repeated their ruse, never suspecting that, although the company cameras couldn't spot them, the one Lucky added two weeks ago, hidden in a convenient I-beam, did.

At two A.M. they gathered in the break room. Lucky opened his lunch box on yet another half-hearted attempt to feed himself. Two minutes in the microwave produced a tomato-sauce covered pulpwood disk the package called pizza. Once upon a time Lucky didn't mind cardboard pizza. Lately he'd been spoiled by freshly cooked fare. He sighed. The night before he'd started working the docks he'd feasted on roasted chicken with brown rice and grilled veggies, complete with made-from-scratch wheat rolls. He missed the cook even more than the home-cooked meals. Not that he'd ever tell the cook.

The crew fantasized how to spend their anticipated ill-gotten gains. "I got a guy lined up who'll pay us a hundred thirty a bottle, five bucks a pop more than last time," Ferret boasted. "That's almost eight hundred for each of us."

Though no fortune teller, Lucky foresaw the guy's future a bit less rosy-colored, but given his insider information that Ferret received one-fifty per bottle, he refused to waste any pity. Slimy fucker not only cheated his employer, but his accomplices as well. A man couldn't trust anybody these days.

"I got my eye on a set on rims," Goose informed the group between mouthfuls of what might have been spaghetti. Dog food smelled better than Goose's dinner.

"I can't believe you guys spend every dime we make as fast as we make it." Christy unfolded a wad of tinfoil to reveal a fried chicken breast. "I'm saving for a new car. I've had it with bumming rides every time mine decides to die on me."

Of the three, if Lucky ever were to develop a guilty conscience or sympathetic streak, it'd be for Christy, the single mom struggling to support her kids. She'd be a whole lot more successful if she'd dump the loser boyfriend who snorted her weekly paychecks up his nose.

Ferret kept quiet about his plans, munching a vending machine burrito.

Lucky ripped a piece of pizza off and tossed it into his mouth. "Don't you ever worry about what we're doing? Aren't you scared somebody's gonna notice?"

Ferret chuckled. "Ain't one damned thing they can pin on us. If they paid us decent money, we wouldn't have to help ourselves. If it makes you feel better, consider it a company retirement program, 'cause these assholes sure as hell don't have one."

"It's not like the fuckers are hurting," Christy chimed in. "You've seen the cars the bosses drive. They could afford to give us more. Besides, we're doing a public service. The good folks of Atlanta will have real nice time this weekend, thanks to us." Yeah, like the woman's jerk-off boyfriend.

Lucky'd heard enough. He poured a cup of coffee from his thermos, tossed his food in the trashcan, and sauntered out the back door to stare up at the night sky. In mid-April, the night still held a hint of the receding winter's chill. In a few short weeks temperatures would soar—summertime in Georgia. He reached up a newly healed hand to scratch an itch where doctors had recently sewn his scalp back together. How he'd love to be home in bed right now, and not alone. Soon enough, soon enough.

He exhaled slowly, breath fogging before his face as he contemplated life—quite a feat for a man declared dead four months ago. A memory danced into his consciousness—dark brown eyes, mischievous smile, tanned skin appearing even darker against white cotton sheets. He'd spent most of his life avoiding weaknesses, not getting involved 'cause the resulting heartache and betrayal wasn't worth the grief. And one man had to go and sneak in under his defenses, reawakening feelings he'd denied himself for far too long.

Where was his weakness now, and when would they meet again? After another long breath of clean air, he returned inside to finish up his shift.

The rest of the morning passed uneventfully, except for the wild pounding of his heart when the hour crept painfully close to quitting time. Quitting time meant show time. Lucky lived for show time.

The morning shift arrived, trading banter and trailing the fresh scent of clean clothes and recent showers. Quite frankly, Goose and Ferret never smelled fresh, which might be how they'd earned their names. Christy hardly fared better after crawling underneath pallets.

Lucky crossed the warehouse on his way to the time clock, passing between the storage racks and stopping by an open box. He lifted six bottles out to slide into the pockets of his cargo pants, and kept on walking. The guard checked his lunchbox on the way out of the door, patted down his jacket, but never touched his shirt or pants. Moron.

With each footstep between the guard and the door, Lucky's heart beat faster. He wiped sweaty palms on his pants. Twenty more minutes. Twenty more minutes and he'd be home free. He stepped out into a gray morning and picked his way through parked cars on the way to Ferret's truck. Gravel crunched behind him, too quickly to be the world's slowest ferret, and too heavily to be Christy. Goose, then. One down, two to go.

He took a deep breath and let it out slowly. In, out. *Breathe normally. Calm the fuck down. Focus!* Everything was falling into place. He needed to keep his shit together a while longer.

"Man, did we ever score last night!" Goose crowed. "We're gonna make a killing off this shit." Further proving his complete ignorance, he hefted one of the bottles. The man's stupidity defied belief.

"Idiot! Put that shit away! Are you out of your fucking mind?" Ferret tried to shout and whisper at the same time. Having watched too many bad spy movies, apparently, he sidled out another door and approached from a different direction, his crouch far more attention-getting than Goose's

6

indiscretion. Christy trotted along behind him, taking three steps for every one of Ferret's long-legged strides.

"Aww...c'mon, Ferret. Ain't nothin' they can do to us now."

Lucky bit down on "stupid-assed mother-fucker" before it clawed a way out of his mouth.

"Let's do this," Christy said on a yawn. "I gotta pick up the kids at Mom's in an hour."

Those kids would still be at Grandma's for a long, long time to come.

Ferret unlocked the toolbox on the back of his truck and the crew reached into their pockets, extracting their night's haul. In mid-motion, a gravelly voice from behind uttered, "Okay, boys and girls. Set 'em down nice and easy and place your hands on top of your head. You have the right to remain silent..."

CHAPTER TWO

Lucky spun on his heels and launched two bottles at the closest officer. When the cop grabbed for the bottles, Lucky dove under Ferret's truck and scrambled to the other side. A wide-eyed Christy crouched by the wheel, chanting, "Oh shit, oh shit, oh shit!" Lucky slithered past her, pausing to listen to the free-for-all in the parking lot. Goose and Ferret weren't giving up without a fight. Lucky took full advantage of the distraction.

When the scuffling escalated to blows, he shot out from under the crew cab, hauling ass toward the chain link fence at the back of the parking lot. "One's getting away!" someone shouted. He didn't look back.

Inhaling and exhaling in time with his pumping arms and legs, he silently thanked the man who'd shamed him into taking up running. He never slowed down, throwing himself at the fence and clambering over. A bone-jarring landing rattled his teeth. He sucked in a deep breath and pounded across a vacant field, a cop in hot pursuit, judging by the fence clattering.

With no clear destination, Lucky zigged and zagged, hoping to tire his opponent rather than evade. A steady diet of doughnuts would leave a man gasping, right? At least two sets of pounding feet dogged his heels. Lucky put on a burst of speed, aiming for a nearby wood.

The huffing and puffing from behind grew closer. What felt like a Mack truck in a blue uniform slammed into him, knocking him to the ground. He rolled and came up swinging. The cop who'd hit Lucky staggered to his feet while his partner played decoy.

"We can do this the easy way or the hard way," the solid mass of muscle forced out between panted breaths. "Choice is yours."

Lucky grinned, not recognizing either man, and eager to break in a pair of newbie officers. Most of the force knew Lucky—enough to avoid him, at any rate. The cop lunged and Lucky ducked, taking advantage of his small size. He wove past the other cop and took off again, aiming directly for the trees. A third cop came out of nowhere, tackling Lucky to the ground. Ow! Fuck!

He landed two good kicks and a solid punch before the three teamed up and pushed him face down in the dirt. "Police brutality!" he bawled. Muscle Boy wrestled his arms behind him and slapped on a pair of cuffs. It took all three to haul him, kicking, screaming, and spitting out grass, to his feet.

"Out of four of 'em, leave it to the runt to give us trouble." A cop sneered, wiping dirt from his face with a uniform sleeve.

Yeah, and it took three cops to bring Lucky down. "Hey! I resent that!" Lucky brought himself up to his full height—and still half a head shorter than any of the officers. "I'm a good six inches taller than the girl!"

"Yeah, yeah. Save it for the chief."

Though trussed up tighter than a Thanksgiving turkey, like hell would Lucky go quietly. He unlocked his knees and let the cop on either side hold his weight.

"We could shoot him for resisting arrest," one suggested.

"I dare you," Lucky shot back. "The video'd go viral before you got back to the precinct." Not that Lucky's boss would allow the exposure. Lucky's face, or any other agent's, wasn't to be shown on any newscast, and not simply as a public service, though Lucky wasn't likely to win any beauty contests.

He had to admit to being slightly impressed once his captors succeeded in dragging him—literally—back to the distribution center. No less than four squad cars sat in the parking lot, along with a couple of unmarked vehicles. Not bad for a two-bit operation like Ferret's, even one used for a training exercise.

He spotted a hysterical Christy making denials in the backseat of one car, pouring her heart out to a female officer and possibly counting on sympathy from another woman, while Goose sat stony-faced in another. Ferret was nowhere in sight. Yeah, figured he'd run.

Squinting toward the loading docks, Lucky spotted an open bay and a handful of workers rubber-necking the action. Fuckers. The boss ought to dock every last one of them. The facility didn't allow cell phones on the premises, or somebody would be confiscating the gizmos to prevent amateur videos appearing on the Internet. Wouldn't be the first time.

Lucky's escorts steered him past the standard issue squad cars to an unmarked Chevy Impala. One cop pushed his head down while another shoved him into the backseat so hard he tumbled over sideways. Hands trapped behind his back, he struggled to right himself, breathing in a mix of sweat, leather, and things he didn't want to dwell on. The vehicle dipped sharply to the right and the distinct aroma of Old Spice chased away the ghosts of prisoners past, along with a scent so heavenly he almost forgot his predicament—coffee, untainted by any scented frou-frou creamers. Gazing up through the crack between the front seats to the passenger side, he remained in prone position, mumbling, "Hello, Walter." A man who'd easily make three of Lucky nodded acknowledgement.

A driver got in, slammed the door, and started the car while craning his neck over his shoulder to back up. "Cuffed and beaten down. That's a good look on you."

Fuck. Of all the assholes in the SNB, why'd Walter have to pick Keith to drive?

The Starbucks cup in Walter's mitt better be a peace offering, 'cause Lucky wouldn't easily forgive his least favorite person on earth catching him like this. Oh crap! Keith specialized in surveillance. "You got video?" Lucky asked, his voice none too friendly.

Keith stopped the car long enough to flash an evil grin. "Does a wild bear shit in the woods?"

"Walter!" Lucky bellowed.

"You know it's standard procedure to record our operations, for legal reasons as well as for training purposes." Bastard Keith sounded far too smug.

Shit. "Training purposes" meant the whole damned department gathered around a big screen TV, sniping catty comments about Lucky's performance. He'd done the same for others' videos.

"Uh...mind freeing my hands?" Though hardly his first rodeo, Lucky's pulse pounded a steady beat in his ears. He sucked in a ragged breath, waiting to be released. The cuffs tightened and he strained against the cold metal holding him captive. What if he'd been arrested for real—again?

"Oh, I don't know, boss," Keith drawled to Walter. "Handcuffed and at my mercy is the right place for ole Simon."

Simon Harrison. Another tacked-on name Lucky'd like to kick the shit out of someone over. Unfortunately for him, he'd gotten stuck with "Simon," at least for the time being. His last big case ended in a bang, quite literally, Richmond Eugene Lucklighter being declared dead and Walter's methods for handing out a new lease on life giving birth to Simon Harrison at precisely the same moment. The drastic measure allowed a former felon who'd served his time to make a new life, free of a criminal record and shady, grudge-holding characters. Tossing guys into prison for a living caused hard feelings, apparently. Some people were too damned touchy about such things. Without the new identity, "Simon" might have suffered a short life span.

To anyone who valued Lucky's opinion, however, he remained "Lucky" unless the situation warranted a little discretion.

"There's a squad car directly behind us, carrying one of your very irate...friends," Walter replied. "We have to keep up appearances a few more minutes."

Lucky lay still, face pressed against the backseat and tried to figure out, exactly, what created the funky smell. Anything to keep his mind off his cuffed hands. Now if he was in bed with a certain brunet and the cuffs tethered to his headboard, he might not mind so much.

Perhaps in retaliation for Lucky having done the same to him, many times, Keith cranked up the radio, rap music firing from the car's speakers. Lucky didn't need the nose-rubbing. He didn't mind rap, but not at such high volumes, and he ab-so-fucking-lutely hated being bested at his own game.

After a near eternity of bass pounding hard enough to rock the car, they slowed and finally stopped. "Do I gotta?" Keith mock-whined.

Through the crack between the seats Lucky witnessed Walter's scowl. "Yes, Keith, and without any further comments, please."

What? Walter bitch slapping Keith down? *Hah!*

Grumbling low, Keith got out, opened the back door, and hauled Lucky upright none too gently. Lucky didn't fight him directly, being under their boss's watchful eye, but he didn't exactly help either.

The cuffs *snicked* free. Lucky jerked his arms in front of him and rubbed abused wrists. Out of Walter's line of sight, Keith mouthed, "Fucker."

Lucky replied, "Yup. Not that it'll do you any good. I have *some* standards."

"Lucky, enough," Walter quietly intoned, handing a Starbucks cup over the seat. "Get some sleep and report in this afternoon." Lucky stepped out of the car while the man he'd never admit to admiring added, "You did good."

Keith gave him the hairy eyeball from the side mirror. Lucky extended his middle finger. The car pulled away, leaving Lucky in front of his duplex, cup in hand.

"Good morning, Simon. Another wild night, I suppose," his landlady commented from the unit next door, where she sat on her porch swing stroking one of about seven cats. Two more sprawled at her feet. Lucky had nothing against pets, but with his job, anything more than a houseplant was guaranteed to die of neglect. Not that he'd actually tried with houseplants, either, unless the occasional sprouting onion or potato in the refrigerator counted.

"Ah, you know me—same ole, same ole." He checked his full mailbox before trudging up the walkway to his front door. Bill, bill, envelope from his sister... "How's things been with you?"

"The usual. Arthritis's acting up, touch of gout. I'm guessing we'll get rain today."

Lucky gazed up at the clear morning sky. "I suppose we might," he humored her. Having had enough small talk for the month, Lucky slogged through his front door and tossed his mail on the coffee table to join a few weeks' worth of flyers and credit card offers. He chugged the cup of Starbucks, hoping

Walter remembered he'd given up caffeine, and discarded the empty cup on the kitchen counter. A little on the cool side, but plenty of sugar, the way he liked his brew, when not under the watchful eye of He-who-insisted-on-stevia.

He stripped off his shirt and gritted his teeth, ripping out hairs in his haste to remove the transmitter taped to his chest. The distribution center didn't allow employees to wear jewelry on the job, or other more easily attachable microphones. Or maybe Keith only told him that for the joy of causing Lucky pain. Asshole should've removed the damned thing before dropping Lucky off. Imagining the unrestrained glee on Keith's face as he jerked the tape off to maximum effect, Lucky grimaced, deciding to keep the gadget for a few days. Let Keith sweat a while when his inventory came up wrong. Lucky clicked the device off.

A few minutes spent under the shower's spray revitalized Lucky some, and he accidentally poured an unfamiliar brand of shampoo on his hair. Oh well, it didn't make a whole lot of sense to rinse and start over.

The shampoo's fragrance invaded his senses, inviting memories of a simmering gaze peering up from beneath a tangle of water-slicked hair while a pair of welcoming lips enveloped his cock. He stroked himself in time with the image's bobbing. God, it'd been too damned long. Reaching beneath his balls, he pressed against the spot sure to bring him off quickly and increased his pace. The warm water falling on his shoulders and his lover's scent spurred him on.

In no time he cried out, spurting against the shower wall. He sagged against the tiles, letting the water rinse away both soap and the evidence of his arousal. *Damn but I want more than a memory to play with.*

Bleary-eyed and the weight of the last few hours pressing down like a giant hand, Lucky dried off and dropped the towel to the bathroom floor. He picked his way over an assortment of shoes and discarded clothes to flump down spread-eagled on the bed. A weary glance at the clock showed nine A.M.

After a while he grew restless, tossing and turning in a vain attempt to get comfortable. He didn't really need his "teddy bear" to get to sleep. No, Lucky didn't actually *need* anyone, but did tend to sleep better with a familiar body lying close by and safe, even if the man snored from time to time. Not knowing "Teddy's" exact location or assignment certainly didn't help Lucky's nervous tension, especially now without his own assignment to occupy his mind.

He recalled the envelope lying on the coffee table, addressed in his sister's handwriting. What was today anyway? The ninth? The tenth? Ah, hell. The eleventh. Entering the pleasant void where sleep and wakefulness shook hands, he muttered, "Happy fucking birthday to me."

CHAPTER THREE

Lucky turned sharply to the right, eyes glued to the rearview mirror. The truck following him turned too. Ah, cat and mouse, huh? He'd rather be the cat. Either role got his heart revving.

He sped up, counting on the driver behind him not to break the speed limit, especially not within city limits. Lucky wasn't above using others' scruples against them. Another turn and two blocks later the familiar pickup once again fell in behind him.

Gunning through a yellow light, he lost his tail, and turned right and left a few more times before driving under a building to the parking garage below. He sprinted from his classic Camaro—that others might call old—to hide in shadows. One, two, three. Yep, all surveillance cameras present and accounted for. Those might prove problematic. A quick look-see inside the elevator showed no units had been added since his last check over two weeks ago. Even in a government building, security saved the cute little "you can't see me" models for when and where needed. He pushed the button to send the elevator to the sixth floor and buy him some time, and dashed out before the doors *whooshed* closed.

The rumble of an engine reverberated against the walls of the parking lot, shutting off in a spot close by. A door opened, then slammed shut. Lucky measured the *click, click, click* of a pair of hard-soled shoes. Tennis shoes were a whole lot quieter. Some guys never learned.

He crouched. The guy strolled right past him without even a glance, and pressed the elevator button. About six foot, dark, artificially highlighted hair, trim build beneath a pressed, button-down shirt. The new arrival wouldn't stand out in a crowd. His most noticeable feature curved impressively behind him,

15

nicely filling out a pair of dress slacks. Hands folded together before him, the understated hunk didn't know what hit him when Lucky slammed against him the moment the elevator doors opened, trapping him against the back wall.

"What the hell!" the man tried to yell.

Lucky cut him off by rising up on his toes and slamming his mouth against his prey's. "Mmmmfff?" the guy exclaimed, finally getting into the spirit of things after a moment's struggle.

Tall, dark, and unwary wound his arms around Lucky, returning the kiss with vigor. "Damn it, Lucky!" he spat when he finally came up for air. "You about gave me a fucking heart attack!"

"Yeah, I missed you, too." Lucky got in another kiss and a grope to the man's muscular backside before turning to face the door. He schooled his face into his normal glower.

Bo Schollenberger, fellow agent and warmer of Lucky's bed whenever possible, lowered his voice to ask, "When did you get back?"

"Just now," Lucky replied. "You?"

"The same."

"Wanna come over later? Have supper?"

"What's wrong with my apartment?"

"My place is closer."

"No it's not."

"Okay, maybe I like having the home field advantage."

Bo snorted. "What are you planning to do, play football?"

Now there's a roleplaying idea! Lucky gave Bo his best sidewise grin. "That's one we haven't tried before. You can run and I'll tackle you. Be sure to wear a jockstrap."

Bo crossed his arms over his chest, tapping out a rhythm with the toe of his shoe. "You tackled me a few minutes ago."

"But you weren't running. Anyway, I'll pick up some portabellas and a bottle of wine, you come over, I'll fire up the grill..." Lucky's stomach rumbled. "Oh, pack an overnight bag, we've got some reacquainting to do."

"Fine, fine. Have it your way. I'll come over." They stood side by side quietly for a moment until Bo broke the silence. "Lucky?"

"Yeah?"

"Are we gonna stand around in this elevator forever, or do you intend to push the button at some point?"

Lucky jabbed the button for the fifth floor, copping a feel as the elevator rose. The door opened, Lucky mouthed, "Later," and they stepped out into the offices of the Southeastern Narcotics Bureau.

"How's it going, Schollenberger?" Keith stood at the reception desk chatting with the receptionist. He raked his eyes over Lucky's choice of attire—T-shirt, blue jeans, and tennis shoes. "Luc...I mean, Harrison. There's such a thing as an office dress code. Ever hear of it?"

Why'd he have to lay eyes on Keith first thing? Lucky's semi-erection wilted. "Yeah, but today's casual Friday."

"It's Thursday, numb nuts."

Lucky forced his most sarcastic smirk. "It's Friday somewhere." He took a step toward Keith. If he slugged the guy now his boss might pass it off as fatigue. Lucky'd only managed about four hours sleep.

Bo neatly inserted himself between Keith and Lucky. "Actually, since it's three P.M., Eastern Standard Time, he's right." To Lucky he said, "Can't you go for five minutes without picking a fight?"

"Hey! He started it!"

The boss's intervention prevented bloodshed. "Ah, Lucky, Bo! Glad you're here. Nice work, both of you." He faced Keith. "I've been looking for you. Would you mind stepping into my office?" With a final nod to Bo and Lucky, Walter strode down the hall. A woman stepped back to allow the man's bulk to sweep unimpeded down the narrow corridor. Keith trailed in his wake. Would a good ass-chewing be too much to hope for?

"C'mon," Bo said, a hand on Lucky's shoulder. "The sooner we get this over with, the sooner we can leave." He nodded to the receptionist. The woman showed all her teeth in return.

They followed in the direction Walter and Keith had taken, down a long hall to the offices and cubicles of the unsung heroes of the drug enforcement world—the SNB's Department of Diversion Prevention and Control. Two desks sat side by side in a cube—one a study in disorganization and coffee cups in various stages of emptiness—Lucky's home away from home. By contrast, the other half of the office appeared pristine: papers stacked neatly, pens organized in an ornate cup. Behind Bo's desk the Christmas cactus they'd used in place of a tree last December while on assignment trailed long tendrils down the sides of a filing cabinet. Why in the hell had Bo kept the damned thing?

Lucky eased down into his chair on the squalid side of the cubicle, a monstrosity of wood and frayed padding famed for throwing the unwary.

"I take it no one's gotten rid of the Hell Bitch yet." Bo jerked a nod toward the chair.

The torture chamber reject had mysteriously appeared in Lucky's cube years ago, probably left by some asshole. Not one to accept defeat, or remain the butt of someone else's joke, he'd learned the furniture's touchy nature and found the orneriness a good match for his own. Besides, every time he left on assignment his coworkers appropriated anything of value left unguarded. No one touched the chair from hell. However, his stapler appeared to be missing.

He leaned over as far as the Hell Bitch allowed, laying his palm out on Bo's chair the moment Bo sat. "What the fuck!" Bo jumped back up, nearly knocking over the orderly stacks on his desk.

"Gotcha!" Glimpsing movement from down the hallway, Lucky busied himself arranging paperclips, wearing a mask of faux innocence. Oh, but he planned to do a lot more than merely grab a feel—later.

"Now see here!" Bo shouted, pausing mid-rant when Walter rounded the corner.

"Hi, Walter!" Lucky grinned. "What can I do for you?" From the corner of his eye he noticed the flush creeping up from the collar of Bo's shirt. Damn, the man looked sexy all flustered like that.

"I realize you've just returned, but I'll need your reports filed by this evening, and I want you both in my office first thing tomorrow."

"Sure thing, boss. Will do," Lucky replied for himself and the apparently speechless Bo. Walter wandered away. Once he left earshot, Lucky sighed. "Damn. I'd hoped for a few days of downtime."

"What's going on?" Bo, with the department less than a year, hadn't been around long enough to recognize Walter-speak for "don't unpack."

"I reckon he's sending us out again." All during his last assignment Lucky had looked forward to a few early morning blow jobs. Walter's cryptic instructions didn't bode well for waking up with lips wrapped around his cock. If he kept jerking off he'd be at the doctor's sooner or later for strained ligaments. Hmmm... Did self-induced wrist sprains count as work-related injuries?

"Damn. I'd kinda hoped for a few free weekends."

"Oh?" Lucky raised a brow. His plans for the foreseeable future included him, Bo, and a bed. "Anything particular in mind?"

"Yeah. The office picnic is this weekend at the park. And I'd like to do a little hiking up near Rabun Gap while the mountain laurels are blooming."

Unease slithered through Lucky's gut. Picnic? Hiking? Bo hadn't mentioned either before. "And exactly when did you intend to tell me you planned to blow me off to go traipsing around in the great outdoors?"

"Blow you... Oh." It started slowly, a twitch at the corner of Bo's mouth. One corner lifted, then the other, a dimple appearing in one cheek. He kept his voice to scarcely above a whisper. "When I made plans, I assumed you'd come with me. You will come with me, won't you? We don't have to hang out all the time at the picnic. No one will think anything of it, if that's what you're worried about."

Lucky didn't reply, merely swiveled his chair around, folding his arms across his chest.

"You do like hiking, don't you?" Bo asked. Fine time to ask now, after he'd already made plans. "North Georgia's great this time of year. We can leave next Friday afternoon if we're both still in town, find us a nice little cabin somewhere, then wake up early and take a day trip up Rabun Bald."

Wake up early? Not Lucky's thing. Bleachers, beer, and a dirt track were the limits of his outdoorsmanship these past few years. Although he did have a pair of hiking boots—somewhere.

Bo sweetened the offer. "There's a great home cooking restaurant nearby. And it's far enough away that nobody'll know us."

Damn, Bo had to bring reality crashing back down, didn't he? The overwrought puppy dog eyes tugged at heartstrings Lucky'd forgotten he had. And the prospect of watching Bo's ass flex beneath a pair of canvas shorts added a whole new level of adventure. "I don't suppose a little fresh air will hurt me." Besides, maybe they'd find a secluded spot for some off-trail action. Lucky wouldn't mind hiking so much if Bo offered enough incentive.

Bo grinned. "I'll make sure you don't regret it, old man."

Old man? Had Bo gotten wind of something? Lucky wasn't one to make a fuss about birthdays, except for his sister's and nephews', and he didn't plan on starting now. "I'm not that old."

Bo glanced down the empty hallway before lowering himself down eye-to-eye with Lucky. "Prove it. Two weeks this summer. You and me. Backpacking the Appalachian Trail."

Lucky fired up his computer. Fourteen days of wilderness? No TV? No Starbucks? No home cooked meals? But if he didn't go, would Bo find someone else to take? *"You have to compromise,"* Lucky imagined his sister saying. *"Sometimes you have to do things you don't want to do for the good of the relationship."*

Relationship? Were he and Bo in a relationship? Sure, they got together whenever time permitted, cooked together, slept together, fucked each other's brains out. But a *relationship?* Gnawing took root in the pit of Lucky's stomach. "Let me think about it."

Bo settled at his desk, and for a time, the steady *click, click, click* of both men typing filled the conversational void, the clicking from Bo's side faster and with less pauses to jab the backspace key. Lucky finished first, noting the time displayed at the corner of his computer screen the moment he e-mailed his report. Five o'clock on the dot. "You 'bout ready?"

Down the hall an office door banged shut. Probably Walter's. "Mount Walter" didn't know his own strength.

Eyes glued to his computer, Bo replied, "I've still got a bit more to enter."

"You sure? I don't mind waiting a while." Actually, Lucky wasn't about to risk something coming up and stealing Bo away for the night. He had plans. Big plans.

"Yeah." Bo tore his eyes away from his computer screen, managing a smile that didn't quite match the weariness in his eyes. "If you don't mind, go on by the grocery store and pick up whatever you want for dinner. I'll be along after I'm finished here."

If he had his way, Lucky would rather shop with Bo, even if they drove out of their way to ensure they didn't bump into anyone from work. Although Lucky had worked off the prison sentence he'd earned for trafficking narcotics and regained his freedom, he'd never discussed the terms of Bo's probation. A pharmacist caught with his hand in the proverbial cookie jar, now Bo's career rested in Walter's hands, the same as Lucky's had. Walter undoubtedly knew that the two agents he'd assigned to play house for a former stakeout continued to "fraternize" long after they'd wrapped up the case—Walter knew everything. Would he make it an issue? Lucky didn't dare find out.

Once when he was a kid, he'd broken his mother's cake plate and run, leaving the pieces lying on the counter. She left them there. He knew he'd broken the plate, and she knew the plate was broken. For a week guilt ate him every time he entered the kitchen, and he tiptoed around his mother, waiting for her judgment. One morning the pieces were gone.

"Seeing you on your best behavior, wondering when you'd be punished was punishment enough," she'd told him.

Walter had to have known Lucky's mom. They employed the same techniques.

"I'll leave you to it, then," he said to Bo.

Alone he wheeled a cart up and down the grocery store's aisles, paying closer attention to his purchases than usual, even resorting to reading ingredient labels. He normally avoided too much information about whatever poisons he shoved into his body. Bo, a long-time vegetarian, lectured with the best of them about the evils of bacon, caffeine, sugar, and any other tasty morsels lurking in Lucky's kitchen cabinets. With Bo performing regular inspections, Lucky finally gave up trying to find hiding spots and learned to eat better, for the most part. He carefully guarded his stash of Oreos hidden in the top of the hall closet— reserved for junk food emergencies.

Trading pork chops for baked chicken and French fries for baby field green salads resulted in ten pounds disappearing from Lucky's midsection. Five mile runs replaced afternoons spent lounging on the couch, egged on by the enticing challenge, "Catch me and you can have me." Lack of caffeine meant Lucky spent far fewer nights staring at the ceiling praying for a little shut eye, and more time actually sleeping. Being screwed senseless before bedtime helped, too. Still, the occasional "not good for me" reward helped make all the leafy green veggies more tolerable.

And then there were portabella mushrooms, the not-quite-vegetable. A little seasoning salt, Italian dressing, and time spent on a grill transformed the humble fungus into food fit for kings. Lucky piled the cart with three times the mushroom caps needed for a single meal. Bo wouldn't mind cooking enough for leftovers, would he? For some reason, Bo's always turned out better than Lucky's. Lucky's mouth watered at the prospect of a morning omelet with mushrooms, or of spaghetti the following night, chunks of portabellas flavoring the sauce.

Once Lucky arrived home, he hurried through a general spruce up. Did he need another shower? Nah. Getting all duded up might give Bo a swelled head—Lucky'd never hear the end of it.

He unpacked the groceries at lightning speed to make up for the time lost to grooming, glancing out the window occasionally to watch for Bo, and replenished his Oreo supply. Hiding spots sparked momentary alarm, and he dashed into the living room to retrieve his sister's letter. He ripped the envelope open and out fell a card and three photos: one of

Charlotte and the boys, and one each of Todd and Tyler, their school pictures. They'd gotten older, but Lucky couldn't tell much from a head shot. They both favored their mother, not their father. Thank heaven for small favors. He read the handwritten inscription.

Richie,
I miss you and am looking forward to the day we can be normal again (or as normal as we get) and you can come for a visit.
Happy Birthday! Lots of love and hugs,
Char, Todd, and Ty
P.S. I'm glad you didn't die, and don't even think about leaving me alone like that!

Damn how he'd love to go north and check on Charlotte and the boys, but how did someone explain that Uncle Richie was now Uncle Simon and "you can't tell Grandma he's still alive" to kids? Instead of making life easier, starting over added complications. Lucky hated complications, nearly as much as he hated not being able to visit his sister.

He stared at his nephews' pictures, the high cheekbones and pointed chins no longer hidden by layers of puppy fat. If he weren't careful, he'd wait too late, and they would be grown and gone, with lives of their own and no time for an errant uncle. He'd love for them to meet Bo.

What? Where the hell did those thoughts come from? Next thing he knew he'd be finding Bo's stuff lying around the house like the man lived here.

A vehicle turned in to the driveway, distracting Lucky, and he dashed outside to toss a match on the grill, pretend he hadn't been glancing out the window every two minutes, anticipating Bo's arrival, and stash the card in the tool shed.

"Hello, Mrs. Griggs," Bo said to the cat lady, voice carrying from the front yard.

"Hey there, handsome. Come to see your fella?"

If Lucky ever decided to disappear again, he'd have to take out his landlady. She knew too damned much.

Noises emerged from the house—the tinkle of keys on the counter, footsteps down the hall, but Lucky stayed put, waiting for Bo to come to him. The sun began to slip behind the horizon, and yet the house lights didn't come on to show anyone inside. The coals glowed, waiting for marinated mushrooms.

Lucky slammed the lid down on the grill. Surely that would get some reaction. Bo didn't poke his head out the door to shout, "What the hell are you doing out there?" No help for it. Lucky gave in and climbed the back steps. He felt his way in the dark, creeping into each room on full alert in case Bo planned a little payback for the elevator ambush. Through the kitchen. No Bo. Living room. No Bo. Spare room. No Bo. Bathroom. No Bo.

Either the man had given up and went home without Lucky noticing or he waited in Lucky's bedroom. Lucky's cock rose. Bo naked. In bed.

He eased the door open. The gentle rhythm of steady breathing came from across the room. "You better not have gone to sleep on me," Lucky warned.

"Took you long enough." Bo switched on the bedside lamp and Lucky stopped in his tracks.

Bo lay sprawled on the bedspread, wearing nothing but a pair of leather chaps and a smile.

Happy fucking birthday to me!

CHAPTER FOUR

Lucky's chest tightened. As casually as possible, he adjusted his cock while swaggering over to the bed. Black leather framed Bo's crotch, an impressive erection rising from a neatly trimmed brown thatch. When they first met, Bo'd kept his body shaved. After a few months together, and a few hints about "love your fingers running through my chest hair" he'd begun to favor a more natural look, though he'd never come over without doing some grooming first. That's simply who he was, and Lucky didn't doubt the man had driven back to his apartment to shower, like Lucky didn't fully appreciate a man's natural scent. Lucky inhaled a libido-amping mix of skin, shampoo, and the cologne he'd never noticed on anyone else.

And tonight added leather to the mix. Damn, did the man ever look good in those chaps. Lucky ran his finger across the tiny flaw that marked the garment as his gift to Bo and not the pair Bo already owned before their first stakeout. For some reason, it mattered which set he'd worn.

"Did you miss me?" Bo asked. *Come hither,* his husky tones beckoned.

Every single moment, of every single day. "Nah, not a bit," Lucky lied.

"Oh." The smile fell from Bo's face. "Well, in that case, I'll be going."

"Leave this room and die!" One moment Lucky stood by the bed, the next he lay on top of his lover, thrusting against a leather-covered thigh. He captured Bo's wrists, pinning them against the bed. Bo gasped and Lucky let go. "I'm...I'm sorry..."

Bo and restraints didn't mix. Lucky rolled to the side. "It's okay," Bo murmured. "It's okay." He reversed their positions, staring down at Lucky. His smile returned. "I don't care if you

25

missed me or not. I've missed you enough for the both of us." He proved his point by thrusting his highly obvious home-coming gift against Lucky's belly.

Lucky's clothes didn't stand a chance, and soon lay on the bedroom floor. Bo reached for the buckle of his chaps. Lucky stopped him. "Leave them on."

They rolled face to face on their sides. Bo cupped Lucky's cheek in the palm of his hand and moved closer, coaxing Lucky into a sensual tango of tongue and lips. He pulled away and flipped Lucky onto his back. Gaze never wavering, he lowered his head and flattened his tongue to blaze a trail from Lucky's navel to his shoulder. Fire burned in its wake.

Licks and tiny nips rained down on Lucky's shoulders and neck. Bo ran caressing fingers up and down his torso, tweaking a nipple, giving his erection a teasing pull.

Lucky thrust up into Bo's hand. Bo laughed and stilled. "My, someone's impatient. I reckon you must've missed me after all." A moan escaped when he shoved his length against Lucky's thigh. "Damn, but I dreamed of this."

Bo nibbled along the planes of Lucky's belly, inching downward. Kneeling back on his haunches, he ran his hand up Lucky's shaft before pausing to take the head into his mouth. When he moaned this time, Lucky moaned with him, rocking his hips and biting down on a plea of "More!" He tried his best not to use force, but damn it, Bo's lips needed to squeeze tighter, and pick up the pace. A finger prodded his opening. Lucky spread his legs wider.

Bo teased without breaching. Damn it! What was taking the man so long? His warmth suddenly disappeared. "Get your ass back over here!" Lucky snarled.

"In a minute," Bo replied. He stood beside the bed and rummaged through the nightstand. "Um...Lucky? We're running low on supplies."

Oh shit! How the hell had he forgotten to restock? "We got enough for now, right?" *I hope, I hope.*

"Yeah. Barely."

"Whew," Lucky breathed out, tension flowing out with the words. "Now get on with it."

26

Bo complied, dropping a bottle and square package on the bed. He slid over Lucky and sealed their mouths together again. The silky smoothness his skin lit a fire wherever it touched Lucky's own.

Lucky grasped Bo's ass and tugged, rearing up to rub their erections together. Ah, the lovely slide of warm flesh against warm flesh, the slightly cooler leather and downright chill of the chaps' buckle adding a sharp contrast. Hot, warm, cool and back again. Ah cold! Lucky jerked away from the iciness of lube against his hole as Bo worked his fingers through slickness to plunge at least two into Lucky's body. "Ahh..." Lucky pushed back, blood roaring a pounding staccato in his ears. He gasped and opened his legs wider still to thrust back against Bo's fingers. They withdrew. What the fuck?

Bo broke the kiss, nestling his cock between Lucky's cheeks and pantomiming penetration. "Yes!" Lucky demanded, ignoring the niggling voice warning of danger. *Now! Yes!*

Once or twice Bo prodded his opening, and he shoved back hard, common sense overcome by unbridled lust. After several moments of teasing, Bo eased to the side, patting the covers to find the condom.

Lucky writhed on the bed. "Stop taking so damned long!"

Bo grinned. "If you insist."

Lightning screamed through Lucky's nerve endings, starting at his overstretched opening and flaring outward. "Ahhh..." His erection fizzled and Lucky panted, riding out jolt after jolt of electricity until the searing ebbed, leaving behind a pleasant fullness. He cried out and locked his legs around Bo's thighs, using the leverage to take what he needed. God, he loved it rough.

Bo hissed through his teeth, "So fucking good!" He groaned and glided his cock fully inside. Slowly, slowly he withdrew, only to shove in again and again and again.

"You say that like it's a bad thing," Lucky replied, the words forced out between panted breaths. He'd have chafe marks from the leather come morning, and didn't rightly give a damn. What was pleasure without a little pain?

Rap, rap, rap, went the headboard against the wall, keeping time with their loving. Lucky breathed in short gasps, unintelligible noises escaping with each thrust. Pressure built in his groin. "I'm gonna come!" he warned.

"I'll be right there with you."

Lucky gripped Bo's head and pulled. Their teeth clacked together. Fighting a battle of tongues, cock riding a sweat slick trail between their bodies, Lucky let go, pulses firing from deep within. "Oh God, oh God!" he mumbled against Bo's mouth.

Bo snapped his hips in a frantic rhythm until he stilled, eyes closed and head thrown back. "Ahhhh..." He trembled, weight held up on his arms, before sinking down on top of Lucky. "Damn, that was good! A little too fast, but good."

Yeah, better than good. *Was I actually about to let him bareback me?* Lucky'd never gone without protection with anyone, not even Victor during the years they'd lived together. Of course, Victor had picked up extra-curricular amusements wherever available, whenever one or both of them were out of town alone.

Hmm... Although they'd never actually discussed the matter, he and Bo were exclusive, right? At least, Lucky hadn't sought anyone else for his bed since the agreement to be temporary fuck buddies during an assignment didn't end with the return to normal life. Maybe the deal worked like his lease, automatically renewed unless one party or the other renegotiated.

Something inside rebelled at the notion of anyone else in his bed. And yet...nothing stopped Bo from cruising. Did he? And even if he did, why should Lucky care? Sure, they'd escalated from fuck buddies to the next level, only, what came after fuck buddy? Boyfriends? Lucky cringed, imagining two twinks making out in the back of the parental car. No way in hell were they boyfriends.

"Stop thinking," Bo rumbled. He rolled to the side and propped on one arm to stare down at Lucky.

"What makes you think I'm thinking?"

"The scent of burning rubber and the smoke leaking from your ears?"

"Ha. Very funny."

"Actually, you started twitching, and you get this wrinkle right here..." Bo tapped a fingertip between Lucky's eyes, in the exact spot where Lucky's father had a furrow deep enough to plant potatoes.

"I do not have wrinkles."

"Yeah, you do. Right here"—Bo tapped the furrow again—"and here"—he ran his fingertip beside Lucky's mouth—"and here." A gentle touch caressed the crow's feet Lucky worked hard to convince himself weren't there.

Shit, a year older. Time to change the subject. Lucky bawled in a bad imitation of the Beatles, "Will you still do me, will you still screw me, when I'm a hundred and four?"

Bo's eyes twinkled. "Yes," he replied, dropping a kiss to Lucky's nose.

What? Mushy moment alert!

Bo changed the sentiment with, "I'll just have to make sure it's your ass and not a wrinkle."

Lucky flipped him off. "Fuck you!"

"You just did. Or is your memory's starting to fade already." Bo quirked his lips in a one-sided smirk. "They say the memory is the first thing to go." Lucky lunged, but Bo hopped off the bed, out of reach. He pulled his hands back to his shoulders and wriggled his fingers. "T-Rex!"

"My arms aren't that short!" Not really. "And I'm not that old!" Not much. Lucky stifled a yawn to prevent comments about "Grandpa" and "bedtime."

"Well, I'm ready for bed, how 'bout you?" Bo asked.

Without a word Lucky reached onto the floor and grabbed the first thing he touched to wipe them down while Bo wriggled out of his chaps.

"Night, Bo."

"Night, Lucky."

Lucky tossed and turned in a feeble play for independence before giving up and spooning against Bo's back. Taking Bo's "Ummm...." as a sign of wakefulness, he ventured, "How'd your case go?"

"Good. I got my man. You?"

"Two men, one woman." *Please don't ask for details.* Telling bleeding-heart Bo about carting a single mom off to jail might mean sleeping alone.

"You always gotta one-up me, don't you?"

"Actually, I two-upped ya."

Bo got in the last words: "This time."

CHAPTER FIVE

The absence of a warm body next to him, the coffeepot bur-
bling, a truck door slamming in the driveway. Lucky stared at
the ceiling and blew out a sigh. So much for a few quiet moments before work, or an early morning do-over of the night
before. Sitting across from Bo all day, pretending to barely
tolerate him for the sake of keeping up appearances, got old.
Sometimes Lucky wished he didn't have an asshole reputation
to maintain. But he'd cultivated his reputation for a reason: it
kept folks at bay.

Moist air curled in foggy drifts from the bathroom, laden
with the scent of shampoo and cologne. Damn. He didn't
usually sleep so soundly, but what a reunion with Bo. Still,
with morning came morning wood. What a shame to waste a
perfectly good erection.

A glance at the clock showed seven thirty. Mornings
sucked, no ifs, ands, or buts—a bit of sucking of another kind
would help. A ding from the kitchen announced the coffeepot completing its job, making morning a whole lot more
bearable even without a good morning blow job.

Lucky strolled into the kitchen, scratching his naked
belly. His favorite mug sat by the automatic drip pot, a
mound of white crystals in the bottom. Stevia. So like Bo
to subtly dictate the way Lucky took his brew, by way of
fixing his cup. At least Bo hadn't insisted on one of those
"pop a cup in, get one cup out" fancy machines like he had
at home, complete with choices like chamomile tea and hot
chocolate. The somewhat skunky aroma of fresh ground
beans scented the air, and Lucky filled the mug, breathing
in the steam. The odd glasses and silverware he'd left in
the sink the night before were now out of sight, presum-

ably in the dishwasher. He might as well hang a sign: "Bo was here."

A quick peek inside the refrigerator solved the mystery of the missing mushrooms he'd laid out for cooking. His stomach rumbled. He'd missed dinner. A dessert of hot man more than made up for the lack.

He showered, grabbing Bo's shampoo again since the bottle was closer, not because it smelled like his lover. No, only sentimental saps did shit like that. And it wasn't to win Bo's approval that he scraped the overnight growth off his face, no sirree Bob. A search of the closet and floor turned up two choices—a wrinkled pair of khakis or faded Levis. Keith's ever-present sneer came to mind. Lucky tossed the khakis back to the floor and pulled on the Levis instead. Screw 'em if they didn't like his fashion sense. Considering Bo's likely reaction nearly made him change his mind, but he'd never worn a leash in his life and didn't plan to now. Well, unless Walter held the other end, giving Lucky legal incentive to toe the line. He'd chewed the collar off last year, and it'd damn well better stay off.

Even leaving a half-hour early put him in the middle of bumper-to-bumper rush hour traffic. He beat his hand against the steering wheel, eyeing the high occupancy vehicle lane. Did he dare attempt to remain unnoticed with only one in his car? Surely the cops wouldn't buy the work emergency excuse again, and even if they did, would Walter cover for him, if asked? Lucky stayed in the right lane, with all the other single riders fighting their way into the city of Atlanta.

He detoured by Starbucks for another cup of Joe, his go-cup only lasting halfway through his commute. When he opened his mouth to order, out came, "I'll have a decaf green tea and a decaf black coffee. Nah, no sweetener. I got my own at the office." Why the hell had he ordered tea? Oh, well, no time to think about that now.

Bo's Dodge Durango sat in the parking garage by the time Lucky arrived at the high rise where he spent his days when not on assignment. No doubt they'd both be in Walter's office soon. What had boss man planned for them this time? Just his luck,

Lucky would wind up in Alabama at some godforsaken drug manufacturer, while Bo pushed pills at a pharmacy in Virginia. Between a lengthy hospital stay and an extended vacation while the world believed Lucky dead, they hadn't gotten to spend a whole lot of time together. As his sister Charlotte would say, *"The key to a good relationship is communication and quality time."* Only, Bo and Lucky weren't in a relationship, and Charlotte's love life, if possible, sucked worse than Lucky's.

No one roamed the department halls that early on a Friday. Many probably assumed "casual Friday" meant "get here whenever you please," the slackers. Strange, though. The perky blonde receptionist wasn't usually late, and where the hell was Bo? Lucky placed the tea on the opposite desk and rambled through drawers, hunting tiny green packs. Bingo! He tore two open and poured the contents into his cup, leaving Bo to fend for himself.

Now, now, that's not nice, he imagined his sis saying. He sweetened Bo's cup as well, for whatever good it'd do if the man weren't around to drink the stuff before it got cold.

An envelope lay face up on Bo's desk, addressed to William Patrick Schollenberger III. William Patrick? Bo's name was William Patrick? The third?

At a quiet "A-hem" he glanced up to find Bo leaning against the wall of their shared cubicle. A dimple appeared in one cheek when he smiled. God, how Lucky loved The Dimple. Bo's gaze dropped to the Starbucks cup. "That for me?"

Damn. Busted. For some reason, being caught sweetening Bo's tea made the act of buying it for him seem more intimate. He might get the idea that Lucky actually cared instead of simply intended to return a favor. "Umm...yeah. You made coffee for me this morning. I figured I'd do a little turnabout."

"Thanks." Bo took the cup from Lucky's hand and sipped from the foul-smelling concoction. "Walter sent me to find you. We're having a department meeting in his office."

"Oh, really?" Everybody? Not just Bo and Lucky? Walter Smith took organization to new heights. Trouble must be brewing for him to call a full department meeting without announcing days in advance and scheduling on Lucky's electronic calendar—

not that Lucky'd checked his calendar recently. "I reckon I better get moving." When Walter beckoned, Lucky followed—usually.

Bo stood his ground when Lucky approached to squeeze through the open doorway of their cube, forcing bodily contact. His smile escalated to a grin and he whispered, "*Dinner last night was awesome, Lucky. Can we do it again tonight, and maybe include actual food this time?*" He turned and drifted down the hall a few steps, tossing a coy glance over his shoulder. By the time he reached Walter's office door he'd returned to business mode.

Lucky watched Bo walk away, reliving highlights from the previous night. After a discreet package rearrangement, he took a deep draft of his coffee and made his way to his boss's office.

The moment he opened the door, all hell broke loose. "Surprise! Happy Birthday!" The blonde receptionist rushed forward, attempting to place a cardboard party hat on Lucky's head. Thank God, Keith didn't appear to be filming the fiasco.

Bo's restraining hand on her arm saved the woman from Lucky's wrath. "Not a good idea," he told her. The blonde's smile wavered a moment before she began Act II of Lucky's worst nightmare, leading roughly a dozen people in singing, "Happy Birthday, dear Simon!"

If a situation ever arose where Lucky needed to fake his death—again—he damned sure planned to choose his own alias. Billy or Bobby or something easily forgettable. He hated the fuck out of "Simon." Someone probably woke up laughing every morning at having named him that. Fucker.

Acid rose in his throat. Coworkers who hardly ever spoke to him wished him well because he'd turned another year older. Keith hovered on the sidelines, chatting with Art, one of the few other agents Lucky tolerated—barely. When the receptionist finally heeded Bo's warnings to find safety before Lucky exploded, he discovered the true reason for the gathering—cake. These folks were too easy, their goodwill bought with a bit of frosting or a box labeled "Krispy Kreme." He cut his eyes toward Bo, wondering what Mr. My-body-is-a-temple-sugar-shall-not-enter would say about Lucky diving into the garishly decorated monstrosity face first.

"A small piece won't hurt," Bo came close enough to whisper. "We can always run it off this weekend."

Much better ways existed to expend excess calories, and none of them involved leaving the house.

Bo wandered away, flitting from group to group. A smile here, a well-timed laugh there, had the mindless sheep eating from the guy's hand. As yet, the rumor mill hadn't spewed anything about the two of them, and Lucky planned to keep it that way. What was he thinking, getting involved with a coworker?

Someone handed Lucky a paper plate that might have had a piece of cake on it. He didn't check. Instead he watched Bo raising a fork to his mouth and sliding a tiny bite of the confection inside. Bo snaked his tongue out to capture a stray bit of frosting. *Oh, baby, I got a place you can lick frosting off of.*

In ones and twos the assembled began to leave. Lucky turned to join them until Walter reminded him, "I need to talk to you and Bo."

Lucky fell back and allowed his coworkers to slowly migrate out of the office, *mmmm*-ing and *hmmm*-ing on a sugar high. After the last retreated, only Bo, Lucky, and Walter remained.

"Have a seat," Walter instructed, helping himself to a huge slab of cake. He settled into his chair, as gingerly as a man of his size could. At six foot six, and approximately three hundred twenty pounds, he towered over Lucky, who often joked about Walter being square, in more ways than one. Six-six by six-six. But he'd been one hell of a field agent in his day, and wasn't too bad as a boss, though Lucky would die before admitting respect for the man out loud.

"Happy Birthday, Lucky...I mean, Simon," Walter paused between bites long enough to say.

Lucky placed his untouched piece of cake and now-empty coffee cup on the edge of Walter's desk and slumped down into one of two adjacent chairs on the other side of the desk. Bo sat beside him.

"You should try it." Walter gestured to the neglected plate with a plastic fork. "Caramel mocha. Amazing!" He moaned and inhaled another forkful.

If left up to Lucky, "Simon" wouldn't get a cake either. What the fuck was it with some people and birthdays? Who needed reminding about growing a year older? Or another snubbing by parents and brothers? Not that they could acknowledge the day now if they wanted to—they believed him dead. Only Charlotte deserved the truth, truth rewarded with a card and pictures.

"You wanted us." Lucky eyed the clock on Walter's desk. He'd better things to do with his time than watch the boss eat.

"Ah, yes. I know you keep up with the latest news, and are likely fully aware of the current drug shortage situation."

He'd seen the headlines at the FDA and Board of Pharmacy websites, more and more products joining the shorted list each week. And he'd heard enough out of Charlotte about the hospital where she worked begging, borrowing, and ready to resort to stealing to keep their pharmacy shelves stocked. A series of unlucky events crippled several large US drug manufacturers, cutting production by as much as seventy-five percent, while demand grew. The problem seemed to happen overnight. Digging out of the hole might take years. Opportunists like Goose, Ferret, and Christy added to the problem.

"Some headway's being made, ain't it?" Lucky asked.

"Yes, but a few critical cancer drugs are nearly unobtainable, which leads to your next assignment. Are you familiar with the Rosario Children's Cancer Center in Anderson, South Carolina?"

Bo swallowed a mouthful of tea and replied, "They've got ads on TV. They're pretty famous."

Walter nodded. "Yes, they're the leading pediatric cancer facility in the southeastern US, which is the primary reason they're being targeted by unscrupulous wholesalers."

Lucky lifted his coffee cup to savor the last three drops, then added his voice. "The drugs're in short supply and buzzards are circling, offering what they need at inflated prices. Am I right?"

"In a nutshell." Walter polished off the last of his cake and ran a fingertip across the plate to gather remaining frosting. Lucky would happily have gone to his grave without a visual of Walter sucking on a fleshy digit.

"But gray markets aren't illegal. Unethical, but not illegal." At one time Bo quoting textbooks pissed Lucky off. Now that conviction inspired urges to the grab the man and haul him off somewhere private. Bo leaned forward in his chair, likely ready to do battle with the bastards who'd dare make a profit from someone else's suffering.

"At the moment, you're correct." Walter gave his finger a final lick. "Recent legislation hopes to challenge the practice. Until the bill passes into law, *reselling* is legal. However deeply the moral issue may affect us as people, as agents, we're restricted to finding who sources these entities and ensuring the necessary drugs remain within the legitimate supply chain. Failing our primary goal, we determine if the products are safe for human consumption."

Lucky's résumé included working for an outfit nestled deep in the heart of the gray market, and he'd diverted his share of meds from the "legitimate supply chain." He'd also served time for that, mostly under Walter's supervision. Now he kept others from succeeding where he'd fucked up. A dirty job, but one Lucky took to like a duck to water. If you wanted to catch a thief, you had to think like one. Lucky *was* one.

"Bo, on Monday, you'll begin your training as an assistant pharmacy buyer at Rosario."

"But I don't have experience as a buyer. I only dispense meds," Bo replied.

"Right now you're in training, putting you close enough to the senior buyer to be contacted by dodgy wholesalers. I want the names of any cold-call contacts—addresses, phone numbers, licenses." Walter reared back in his chair, folding his hands over his generous belly. His crisply pressed dress shirt stretched, flashing bits of T-shirt where the front gaped open. Lucky expected one of the buttons to pop off at any second. "We're working in cooperation with the hospital administrator. However, the senior buyer isn't aware of who you are."

"Is he under suspicion?"

"At this point, anyone with any access to the supply chain of the center is under suspicion."

"But if the drugs are in short supply, shouldn't we do whatever it takes, at whatever cost, to get them?" Bo's voice rose a bit higher, well on the way to righteous indignation. The rookie still had a lot to learn.

At a nod from Walter, Lucky set the guy straight. "In the gray market, there's no telling where the drugs have been. Some states have pedigree laws to track a drug from manufacturer to end user. Ryerson's was nowhere near as bad as it gets." Bo and Lucky had first teamed up to take down an unscrupulous supplier who'd changed lot numbers and expiration dates and resold outdated, low-potency drugs as the real thing. "Certain drugs meant to save lives turn to poison if they're not handled right, get too hot or too cold, and folks like Ryerson only care about the bottom line, not quality."

Walter picked up where Lucky left off. "With high demand generics, you normally have several manufacturers to choose from. If one facility shuts down, or suffers manufacturing problems, the others pick up the production. Cancer drugs aren't produced in the same quantities as, say, over-the-counter cough syrup, and they're difficult to manufacture. Only a handful of companies in this country produce them, and many of those are branded, single-source items. Due to a variety of different causes, several manufacturers suddenly found themselves unable to keep up with orders."

Walter glanced from Bo to Lucky and back again. "Not only are we at risk of gray market sellers, doctors have become desperate, illegally importing products, some legal in other countries, but not approved for use here. And some are counterfeits. At Rosario, you'll be in a key position find out who contacts them, and what's being offered."

"What about me?" Lucky asked. He and Bo had shared a house during their last joint assignment. Sleeping in the same bed every night without navigating the awkward "want me to stay?" dance worked for Lucky. "You called me in here, so I guess I'm involved in this too."

"As before, you'll be the go between, since Bo will be high profile. You'll be his contact, though not openly, working in shipping and receiving. Keep a record of any suspicious deliveries."

Walter slid two manila envelopes across the desk, one toward Lucky, one toward Bo. "Keith provides surveillance. Whatever you need, he'll handle it."

Should Lucky mention the wire lying on his bathroom counter back home? Nah. Let the bastard sweat it out a bit longer. Lucky peeked into his envelope and pulled out a Rosario Children's Center ID, a South Carolina driver's license, and a credit card in the name of Reginald Picklesimer. What the fuck? "You're kidding me, right? Picklesimer? What'd I do to piss off whoever's in charge of IDs?"

Walter's lips turned up into a devious smile, a look more shark than saint. "You? Piss someone off? Never!" He laughed far too long and hard. "I have it on good authority that identities are carefully chosen by location, based on local family names."

"If I'm trying to keep my head down, don't you reckon 'Reginald Picklesimer' might raise suspicion?

The mirth left Walter's face. "I'd never let personal feelings endanger one of my agents." His scowl sent prickles racing down Lucky's spine. Yep. The friendly-looking hound dog still had his bite. "While John Smith would certainly be easily lost among a sea of John Smiths, a local family name brings instant acceptance. And who'd suspect Picklesimer of being a pseudonym?"

Walter did have a point, however— "And what happens when they ask me 'how's yo momma an' dem?'"

Walter graced Lucky with a smile only piranhas might find charming. "Lucky, are you backing away from a challenge?"

Lucky *hurrumphed*. "Okay, if I'm Reginald Picklesimer, who's Bo?"

Bo dumped his new identity out onto his lap. "Eric Scott," he read from a badge.

If looks could kill, Walter's last meal would have been cake.

CHAPTER SIX

Normally, between field assignments Lucky utilized the department's "Wheel of IP Addresses" program to contact Internet companies offering prescription meds without a prescription. He'd make the buy and have the goods analyzed. If they turned out to be valid, the seller faced charges for dispensing drugs unlawfully, and usually without a license. Fake drugs piled on counterfeiting charges as well. Illegal imports carried international ramifications.

Checking with government agencies for current licenses came next. Saps who'd tried to rip the public off wound up out of business—a task as soothing to Lucky's nerves as popping bubble wrap, and far less annoying for his cube mate. But for every illegal Internet pharmacy taken down, two more cropped up, a never-ending cycle. And job security.

Today, with one case following closely on the heels of another, Lucky surfed the Internet, not for Viagra ads, but for information on the life-saving drugs no one seemed able to find. Three main manufacturers, one closed due to process violations caught in a random FDA audit, another in the middle of major renovations, and the third struggling to keep up with increased demand from the other two's customers. A shipment of raw materials held in customs. A warehouse fire. Contamination found in a batch of bottles. No damned wonder the US found itself in the middle of the worst drug shortage in decades.

Lucky printed out a listing of unavailable drugs for later use. A forceful sigh called his attention to Bo, doing research at the next desk.

"Why didn't you tell me it's your birthday?"

Lucky paused reading an analyst's opinion of the drug crisis. "It isn't." Damn, the showdown he'd hoped to avoid.

"Oh? Do you expect me to believe Walter, who has access to your personnel files, got the date wrong?"

"Yup."

Bo kicked his bristling down a notch. "Then when is your birthday?"

Lucky turned his full attention to his partner and braced for a fight. "Yesterday."

"Yesterday? You mean, you let me come over and didn't bother to tell me it was your birthday?"

Why did people have to make such a big fucking deal about birthdays? "What difference does it make? You came over, right?"

"What difference does it make?" Bo repeated Lucky's words, three octaves higher. "What if I'd wanted to take you out? Buy you a gift? Get you a cake?"

Lucky snorted. "It's no big deal. It's just another day on the calendar." He strained his ears. Was Walter calling him? At the moment, he'd even accept a distraction from Keith.

"We've been dating since before Thanksgiving. Don't I deserve to know these things?" The anger fled Bo's face.

Dating? "We're not dating." Lucky'd rather deal with anger than have a kicked puppy peering up at him from beneath a fringe of soot-black lashes. Anger didn't trigger guilt. "We're...we're *seeing* each other," he amended.

Bo leaned back in his chair, arms folded across his chest.

"And do you mind keeping your voice down?" Lucky thanked the gods of ornery behavior for having a desk located outside of hearing range of the nearest other cube. His anti-social ways had earned him banishment years ago to the far side of the supply room, separated from the rest of the department by a bank of industrial-sized file cabinets. The best cube in the house. No way in hell did he want busybodies underfoot, prying into his social life.

Spying the envelope on Bo's desk, Lucky turned the tables. "How about this, Mr. William Patrick Schollenberger III? Don't you reckon you shoulda told me your name? I'm not in

41

the habit of sleeping with strangers." Lucky shut up before Bo called him on the lie. Of course, pre-Bo fucks shouldn't count.

Bo emitted a snort. "I thought you did."

Damn, Lucky should've used that answer for the birthday question.

"It's not like I've hidden anything from you," Bo argued. "If you ever spent time at my apartment, you would've noticed my mail by now, and even an embossed family Bible with my name on the cover."

Not the "apartment" thing again! Lucky opened his mouth, ready to make the usual denials. Bo cut him off. "Which brings me to my next point. You don't seem to have a problem being together as long as no one finds out and it's at your house."

"What we do outside of work is nobody's damned business but ours, and I'm comfortable at my place. Don't you like it?"

Bo produced a half snort, half sigh, the kind of noise Charlotte referred to as "long-suffering." "Your house is a pig sty, Lucky. I can barely walk from one room to the next without tripping. Me coming over requires a trip to the grocery store, 'cause you never keep food on hand. And don't flatter yourself that I haven't figured out why you bought the store out of mushrooms last night. It's so I'd cook them and you'd keep the leftovers." He dropped his voice to hiss, "Damn it, Lucky, I'm your lover, not your maid."

Visions of steamy sex, following an actual meal this time, began to fade. "Come over, tonight. We'll talk about it."

"No, if I come over, we'll fuck, we won't talk."

Sounded like a plan. "And you don't like fucking because?"

"Am I just a fuck to you? And a cook? Is that all I am?"

"No! You're an *incredible* fuck!" Lucky's intended joke missed the target.

Redness crept up from Bo's collar. He glared at Lucky, chest swelling with each breath, and in a voice so low Lucky strained to hear, muttered, "Sorry, but I have other plans tonight." He stood, snatched up his jacket, and headed down the hall.

"What the fuck got his knickers in a twist?" Lucky asked a dirty coffee cup. He'd only allowed a handful of men to stick around longer than one night, and of those, Bo alone recognized him for who he was, warts and all, and didn't try to change him—unless forcing him to take better care of himself counted. Bo gave, expecting nothing in return. In return, Lucky gave nothing.

He spied Bo's manila envelope containing a new identity, apartment keys, and other pertinent information lying on the desk, along with the letter addressed to William Patrick Schollenberger III. Well, the nice thing to do would be to remind him he'd left them, right? Wait a minute, though. Lucky didn't do nice.

Was Bo asking too much for Lucky to come over every now and then? Lucky stared at a glass watering ball protruding from the Christmas cactus's soil. Sometime during the last few months, an ornate ceramic pot had replaced the cheap plastic container that'd come from the store. No brown marred the plant's glossy tendrils, no dead blooms. A plant. A damned, fucking plant, still green when most of the cactuses it'd shared a shelf with at the nursery probably hit the trash the moment Christmas ended, or died of neglect shortly thereafter. Bo cherished everything, whether or not it cherished him in return. A plant. The man cared so much for a damned plant. How much more did he care for people?

Jade gave way to rust, the tender shoots withered to blackened husks hanging over the sides of the pot, forlorn lovers cast aside. In Lucky's imagination, the beautiful ornamental shuddered and died. If Bo ever stopped caring...

Lucky took a deep breath and let it out slowly. His choices lay before him. Go home, sulk, and hope Bo continued to water him on occasion, or make things right.

"You look like shit, boy!" Lucky growled at his reflection. He put aside a comb in favor of a brush. A few strokes didn't improve matters. "Now you look like better-groomed shit." No help for it, he needed to wash his hair. Ten minutes later, he swiped away a cloud of Bo-scented fog to try again.

"You still look like you, but cleaner." No help for it. Some people were born gorgeous, others weren't. Lucky sure as hell hadn't won the genetic lottery. Maybe Bo suffered from poor eyesight.

He squeezed an unfamiliar tube of toothpaste from the middle. Minty freshness exploded on his tongue the moment the brush hit his mouth. Not bad. Not bad at all. He rinsed and dropped his old fashioned toothbrush in a glass next to Bo's battery operated model and wiped a layer of dust off a bottle of mouthwash. No, he wasn't trying to impress Bo, not really, but it was here. He could do a taste check.

What if he'd driven the man away? Sex aside, he enjoyed the company, and quiet evenings watching TV or fixing supper. Truth be told, he wouldn't mind those evenings happening on a more regular basis, but wasn't yet ready for the whole live-together thing. Besides, if anyone at work found out...

Bo had been right in Florida when he'd mentioned the "no fraternization" department policy, and more than one office affair ended with both parties being fired. And while Walter didn't tolerate his team bad-mouthing each other, the SNB wasn't immune to gossip. Lucky didn't give a rat's ass about what folks thought of him. In fact, he didn't like them much so why should they like him? Well, except for Walter. Lucky squeezed his eyes shut. While Bo had sneaked past Lucky's defenses, Walter had merely chiseled patiently away, spending years wearing a hole in Lucky's armor.

Push come to shove, technically, Bo and "Simon" were already in a relationship the day Simon Harrison joined the department. Their preexisting relationship overrode policy, in Lucky's eyes. But how about the rest of the department's? Or Walter's? Or the big dogs Walter answered to? And would the receptionist's smile turn to a sneer if she knew Bo left work in the afternoon to head over to Lucky's and do the nasty?

He propped against the sink, opening his eyes to glare at the mirror. "You're a free man now," he said. "Walter can't say a whole lot about what you do on your own time." But Walter did have a say about Bo. Bo fell onto Walter's team the same way Lucky did—by fucking up royally in the outside world. Lucky'd never asked how long Bo had to work off, or the probation details, because he sure as hell resented talking about his. If anyone found out they'd shared more than a house together while on assignment, the shit would hit the fan—and ricochet back on Bo.

What the hell did Bo want with Lucky anyway? Regardless of a new name and expunged criminal record, deep down inside dwelt a two-bit felon, whose own family kicked him out.

"Would you stop looking a gift horse in the mouth?" he heard Charlotte say, imagining a swat upside the head for good measure.

"Yeah, yeah. I hear ya, girl."

He stopped brooding to get dressed. Which T-shirt? The blue or the green? Bo said the blue brought out Lucky's eyes. Lucky put on the green. Bo might read too much into the blue. Boxers, jeans, socks, and tennis shoes completed the outfit.

He loaded up two grocery bags with last night's leftovers and pushed aside Starbucks cups to put them on the passenger seat of his car. Damn, he'd left the envelopes at work. Oh, well, he'd have to come up with another excuse to drop by unannounced.

Despite Bo's jab, Lucky had been to Bo's apartment—twice. Once to drop Bo off after work when Bo had taken his truck to the shop, another time to help him set up a bookcase. Lucky stayed long enough to get laid both times and left. Something about sleeping in someone else's house gave him the creeps. Bad enough he spent nights alone in hotel rooms and rentals while working. To stay where a person lived, though, didn't sit well. Maybe he'd never gotten over his feeling of not quite belonging when he'd lived with his rich lover, Victor, the one who'd taught Lucky the value of a hard-stolen dollar. While he'd become spoiled by the kind of lifestyle Victor provided, a paid-for car, a low rent duplex, and being in control of his own life allowed him freedom and a sense of security. No one needed the power to yank the rug out from under Lucky's feet.

He parked his car near Bo's truck and trotted up to the door. Wouldn't Bo be surprised? The door didn't budge. Damn. He'd have to alert Bo anyway, to buzz him up. An elderly lady approached, leading a yappy little mutt on a leash. She swiped a keycard through the reader and Lucky opened the door, squeezing through behind her. The dog sniffed his leg but decided he wasn't a tree or a hydrant. Smart dog.

Lucky rode the elevator, ignoring the woman's inquisitive gaze. If she didn't ask, he wouldn't tell.

He got off on the second floor. A dozen doors lined the hall. A baby wailed from the first apartment, and a "A Packers' Fan Lives Here" sign adorned the door of another. Lucky rapped knuckles against the forth and held his breath. Not a sound came from within. His heart fell. Had the guy been serious when he'd claimed earlier plans?

Looked like Bo wasn't at home, despite his truck in the parking lot. Lucky shuffled his feet away from the door until it opened and a bleary brown eye peered through the crack. "Lucky? What're you doing here?"

Hallelujah! Lucky sagged against the doorway. "You gonna let me in?"

"Wha...? Oh, sure." Bo stepped back, opening the door wide. Though barefooted, he still wore his work clothes, slightly rumpled now, and his normally styled hair appeared sleep-tousled.

Lucky dropped the grocery bags to the floor and ran his fingers through the waves at the back of Bo's head, pulling him down for a kiss. Bo's anger seemed gone, for he returned Lucky's greeting.

"Mmm... Good to see you, too," Bo mumbled after pulling away. "But you said you weren't coming."

Lucky bit down on his tongue before "I intend to *come* all right" escaped. Canning the asshole remarks just once might keep Bo from saying anything more about being just a fuck. "I changed my mind."

He locked his mouth with Bo's once more and danced them toward the couch. Once step, two steps, three steps... What the fuck? The back of the couch shot backward and Lucky crashed to the floor, clawing at empty air. Bo landed on top of him, laughing. Lucky cracked an eye open and glared up at a brown recliner.

Where was the old tan and gold sofa with the springs sticking out? "New couch, I take it."

"Not brand new. I got it about a month ago." Bo struggled to his feet and extended a hand to help disentangle Lucky from the Hell Bitch's second cousin. "It's only two sections, and both sides recline." He demonstrated by plopping down on the monstrosity. Two pillows and a blanket lay on the floor. "It sleeps good, and will be nice and comfy for us to lay back and watch TV."

That's right, Bo hated sleeping alone and preferred couch to bed if Lucky weren't there. How many nights could he have been here, both of them sleeping better, if he weren't so dog-gone hardheaded?

Lucky eased down next to Bo, ready to jump up if the couch tried to wrestle him again. "It's real nice, Bo. Or should I say, 'William.'" Bo's smile vanished. Damn it, why did Lucky always have to put his foot in his mouth when things were otherwise going great?

"William's my dad. I'm Bo."

Bo's dad. The no account asshole who'd tied Bo to a head-board and gone out drinking, leaving his son convinced the house was burning down around him, and too traumatized to sleep in a bed alone afterward. Not to mention backhand-ing the kid every chance the bastard got. While Lucky wasn't much on meeting family, he'd sure like some time alone with Bo's dad. In his travels for Victor, he'd explored some wide-open spaces where he'd driven for miles without running across a single house. They'd never find the body.

And Richmond Lucklighter, Simon Harrison, Marvin Barkenhagan, Reginald Picklesimer—yeah Lucky could relate to hating a name. "I can't say that I blame you. I bet you didn't learn to spell your name until, what? The tenth grade?"

Lucky half-hearted attempt at a joke brought a chuckle and a hint of smile back to Bo's face. "What's in the bags?" Bo gestured to the two sacks sitting inside the door. "You bring dinner, or you moving in?"

Crap. Lucky hadn't even packed a change of clothes. Bo must think he planned to fuck and run. "I just put these on. If you suddenly decide to lock the door and not let me leave tonight, I can wear 'em again in the morning."

"Look, Lucky. About that—"

Not good. This early on a Friday night left plenty of time to get up to mischief. Maybe Bo hadn't been lying about having other plans.

"I'm sorry about what I said. You've been a private person from day one. You've got your issues, I've got mine. However..." Bo drew in a deep breath. "We've been seeing each other six months, and I don't know you any better now than I did when we shared a house in Florida for work. Don't you find that odd?"

"Four months," Lucky murmured. He perused the apartment, noticing the little touches added since his last visit. The bookcase he'd helped assemble held a variety of books and sculptures, mostly of dragons and gargoyles, perfectly aligned with talons and toes all facing forward. Bo had a fantasy fetish?

"What?"

"Four months, if you take two off for me being an asshole and playing dead. And if you subtract the time we spent apart working separately out of town, three months." Lucky scoped out the rest of the living room. Nothing out of place but a pillow, a blanket, and maybe Lucky.

"Yeah. Okay, we've seen each other for *three* months. But even at three months, haven't I earned the right to take you out for your birthday? Damn it, Lucky! Cut me some slack here."

Actually, Lucky didn't find anything odd about *not* flopping down on a couch and confessing his life history. Victor had certainly never asked a lot of questions. Of course, Victor had ways of finding out without asking. Lucky had come home one day to cake, a brand new Mustang, and plans for a weekend in Vegas, Victor's gifts to him, back before Lucky swore off birthdays. He never bothered to wonder how Victor found out the date or what he wanted. Victor paid people for information. Bo, apparently, expected to be told directly.

"It's not like I'm holding back on you or anything. I figured if you wanted to know something, you'd ask." Or do as Lucky did and Google. And if Google didn't cough up the answers, well, there were reasons Walter assigned Lucky to teach Bo to track suspects. Only, Bo's sense of honor wouldn't allow him to practice the skills without a professional reason. The "scruples" thing again.

"Back home that's called prying," Bo said.

"Not at my house. My folks called it 'forewarned is forearmed.'"

Bo tilted his head to the side, the wrinkles on his forehead relaxing. "Where's home?"

Lucky paused before answering, seeking ulterior motives for the question. *Lighten up, dude, he only wants to know where you grew up.* No harm in the truth. "Tobacco farm north of Raleigh. Mom and Dad still live there. My youngest brother's probably still there, too."

"You don't talk to them?"

"They disowned me ten years ago, after I got busted."

"Sorry."

"Don't be. They're not." Lucky swallowed past a lump in his throat. "They were told I died last December."

Bo's mouth dropped open. "You let them believe you're dead?"

"I don't see a reason to tell them any different. Do you? Besides, I made a few enemies in my day. Knowing I'm alive and where I am would put them at risk." Please let Bo buy the half-truth and turn a blind eye to the needles digging into Lucky at the mention of parents who wouldn't talk to him. One phone call, with enough time to plead his case. That's all Lucky had wanted. After the third time they'd picked up the phone and slammed it down without even saying hello, he'd learned his lesson.

Bo scooted closer. "I guess you did the right thing. But it's gotta hurt. I mean, even after the shit my father did to me, he's still my dad, ya know?"

Lucky shrugged off Bo's sympathy. He'd gotten good at pretending not to care about the loss of his family. "Life hurts. I'm used to it. I still got Charlotte and her boys."

A laugh lifted Bo's features. "Yeah. Tough lady. Looks a lot like you."

Lucky shot Bo a puzzled glance. "How do you know?"

49

Bo gave Lucky an "Oh, please!" eye roll/scowl combination. "For one thing, you keep a picture of her on your desk whenever it's visible beneath the clutter. And remember, I tried to find you once I figured out you weren't dead. She ran me off with a shotgun."

Oh yeah, Lucky'd forgotten. Sounded like Charlotte—now. Why she couldn't bring herself to stand up to her abusive ex remained a mystery. "Sorry 'bout that," Lucky said.

"Sorry your sister pulled a gun on me?"

"I'm sorry I left without telling you bye. It seemed the thing to do at the time."

"That's okay. I found out better." Bo wove their fingers together and leaned farther back on the couch. He held tightly, the grip nearly painful. "My mom always said I'd go to any length to get the last word in."

A weight gathered in Lucky's chest. How he wished he'd handled that whole situation differently instead of leaving Bo high and dry. "For what it's worth, I wrote you half a dozen e-mails. I never had the guts to send them." Lucky winced. A few beers and a computer keyboard and he'd pecked out a bit of unprecedented mushiness. Thank God, he'd trashed the drivel before he'd hit "send."

"Why not?"

"Why not? Look at me. I'm a low-life ex-con not good enough for his own kin. You're a college educated hotshot going places."

"You forget. I've staggered down dark alleys, too."

"But somehow you managed to scrape it off." And there, in a nutshell, was the single quality that drew Lucky to Bo, the flame Lucky warmed himself by. Bo didn't dwell. He got over the little shit and moved on. Maybe Bo could teach him how to pull that off.

"I choose to learn from the past and live in the now."

Lucky chuckled, releasing a pent-up breath. "Now that's exactly the kind of new age crap I expect from you."

Bo stiffened. Lucky gave him grief often enough about his free-spirited logic. "You should try it sometime."

"Nah, that's what I got you for. You wouldn't want to be

outta a job, would you? My own personal new age guru."
Lucky pursed his lips. "Muwhaa!"

"And dietician. Don't forget dietician." Bo grinned.

Lucky attempted to kiss the smart-assery out of the man.
A slow play of tongues, unhurried caresses, stoked the flames
higher than a passionate encounter with anyone else. Who
needed supper? Hell, who needed to even breathe?

Bo wasn't finished talking. "Let me ask you this... You're
not used to being part of a couple, are you?"

Part of a couple? Even during his years with Victor Lucky
hadn't considered himself part of a couple. "I told you I lived
with Victor, but we did our own thing when we weren't together. I didn't answer to him, 'cept about work, and he sure
the hell didn't answer to me. You?"

"I had a few boyfriends in college, nothing too serious.
Mostly frat boys out for a good time. We may have been close
in age, but worlds apart otherwise. And I developed a hopeless
fascination for a straight guy while in the Marines. So I guess
we're both two blind squirrels hunting a nut."

Once more Lucky bit down on a snappy comeback involv-
ing "nut." Intimate moments probably weren't the right time,
although he hadn't had much experience with intimate moments. They lay in silence for a while until Bo contracted the
couch. "C'mon, I'm hungry. Let's fix dinner. We can finish the
conversation in the kitchen."

Bo's kitchen matched the rest of his current life—tidy
and organized to the point of obsession. The few canned
goods Bo allowed—he usually didn't abide tinned vegeta-
bles due to complaints of excess salt—sat neatly arranged
in the pantry, labels facing out at precisely the same angle.
Silverware lay tucked into compartments in a drawer, unlike Lucky's own silverware drawer where he simply threw
in spoons and forks and untangled them the next time he
needed one.

While Bo prepared the marinade, Lucky cleaned and
stemmed the mushrooms, scraping out the gills like he'd been
shown—the reason his earlier attempts at grilling portabellas
didn't turn out like Bo's. His still didn't, but why cook them

himself and risk less than perfect results when Bo got them right every time?

"These would have been better over charcoal last night," Bo commented, while tossing a few veggies and some tofu cubes into a saucepan to stir-fry.

"I've no complaints about last night." Nope, not a one.

"Anything else you want to ask?"

Was there? What should Lucky know about the man he slept with? Walter eliminated most of the biggest issues with a thorough background check, though only the extremely paranoid would ask about any criminal history worse than a misdemeanor, right? What kind of questions would *normal* people ask? "Where'd you grow up?" That was a normal question, wasn't it?

"Pine Bluff, Arkansas. Now my turn. Did you have any pets when you were a kid?"

Lucky rinsed and patted the mushroom caps dry before passing them to Bo to marinate and place on the indoor grill. "I lived on a farm with plenty of animals, but you probably wouldn't call them pets."

"You didn't have a dog or a cat?"

"At any given time we'd have a dozen or more barn cats hanging around, but we kids weren't supposed to tame them." A memory came to mind of a much younger Lucky trying to sneak a kitten into the house. His father hadn't approved. "If you tamed 'em they'd hang out on the back steps begging a meal instead of chasing mice in the barn. Of course, Mom always kept one cat in the house as a mouser."

"Cats, huh? You strike me more as a dog person."

"We had those too. We always kept a pair of Great Pyrenees to watch the goat herd, keep foxes and coyotes from picking off the kids."

"Cool. I've never seen one of those before."

"Beautiful animals, easy going most of the time, but they'd kill a fox in a heartbeat."

Bo sighed. "I miss having pets. I'm not home enough these days to take care of one."

"I'm sure old lady Griggs wouldn't mind you cuddling one

of her critters if you wanted." Lucky envisioned Bo, sitting on the landlady's porch with a lapful of cats.

Questions about school and old friends occupied their meal, and they'd moved on to early loves by dishwashing time. Bo elaborated on having fallen madly in love with the straight fellow Marine who'd broken his heart by getting married, and Lucky made it a point to avoid overanalyzing any encounters lasting longer than twenty-four hours. Not that he'd tell Bo. The past should stay in the past.

Lucky stepped up behind as Bo stood at the sink, elbow deep in soapy water. He rose up on his toes and whispered in Bo's ear, "You like my mouth on you, don't ya?"

Bo moaned a response.

Lucky exhaled against Bo's ear. "And you like riding me, but what else turns you on?"

He blew another puff of warm breath across the back of Bo's neck. Bo shivered and answered without turning around. "Why do you think I've been trying to get you to come here?"

Leaving the dishes half-washed in the sink, he dried his hands on a dishtowel and silently left the room. Lucky didn't hesitate to follow down the hall to the lone bedroom.

"Sit," Bo commanded, pointing to the bed.

Oh, so rookie boy wanted to call the shots? Maybe not all the time, but tonight Lucky'd turn over the reins. He relaxed onto the bed, keeping an open mind about where the night might lead.

Bo lit two candles and turned out the overhead light. He flipped through a few CDs and picked one to slide into a player that doubled as the bedside clock.

An electronic dance mix started and Bo turned around, suddenly transformed into someone far more self-assured and even a bit cocky. The blood rushed from Lucky's brain for a vacation south of the beltline.

Bo flexed and strutted to the beat, not the timid "Hey! I'm moving my hips!" dancing of the insecure, but a bumping, grinding, vertical sex scene for one. He humped the air, lips set in a thin line and a smoldering gleam in his eyes. His normally mild mannered persona slipped to the floor along with an apron.

In perfect time with the pulsing beat, he slowly opened his shirt. One button at a time, Bo flaunted glimpses of skin before covering them up again. When the shirt fluttered to the floor, Lucky barely contained a shout. "Yeah, baby, take it all off."

Bo fumbled with his belt buckle and flashed Lucky a smile of pure seduction, while unfastening and pulling the woven strip slowly from each loop. The belt joined the shirt and apron. He swiveled his hips in exaggerated fashion, slowly rotating to give Lucky an unobstructed view of his ass.

As Bo's firm cheeks bounced and wriggled, he lowered his pants, twin globes peeking over the waistband. Lower and lower, inch by inch, Bo revealed his stunning bubble-butt. *Hello, there, boys! Did you miss me?*

Lucky reached down, palming his cock through the denim of his jeans. How long was this damned song? Shouldn't Bo be naked by now?

The world's longest remix played on, Bo teasing Lucky to the point of pain. He let the pants fall and kicked them out of the way. The dance continued, his hip thrusts more suggestive, more primal. Bo's runner's build wasn't as bulky as some dancers Lucky'd watched over the years, but damn if he didn't have the moves down.

"I stripped some in college to make a few extra bucks," Bo said, beginning to pant. He ran his hands up and over his sweat-slicked chest. "Guys used to shove dollar bills in my thong." He reached down, caressing his cock, now tenting out the thin cotton of his boxers. He dropped to his knees and pumped his hips, mimicking plunging into a lover.

"Ever go home with any of them?" Lucky's groin ached for a hand, a mouth, or any other willing orifice. He rubbed himself harder.

"On occasion." Bo's gaze met Lucky's. "Never for money. Some of the other guys did, but dancing got me hot."

Sweat gleamed on Bo's skin in the candlelight, and he moaned, releasing himself suddenly. He gave Lucky a sheepish smile. "Got a little too close to coming there."

Music apparently forgotten, he crawled forward on his

hands and knees and buried his face in Lucky's crotch, mouthing Lucky's erection through denim.

Quiet, unassuming Bo, half naked, surrounded by faceless strangers, all wanting him for the night. Some had him, some never would. Tonight he was all Lucky's. Lucky's hell cat. Wait a damn minute! *Mine?*

Bo unzipped Lucky's jeans and Lucky's brain fuzzed out. He fell back on the bed, letting his own personal stripper take control. Jeans and boxers around his knees, Lucky watched his cock disappear into Bo's wide-open mouth. Oh sweet mercy!

Hot, tight pressure, slip-sliding over Lucky's cock. Not hot enough, not tight enough, not fast enough. *Oh please, suck me harder!* Bo ran his tongue up and down Lucky's shaft in slow motion. That fantastic mouth withdrew and Lucky stifled a whimper. Bo made short work of shoes, socks, jeans, and boxers. Lucky recovered enough brain cells to strip off his own shirt—halfway. Bo took over from there.

The music changed from hard and driving to a slower one-two rhythm. Bo pulled open a drawer on the bedside table. "You asked me what I like," he said. "Let me show you."

CHAPTER SEVEN

Lucky expected condoms and lube, but not the oblong box Bo removed from the drawer. Avoiding Lucky's eyes, Bo opened the box. A flesh-tone rubber phallus lay inside, about seven inches long.

Lucky seized the base of his cock, fighting back the sudden jolt of arousal. Holy shit! That dildo, sliding in and out of Bo. Fuck! What an image.

He started to speak, but Bo flinched. *Shutting up now*. The snarkmaster shouldn't say a damned thing. Bo likely expected sarcasm, and yeah, not so long ago, he would have been right. The man was taking a big chance with his toy and Lucky's absence of a brain-to-mouth filter.

Lucky weighed several possible responses, settling for, "You want me to use this on you?"

Bo nodded.

Holy shit! Lucky must've fallen asleep and started dreaming his favorite fantasy. Mouth suddenly dry as dust, he managed to get out, "Lie down."

He moved over, allowing Bo to stretch out on the bed. Bo's erection faded, and the poor guy still wouldn't meet Lucky's eyes. Lucky bent down and kissed him, taking the box from his hand and placing it aside. "I'm gonna make it good for you," he promised.

Flickering candlelight played over Bo's sheened muscles. Lucky wrapped one hand around the base of Bo's cock and worked the foreskin up and down the shaft. Faster and faster he went while Bo moaned and squirmed. "Stop!" Bo cried, "I'm too close."

Lucky released his hold and nudged Bo's legs apart to settle between. He squirted lube onto his fingers and massaged Bo's

Keith will be back any minute to get me, and I'm due in Atlanta by morning. Keep up the good work."

Lucky lay on the couch a long time after Walter left. He and Bo worked well together. They made a good team. Damn it, he hated when Walter was right.

"Fluorouracil! Do you have any idea how much these are worth?" Bo ran his hand lovingly over the vials.

"A lot more than they should be. You need to switch those off with tomorrow's shipment. Then I'm heading back to Atlanta with the goods." *Thumpa, thumpa* pounded in the background, the wanna-be disco next door back in full swing. Damn it.

"You're leaving?"

"Are you kidding? I can't wait to get out of here. To date, we've been able to track down most of the suppliers you've given us. The others are only a matter of time."

Bo paused, more questions in his eyes than what he finally voiced. "That's it?"

"What's it?"

"We close them down? What happens to the people who need those drugs?"

"That's not our problem."

"Not our problem?"

Lucky should have gone up in a puff of smoke under Bo's glare. "Once we close down a few shady dealers, it's only a matter of time before the law goes into effect, making gray markets illegal. After the shysters are gone, the legitimate supply chain will start working again." He quoted the department's official stance. No need telling Bo that he'd already asked Walter for help for Rosario.

"Damn it, Lucky! Are you always this cold?"

"What?"

"Don't you give a damn about anything?"

Where the fuck did that come from? "Of course I do!"

"What if it was one of your nephews lying in a bed at the center? Would you be so quick to dust off your hands and walk away?"

"Bo..." Lucky sucked in a deep breath. He held out a hand.

Bo backed away. "I've got what I came for. I'm leaving now." He pulled out his cell phone and yelled Lucky's address over the neighbor's chaos. "I'll be back tomorrow with the samples," he said after hanging up his call, and left without saying goodbye.

At two in the morning Lucky lay staring at the ceiling, imagining one of Charlotte's boys lying in a bed at Rosario. He pictured Stephanie, her big eyes and bright smile, despite fighting a battle with cancer. A weight bore down on his chest. He wanted to punish the people who valued Ben Franklins over Stephanies. He wanted to fix the broken system that allowed such opportunists to flourish.

"Lucky," he groused to himself. "You're getting too fucking close."

"Here ya go!" Lucky offloaded the last package from his cart in the gift shop.

A customer approached the counter, carrying a few magazines and a box with a smiling baby on the cover. "Will you gift wrap this for me, please?"

"Can you wait a minute?" the middle-aged clerk asked Lucky. "I'll be a few minutes. I need to check these in before I sign."

Lucky grunted what he hoped sounded like an "Okay."

Instead of hurrying about her chore, the clerk asked about the customer's family, job, and a million other things. Apparently, the owner of the shiny platinum credit card was a personal friend with lots of gossip to share.

Lucky bit down on several choice words he'd like to say. He'd love to vent his spleen on the molasses-slow clerk. He'd never been known to idle well, and he rambled through the store, inspecting an item here and there to keep himself occupied. Why the hell would anyone pay those kind of prices when the same stuff was sold elsewhere for a lot less?

He rounded a corner and halted. Green eyes caught his attention first, followed by whiskers and yellow fur. Lucky opening, pressing harder and harder until the tips of two digits popped inside. In, out, in, out, add more lubrication, in, out...

He paused long enough to fumble the dildo out of the box, slick the sides, and line the bulbous head up with Bo's hole. Bo emitted a long, low hiss as the rubber breached his body.

"That is so fucking hot," Lucky murmured. He held his breath, watching Bo's pucker stretch to allow the intrusion. *That's how he looks when my cock's in there.*

Lucky shuddered. If he gave in to temptation, he'd toss the dildo onto the floor, crawl on top of the man, and mindlessly pump to completion. But this wasn't about Lucky. This was Bo's fantasy. With the fake cock seated as far as Lucky dared, he slowly pulled it back until only the head remained inside, then slipped it out completely. Bo's ring quickly contracted. Lucky reinserted the toy, thrusting more forcefully.

"Oh, hell yeah," Bo moaned.

Faster and harder Lucky stroked, glancing up at Bo's blissful smile. Knees spread wide, Bo rocked on the bed, urging Lucky on. "Suck me!"

Lucky wrapped his lips around Bo's cock, bobbing in time with the rhythm of his thrusts.

"Oh God, oh God!" Bo chanted.

Lucky pulled off, replacing his mouth with his hand to watch Bo's face.

Eyes unfocused, Bo convulsed, barely human sounds emerging from his throat. Lucky desperately wanted to jerk the dildo out and fill Bo's body, but waited. A jet of white shot from Bo's cock and Bo grabbed Lucky's hand, forcing a tighter grasp. Come spattered his chest.

"Ah, ah, ah!" Lucky chanted. He removed the toy and flopped onto his back, one hand racing along his cock, the other gripping beneath his balls. Seismic charges detonated, shock waves pulsing outward from his groin.

At some point Bo moved, for Lucky came to himself plastered to the man's chest, wheezing out shaky breaths. "That was...that was..."

"Fucking amazing," Bo finished for him.

Lucky floated in a contented haze and woke much later to full darkness, his head on Bo's chest. The scent of sex sent a meager shudder through his cock, egged on by the aroma of lube, latex, and Bo. He nudged Bo's hip. Bo muttered something that might have been, "Don't even think about it." Lucky drifted off with a smile on his face.

"What are you doing?" Lucky stood in the doorway of Bo's kitchen. Had he slept through a party? Except for a few dishes soaking overnight, they'd left the room nearly clean. Now, a few hours later, potato peelings lay mounded in the sink, pots of boiling water sat on the stove, and Bo dashed about the tiny space, stirring, slicing, tasting. Something mouthwatering scented the air, along with the rich aroma of coffee from Bo's tiny little one-cup-at-a-time machine.

"Did you forget? The office picnic is today." Bo shrugged, one side of his mouth lifting and bringing out a brief appearance of The Dimple. "I'd planned to make potato salad and baked beans last night, but got distracted." He shuffled over to the coffeemaker and wrapped Lucky in a quick one-armed hug while passing over the brew. "What are you bringing?" Something *dinged*, and Bo dashed back to the stove.

Lucky vaguely remembered a memo. And an e-mail. And a few flyers posted. And Bo's recent reminder. He'd ignored the random department get-togethers for eight years. He spent enough time with coworkers already, why volunteer to give up free time to spend more? "Actually, I'm not going."

"What?" Bo stopped mid-stir. "Why not?"

Why not? *Let me count the ways.* "Bo, they don't like me, I don't like them, why spend more time with them than I already do?"

"Has it occurred to you that if you *did* spend more time together y'all might like each other more?"

Ah, the young and naïve. "And what if more time winds up meaning we like each other less, huh?" Lucky sipped his coffee. Wait. Bo planned to go to the picnic, Lucky didn't. Lucky'd also planned to spend the day together. What would it take to get

Bo to blow off the picnic for some one-on-one time, sans nosy coworkers? "Why don't you pack all that stuff away and let's go somewhere else instead?"

"I can't. I promised I'd be there and bring food."

"You can always drop off the dishes and come back home. I'll make it worth your while." Lucky waggled his brows. Bo liked cute. If cute headed off an argument, Lucky would give it a try.

"Why? You might not like social functions, but I do. I like people, Lucky. I'm curious about them. I want to meet Lisa's husband and new baby. I want to swap war stories with Art. He served in Afghanistan too."

Art, Lucky knew, but, "Who's Lisa?"

Bo gave Lucky an "I know you didn't ask me that" glower. "The receptionist you walk past every morning to get to your desk."

"She had a baby?" She had put on a bit of weight there for a while, hadn't she? But...babies? Lucky shuddered. They screamed and cried for no apparent reason, pooped and barfed on you. Charlotte had once handed him a squirming bundle named Todd. He'd taken in the tiny little nose and mouth, marveled at the miniature fingers closing around his. Then the bundle screamed. He'd handed the bundle back.

"You didn't get her a gift, did you?" Bo's pursed lips didn't bode well for ducking arguments.

"Why would I do that?"

"Because it's the nice thing to do."

"I don't do nice."

"Obviously not. Anyway, why won't you come hang out with me? You'll have fun, I promise. I'm in charge of the face painting. I wouldn't want to disappoint the kids. And we're coworkers. I promise no one will think anything of seeing us talking. Beside, there'll be horseshoes and Frisbee. Accounting and logistics are planning a grudge match tug of war."

The entire SNB in one place at one time, with their families, disapproving stares firmly in place, or worse, turning a cold shoulder whenever Lucky approached. Lucky shook his head. "I can't. I've got things to do around the house."

"But not two seconds ago you asked me to go do something with you. Where were those plans then?"

Damn but Lucky hated verbally sparring with someone who wouldn't back down. "I don't want to go, okay? End of discussion."

"Well, I'd really hoped to spend the day with you, but if you're not going, I suppose I'll see you tonight, *if* you're not too busy. Then again, if what you've got to do involves cleaning, maybe you won't be done for days."

Together they loaded containers into Bo's truck. Bo asked once more, "Sure you won't change your mind? I mean, I hate leaving you on your birthday."

"It's not my birthday, and yes, I'm sure."

Bo kissed him, in public. Lucky didn't do public displays of affection. He darted a glance around the parking lot. Good. No witnesses. "I'll see you tonight," Bo said. "The picnic's from twelve to five, and I promised to stay and help clean up. Why don't you come over around seven?"

Lucky didn't respond fast enough to suggest his place instead. Bo drove off, leaving Lucky to drive back to his duplex and spend the day alone.

He made a halfhearted attempt at cleaning, washing laundry in preparation for his trip, and then sat on the front porch with a couple of Mrs. Griggs's cats for company.

"I don't get Bo sometimes," he told them. They didn't answer, though the fat tabby chirped, lifting its head for a good chin scratching.

What to do with his day? He could call his sister, but he'd always made a habit of e-mailing. What if she were at work? What if she didn't have time to talk? What if she didn't want to talk? What if one of the boys answered? Besides, hearing her voice would make him all the lonelier.

To avoid appearing overeager, he didn't get to Bo's place until seven thirty, for a dinner that tasted pretty good for being picnic leftovers. Lucky wasn't going to admit they might have tasted better when they were fresh, when the people Bo kept going on about were there to talk to. He'd ignored them this long, hadn't he?

***

60

Lucky poked his head out from underneath the covers and sniffed. Was he dreaming? No! There it was again! The tantalizing aroma of—bacon! He opened one eye, expecting to fully wake up disappointed. But no, Bo stood over him, tray in hand, wearing nothing but a smile. Damp hair, slicked back, told of a recent shower.

"Wake up. I brought you breakfast in bed." Bo sat the tray down on the nightstand.

Lucky scooted upright, taking in Bo's offering—crispy strips of something Bo had sworn never to cook. "Is this a test or something?" Two eggs sat sunny side up beside dry wheat toast and orange slices, the bacon beckoning. "Umm...you didn't cook naked, did you?"

"I wore an apron. And nope, no test. Since it's your birthday, I thought I'd compromise. It's turkey bacon. Still high in salt, but less carcinogenic than pork."

Oh, that again. "It's not my birthday."

"It's not? Okay, I'll take this away." Bo reached for the tray.

Lucky grabbed the plate before Bo could snatch it away. "Touch it and die."

"Can I wish you happy birthday, even if it is a few days late?"

Lucky shifted his gaze from Bo to the plate and back again. Bacon. Bo'd cooked him bacon. "If it makes you happy." Keeping an eye on Mr. Healthy lest he change his mind, Lucky bypassed the fork on the edge of the plate and lifted a strip of crispy goodness to his mouth. "Oh damn. That's almost better than sex." It didn't matter if it came from a pig or a turkey—the mouthwatering morsel looked like bacon, smelled like bacon, and with a little imagination, tasted like bacon. Lucky entered blissed out, bacon heaven.

Bo scowled, folding his arms across his chest.

Lucky couldn't resist yanking the guy's chain. "I said *almost*. Actually, real bacon's almost better than sex. This stuff's more like looking at porn. Kinda reminds you of the real thing, and will tide you over, but nothing beats honest to goodness bacon." Lucky broke a yolk with his fork, dipped a piece of toast into the mess, topped the egg with a slice of bacon, and popped it into his mouth. He moaned, he couldn't help himself. Mixing with egg made the wish-it-was-bacon taste more like the real thing. At least it wasn't soy bacon. *Brrr*....

"Turkey bacon or porn?" Bo flexed, pumping his cock to semi-erectness. "Well, imagine *this* on the page of your favorite jerk-off mag. Okay, keep chewing, and compare it to *this*." Bo spun around, bending over at the waist.

Lucky spewed a few toast crumbs, but not the precious bacon.

Bo exaggerated a put-upon sigh. "Have it your way. I'll be right back with your coffee."

"You do that," Lucky replied, words coming out "Mmmm mu mmaaht" due to a full mouth. Bo reappeared and set a cup of coffee on the nightstand before dashing out the door again.

Lucky mopped up the last of his breakfast with a piece of toast. Bo returned, carrying a package the size of a shoe box, wrapped in garish red, white, and blue paper covered with smiling boats, airplanes, and trains, more suitable for a kid's gift than a lover's. A very young kid. "Sorry 'bout the paper. I got there late and the gift shop had nearly run out. My choices were this"—he indicted the grinning vehicles with a wave of his hand—"or Hello Kitty."

"Good choice," Lucky replied. Bo got him a gift? Suddenly, birthdays didn't seem half bad. Except for the annual card from Charlotte and the boys, nobody'd gotten Lucky an actual present since Victor. A shadow fell over Lucky's mood. Who'd wound up with his Mustang, the nice watch, and the other presents he'd gotten, all seized after Victor's arrest? Lucky could've sold the rings and chains Victor'd given him and lived comfortably for years. Gone now. *Don't look back.*

Bo placed the package on the bed and took the plate away. "It's just a little something. I hope you like it."

Lucky shook the package. What'd Bo get him? A brick? Damned thing weighed a ton. He ripped open the paper, finding a white paper box inside, and lifted the lid on... A dragon? He hefted it out of the box for a better look. "I... well... gee... I mean..."

Bo's nervous smile vanished. "You don't like it."

"I do. I mean..." A dragon?

"It's for protection and luck. It's Chinese."

Well, at least Lucky could honestly say Bo'd surprised him, with the bacon and the gift. "Thanks, Bo. I like it. I really do." He didn't know what to do with the darned thing. It'd make one hell of a weapon, all wrought iron with sharp ridges. Why couldn't he have had it while in prison? He'd have slept a whole lot safer.

"Since I only found out Friday, I didn't have time to special order, but it's your birthday—I wanted to get you something. The moment this case is over, I'm taking you away somewhere. You and me, the whole weekend, no distractions. How does that sound?"

"You didn't have to get me anything."

Bo sat the plate on the nightstand and lay down on the bed. "Yes, I did. And unlike you, I love birthdays. Come September, be prepared to spoil me rotten. But today is for you, or rather, until we have to go to work." He rolled to his side and nibbled Lucky's earlobe. "I'll make your birthday a day to remember."

"Not my birthday," Lucky mumbled, instantly distracted when Bo shimmied down the bed to take Lucky's cock in his mouth. First bacon, now a blow job? "Given time, I might learn to like birthdays!" Lucky moaned.

Bo chuckled, uttering what sounded like, "Anything you say, bacon breath," around his mouthful.

Lucky slumped farther down on the bed, eyes drifting closed. He cupped the back of Bo's head, lending a helping hand to control the motion. Nothing beat a good morning blowing. Not even bacon.

Bo groaned and Lucky opened his eyes, observing while his lover applied suction. Damn. Just damn. "Lay on your stomach," Lucky ordered. Maybe something did beat a morning blow job after all.

Bo fell to the side and arched his back, raising the most tempting ass this side of the Mississippi. Lucky rolled over, palming one firm mound. Damn, what a body. Not too bulky, not too skinny, packed with lean runner's muscles, and liberally sprinkled with freckles, the occasional mole tossed in for good measure. Lucky sank his teeth gently into flesh while kneading the other cheek. Bo gasped, pressing into the contact. Nature had given Bo a nice butt because he totally got off on attention paid to that particular area, apparently.

Lucky ran his rough fingertips over silky skin, blowing out a puff of air. Gooseflesh gathered in the path of the breeze. Nice. With tongue and teeth, Lucky worked his way up to Bo's shoulders and back again to the twin globes that haunted his dreams. He eased his hands down, parting flesh and swiping Bo's pucker with his tongue. Bo wriggled and let out a whimper. Lucky took that as permission to explore freely.

He lavished attention to Bo's balls, hole, and the area in between. Soap and man and arousal filled Lucky's nostrils, and he worked a hand under a thigh to grasp Bo's shaft.

"Damn, that feels good," Bo gasped.

Lucky swirled a finger against saliva-moistened skin, pressing in until the barest tip pushed past Bo's muscled barrier. Should he ask for the toy, repeat their play from Friday night? Bo wriggled, moaned, and chanted, "Oh yeah, fuck me, Lucky." No time for toys now.

Who'd moved the nightstand? Had it always been so damned far away? Lucky stretched to reach the drawer. He yanked too hard, sending the contents crashing to the floor.

"Get what you need and leave the damned drawer," Bo growled, sliding a pillow beneath his hips.

Hanging halfway over the bed, Lucky snatched up a box and a tube. He fumbled with the condom pack, dropping it twice. "Hold still, damn it!" The cellophane pack refused to rip.

"Hand it here." Bo ripped open the pack with relative ease and handed back a latex circle.

Lucky rolled the condom on in record time, dabbed on a touch of lube, and plunged into sweet, tight pleasure. Ahhh... Like coming home. Bo answered his blissed-out moan with one of his own. A series of sharp thrusts later, Lucky's groin rested against Bo's ass. He bent to place a kiss between Bo's shoulder blades. Arms wrapped securely around his lover's chest, Lucky turned them into a spooned position, dropping one hand to Bo's cock.

He worked himself in and out of Bo's body, matching his

thrusting with the pace of his hand. A shoulder proved too tempting, and Lucky trailed his tongue over taut muscle.

Bo rocked back against Lucky, impaling himself, emitting breathy little grunts. Lucky pumped a steady rhythm. Bo's muscles tensed.

"I'm gonna come," Bo warned. Lucky snapped his hips, driving in and retreating at a frantic pace. High pitched noises harmonized with huffed breaths, squeaking bedsprings, and a string of cussing muffled by a pillow.

When Bo's channel gripped tight, Lucky stilled and let loose, releasing pulse after pulse. Slickness coated his hand. He panted through the aftermath, holding Bo to his chest in a vise grip. Damn but they were good together.

They lay in silence, Bo skimming his fingers up and down Lucky's arm lying draped over his chest. "Still think bacon's better than sex?" he asked.

"I said almost."

"Okay, is it still almost better than sex?"

Lucky mumbled something low. Bo could imagine it to be whatever he wanted to hear.

"What's that? Can't hear you!"

Lucky mumbled again. Damn. The man didn't play fair.

"Still can't hear you."

"Oh, all right. Sex is better than bacon."

"You bet your ass it is. Better for your health too. Now, while I hate to break up the party, we need to get moving."

Lucky's cock slipped from Bo's body, and he lay boneless and recovering while Bo returned the drawer to the nightstand. Something poked at his calf, and he looked down into the dragon's red eyes. Though he'd never been accused of being overly observant outside of work, he recalled similar figures in the living room. "Bo?"

"Yeah?"

"What's with the dragons?" With its weight and size, Lucky figured to use his for a doorstop. That is, if he didn't trip over the damned thing and break a toe.

"I told you. It's for protection."

"Yeah, but what about all those of yours in the living room?"

Bo sank onto the edge of the bed and peered down at Lucky, eyes dark and serious. "You remember me telling you what happened with my dad, right?"

"Uh-huh?"

"And how I couldn't sleep in a bed?"

"Uh-huh."

"After I went to live with my aunt I woke her up a lot with nightmares. She bought me a gargoyle because she said that's what old cathedrals used to keep evil away. My brother bought me a Chinese dragon figure for Christmas that year. I've been collecting ever since."

"Just dragons and gargoyles?"

"I've got other things I've added over the years. Coins, amulets, mostly given to me by my aunt and brother."

Interesting. "Do they work?"

"They keep me company."

"You don't like being alone?"

"Stop asking questions, we need to get ready. We have to get to Anderson and settle in before tomorrow."

"But you said we needed to learn more about each other."

"Later. Now get up and take a shower. I still have to pack."

Liar. Bo's packed suitcase sat by the bedroom door. Why did the man suddenly want to be alone, especially when he didn't seem to like it much?

"Here, why don't you take some of this with you?" Bo loaded plastic containers filled with potato salad, beans, and leftover mushrooms into a mini cooler.

Lucky would have preferred a few more days off to discover what else about Bo he'd missed out on, and why Bo wouldn't answer the question about being alone. In a few short hours, they'd be back to square one, coworkers who, in this case, couldn't openly acknowledge one another.

Bo dragged his suitcase into the living room. Maybe he'd packed the rubber dildo. Lucky adjusted himself when his cock took notice of gutter-worthy thoughts. Come to think of it, he hadn't seen it fall from the drawer earlier—not that he'd been looking. He'd never be able to look at the man again without picturing the uninhibited creature from Friday night.

He sighed and studied his watch. If only they had enough time for another round, and maybe a chance to use Bo's toy again and further discuss what else lit the man's fires. "I hate to run," he said, meaning every word, "but I need to get home, get my shit together." Why hadn't he brought his duffle over last night?

"Okay. I'll bring the cooler and meet you at the office to pick up our cars."

In the light of day, Bo seemed bashful, reserved. Was he still pissed at Lucky for not attending the department get-together, or mentioning his birthday? Stepping up from behind, Lucky wrapped his arms around Bo's waist. They couldn't part on a bad note. "You are so fucking hot." He trailed his lips across Bo's neck.

"Really?" Bo nestled back into Lucky's embrace, releasing a deep breath.

"Really. And first chance we get, we're gonna explore what else you've been keeping from me." After a parting pat to Bo's backside, Lucky retrieved his gift from the coffee table and sauntered to the door. If he looked back, he might never leave.

CHAPTER EIGHT

Lucky and Bo followed a young woman in Sunday-go-to-meeting-clothes across the parking garage. "Here's yours." She handed Lucky a set of keys. "Sign here, please." Oh dear God, no! Who in their right fucking mind deliberately painted a car chicken shit green? And not any old garden-variety chicken shit green either, but a fucking ugly-assed, glow in the dark chicken shit green, like a Rhode Island Red ate radioactive corn or something.

Scowling at the Pimp Daddy Special Chevy Malibu, Lucky scribbled a signature on a clipboard-bound form. He gave a rim an experimental tap. Spinners? Who the hell had owned this piece of shit? "Toss in a pair of fuzzy dice and a hooker or two, and I'll be set. Is this the best we got?"

"Well," the lady answered with feigned sweetness, "we had a pretty decent Mazda, until *somebody* totaled it last year."

"Now wait a doggone minute! I—"

"The car is fine," Bo said, cutting Lucky off.

"Oh, that's his vehicle. Yours is this way." She clip-clopped on impossibly high heels around a column, Lucky and Bo trailing behind, and handed Bo the keys to a late model Acura RDX. "Now you better take good care of this one. It's a seizure from a raid and scheduled to go up for auction next month." Bo signed on the dotted line, a little more readily than Lucky had.

"Why do I get a piece of shit, and he gets an Acura?" Lucky pointed at the deep burgundy SUV.

"Him, hospital big-wig. You, basement-dwelling package wrangler. Any more questions?" She flipped a strand of chestnut hair over her shoulder, smiled pleasantly at Bo, and stalked off.

"What'd you do to piss her off?" Bo asked, leading the way back to Lucky's car.

"Hell if I've ever laid eyes on her before. Is she new?"

"Judy? She started about a year ago. From her reaction I figured you'd had a run-in at some point. She sure doesn't seem to like you much."

Lucky cut a sharp glare at Bo. "Judy? Been getting friendly with the staff?"

Bo's eyebrows rose, the corners of his mouth fell. "I need cars for assignments. She gets them for me. She and Lisa look after the cactus when I'm away. Yes, her name is Judy, she's twenty-seven, has a two-year-old daughter, and loves Braves baseball. It's called conversation. Two people talk and learn things about each other. You'd know this if you'd come to the picnic yesterday."

Why did the rest of the world care about other people's business? Lucky didn't flat give a damn what others did. Not usually, anyway. Bo gave the pimpmobile's rim a nudge with the toe of his shoe. "It's certainly not much to look at, is it?"

Lucky didn't feel the comment answer-worthy. Instead he popped the trunk and loaded two duffels from his Camaro, while Bo schlepped a Pullman case to the Acura. The cooler containing supper warranted a spot on the front passenger seat, along with a backpack carrying his laptop.

He finished arranging his bags to find Bo standing beside him. "Sure you don't wanna stop by and find out where I live?" Bo asked.

"I'd love to, but by the time we get settled in, it'll be time for bed. And we both gotta get up in the morning." No need to draw out the inevitable, or risk blowing their cover on day one.

Their gazes met and held. What should Lucky say? *Take care, we'll fuck when we can?* Or maybe, *Bye dear, have a nice day?* In the end he managed, "Take care of you."

"Take care of you too," Bo replied.

They bumped fists and Lucky climbed into the Malibu. He followed Bo out of the garage, eyeing himself in the rearview mirror. "'Take care of you?' Damn, I'm lame."

***

"It's the seven levels of hell!" Lucky stared up at the apartment building, double-checking the address. Nope, no mistake. While he hadn't exactly been raised in the lap of luxury, his parents' farmhouse beat this rundown crack house by a country mile.

A skinny, twenty-something man in blue jeans and nothing else lounged in a folding chair outside the main entrance. Lucky shivered. Why didn't the guy at least have a shirt on? They may be in South Carolina, but April wasn't exactly balmy. Especially not in the shade.

He slung the straps of both duffels over one shoulder and grabbed the cooler and backpack, lugging it all in one trip in case the Malibu wasn't there when he got back. This didn't look like the safest of neighborhoods. After fighting traffic for three hours, he didn't rightly care. Maybe the original owner would steal the ugly-assed piece of shit back.

"Which way's the elevator?" Lucky asked the man displaying his body in sixty degree weather. Not that he didn't have a nice body. Not as nice as Bo's, but the guy probably didn't sleep alone unless he wanted to.

Mr. Shirtless laughed. "Elevator? Where do you think you are, The Ritz? The *stairs* are that way." He jabbed a finger at the building's front entrance.

Loaded down, Lucky trudged up seven flights of stairs. "Motherfucking job, motherfucking apartment, and motherfucking whoever the hell found this place. Probably the same woman gave me the piece of shit Malibu." A palmetto bug scurried out of his way. Oh shit! Only right that hell came equipped with the nasty fuckers. If they lived on the landing, chances were, they weren't above invading apartments. Great, just great.

It took Lucky a few tries to wrestle open the door to apartment 7C. He dropped his belongings and hurried through the apartment, flipping on lights to flush out uninvited multi-legged guests. He searched the tiny living room, shoe box sized bedroom, bathroom barely big enough to turn around in, and finally the kitchen, which was more a closet someone managed to squeeze a refrigerator and a stove into that opened onto the living room. No creatures scuttled away, but the mouse trap under the kitchen sink didn't bode well for pest-free living.

Somewhere a Salvation Army Family Store was missing furniture, but otherwise the place appeared livable. He pulled out his work cell phone and texted news of his arrival to Walter. Duty done, he typed out a message to Bo on his personal phone. *"Hope yr place is better n mine."*

With no microwave in sight, Lucky reheated his beans and mushrooms in the oven, and munched a barely edible dinner, the beans too cold and the mushrooms too hot. He jumped when his phoned chimed. Screw dinner—he dashed into the living room to read: *"S ok. Wish U were here.'"*

Yeah, I do, too. Lucky caught himself smiling at the phone in his hand. What the hell? A few good mind-blowing fucks and now he behaved like some love-sick teenager? Okay, more than a few.

He fired up his laptop, thanking the gods of Internet connection for a signal. Hmm... What to say? Three drafts hit the recycle bin. The fourth attempt showed promise.

Char,
What's the early warning signs of a relationship?

After a few minutes spent unpacking and settling in, he returned to his laptop to find an answer.

Does he have a toothbrush at your place and do either of you ever cook for the other? Is he your one and only or are you still fucking around?
Toothbrush + you in a kitchen + monogamy = relationship.

Lucky reread Charlotte's reply three times, adding up the equation a bit differently. Toothbrush plus him and Bo in a kitchen plus monogamy equaled complication. He closed his eyes. Candlelight played over Bo's whipcord lean muscles in a memory. Maybe Bo was a complication worth having. But hell if he'd tell Bo.

***

71

The Malibu survived the night on the street in front of Crack Central. Its rims and tires, however, did not.

"There's gotta be a special place in hell for assholes who make me call the keeper of the cars this soon," Lucky snarled. Maybe he should let Bo do it, since he'd gotten friendly with the woman. The guy who apparently owned no shirts sat by the front door. "You see who did this?"

"Nope."

"No, of course not." Day started on the bad note, Lucky left the car on cement blocks like he'd found it and called a cab, trading one hell for another—a nine to five job.

He e-mailed the theft report to Walter. Let him deal with it.

"Yo! Reggie! Get over here!"

Reggie, get over here. The bastard went on and on like some broken record. Lucky trotted over to his coworker's side. Was the smoke pouring from his ears enough to set off the fire alarm?

Sammy, a heavyset, pimply-faced kid who couldn't have been old enough to legally drink, handed a clipboard back to a man leaning against the door of a delivery van. The van driver watched like a hawk as Lucky and Sammy unloaded generic-looking gray totes. None were the double-sealed variety used to transport controlled substances.

They loaded their bounty onto a cart. The shipping clerk stepped out of her mini-office and snatched the paperwork off the totes, logged in receipt, and returned the forms to Lucky.

"Take this up to the pharmacy." Sammy probably enjoyed the hell out of ordering around the new guy.

Lucky squashed down a smile. It wouldn't do to show eagerness to a supervisor younger than most of his socks. If the guy knew how badly Lucky wanted inside the hospital to catch a glimpse of his partner, he'd probably wind up leg-shackled in the basement. He rode the elevator up to the second floor and scanned for tall brunets while wheeling the cart down the hallway to the pharmacy.

"Got something for us?" a too-perky woman asked when Lucky scanned his ID badge and let himself in, as he'd had to do in other areas of the hospital. Fort Knox had nothing on this place, security-wise. Lucky approved.

"Danvers?" He called out the name from the packing slip.

A balding man approached, wearing a white jacket similar to the one Bo'd worn while playing pharmacist at a bogus pain clinic in Florida. His pale skin nearly matched his jacket. Sheesh, did the guy have something against getting outside every once in a while?

"You won't find Mr. Danvers down here with us mere mortals," the pharmacist drawled. "He doesn't leave the crystal palace unless he has to."

"The crystal palace?"

"The fourth floor," the woman explained, her pink smock marking her as a pharmacy tech, if Bo's explanation of the color-coded pecking order in pharmacies held true. Pharmacists wore white, techs didn't. "He's in purchasing and doesn't come down here often."

The pharmacist sniffed. "Probably won't come down at all now. Did you get an eyeful of his hot new assistant?"

"Yeah. If I worked with the guy instead of you, I'd never be late to work. He's got a body that'd stop a truck." The woman grinned, teeth flashing against her dark skin. Lucky wanted to grab them both by the back of the neck and clang their heads together. She redeemed herself slightly by adding, "But Danvers is too straight to notice the hottie. Me, on the other hand? I appreciate the Lord's bounty in all flavors and colors."

"Honey, back in the day, I'd have that lovely man wrapped around my little finger." The pharmacist signed for the cartons with a flourish and traipsed off. Two more pharmacists and another tech milled behind a counter.

In your dreams, shithead.

"Don't mind him, he's harmless," the woman said. "I'm Ava, and he's Martin." She hiked a thumb in Martin's direction.

"I'm Reggie. Just started today." Reggie! Bah!

"Nice to meet you, Reggie. Don't let Sammy give you too hard a time down in receiving. He likes to pretend he's more than he is if you get my drift. Stand up to him. He'll back down."

Imagining Bo's elbow nudging his ribs and a hissed *Be nice!* Lucky managed a semi-sincere, "Thanks."

"Don't mention it. Now if you'll excuse me, I've got syringes to fill."

The hours ticked by, with Lucky hauling cases up to the pharmacy, kitchen, or general supply department.

He clocked out at five P.M. What time did Bo get off? A text message waited on his cell phone. *"Dinner w/ salesman. TTYL."*

Shit. Another lonely night. Had Bo learned anything yet? What about the dinner meeting? Maybe he needed Lucky to tag along to keep an eye on things. *And that's the only reason you want to go?* his conscience asked.

While some jerkoff wined and dined Bo, Lucky munched Chinese takeout, parked on the couch in his tiny apartment. *Thumpa, thumpa, thumpa* from the apartment next door shook the walls. "Hey! Turn your fucking music down!" he bellowed, banging the wall with his fist.

The volume fell for a full ten minutes before ramping up again. "Crack heads." He perched his laptop on his knees. No new e-mails from Walter or Bo. Nothing from Charlotte. Another damned office get-together in the works. Two new shortage drugs added to the FDA website, none removed. He sighed. A quick run to the border back during his time with Victor and he'd have scored enough meds for the center to run for weeks. They might not be FDA approved, but he'd have gotten them.

Where did the salesman take Bo? Joe's House of Pizza? Or some swanky place with linen napkins and crystal goblets. The kind of place Bo always wanted to go but Lucky said no. Was the salesman a fussy old senior, or some red-hot yuppie-type fresh out of college? Lucky formed a mental image of a charmed Bo, laughing at some two-bit pill-pusher's flattery. Maybe Lucky shouldn't follow Bo to his meetings. If he did, he might smash in a face if the sales rep so much as looked at Bo with intent. Not that he'd be able to follow even if he wanted to, with his damned car still up on blocks while someone in accounting wrangled with insurance and paperwork issues. And with a car checked out, he'd pay hell getting reimbursed for a rental. He'd take cabs.

With nothing to occupy his time, Lucky ambled off to bed. He tossed and turned. The moment his eyes closed, a *Boom!* from next door jerked him awake. Meth lab explosion? *Sniff.* No smoke. No sirens. He turned on the bedside lamp and texted Walter. *"Get warrant, arrest my neighbors."*

CHAPTER NINE

"Is that all?" Sammy peered into the back of the delivery van.

"Three cases." The driver pointed at three Styrofoam coolers nestled near the van's door.

The clerk checked the inventory in and disappeared back into the office. Two days on the job, and Lucky had yet to hear the woman speak.

"Damn." Sammy unloaded the coolers onto a cart. "Reggie, take this up to the pharmacy. They ain't gonna be happy. That's half as much as we usually get."

Lucky rode the elevator up, staring at the coolers. Regardless of the contents, three packages of anything seemed too little for a two-hundred bed hospital specializing in pediatric cancer treatment.

The door opened and his throat tightened when a familiar head of brown hair caught his attention. Bo. Hand on the small of Bo's back, a handsome older man steered him out of a conference room.

Bo hung his head and swiped a hand though his hair. Lucky tamped down his protective instincts. Storming down the hall, knocking the man's hand away, and demanding, "What's wrong," wasn't the way to stay uncover. Others followed Bo from the room. Not a smile or even a hint of one marked any of their faces.

A woman stepped between Bo and Lucky, and when she moved, Lucky found himself staring straight into Bo's eyes. Their gazes held momentarily, Bo glancing away first when someone spoke to him. He moved in the midst of a group past Lucky and down the hall. What the hell was going on? Did somebody die?

The rest of the day Bo plagued Lucky's mind. That evening he took a cab to his apartment—he refused to call it home—to find new tires, new plastic hubcaps, and the same old Malibu. While heating a can of soup on the stove, he checked his personal cell phone. A text from Bo said, *"Coming over."*

Lucky showered and shaved. He waited until nine P.M. before a knock penetrated the heavy thudding from the neighboring apartment. Lucky opened the door and Bo grabbed him, cutting off Lucky's air. "Oh my God. It's fucking awful!"

Lucky guided Bo inside. "You didn't park on the street, did you?"

"Are you kidding? In this neighborhood? No, I called a cab. I barely found the place, and when I got here, the driver asked me four times if I was sure I wanted out." Bo wiped his eyes with his sleeve.

"Good God, Bo! What happened?" Lucky led Bo farther into the living room and dashed into the kitchen area for a handful of paper towels. Bo sagged down onto the couch.

Lucky plopped down beside him. "Now, tell me. What's wrong?"

Bo rubbed his face with an offered towel. "I had no idea what we were getting into. It's a whole lot worse than I imagined."

"What do you mean?" Surely things hadn't gone south already. They'd only been on the case two days.

"Today I sat in a meeting and explained to a panel of doctors and nurses why the drugs they need aren't available through legitimate suppliers, at any price. And then they decided patient by patient who gets what little we have, who gets less effective substitutes, and who might get nothing at all." He slammed his balled up fist against his thigh. "We're talking about children, Lucky, innocent lives, and we're triaging and rationing like on a battlefield. One of the best cancer centers in the country and we can't come up with enough drugs to even keep the patients comfortable, let alone save them.

"We don't have enough. We don't have a fraction of enough, to give those kids what they need." Tiny clear droplets glittered on Bo's lashes. He collapsed against Lucky's shoulder. "What's the world coming to when a hospital can't even get morphine?"

"What about your salesman last night? That didn't pan out?" Lucky wrapped his arms around his partner. Bo's shudders rocked them both.

"Smoke and mirrors. He works for a distributor. His company wants to keep our business, but everything we ask for goes straight into backorder. Calling the manufacturer directly doesn't help either. They have no idea when they'll get the facility up and running at full speed again."

Lucky gave Bo's arm a few awkward pats. Charlotte always knew the right thing to say when folks cried. She got the comforter genes in the family, leaving Lucky to inherit all the asshole tendencies. He stayed quiet, holding Bo and rubbing circles against his back.

"I've been worrying all afternoon, and have no earthly idea how to make this right." Bo sighed.

Uh-oh. Time to draw the line between personal feelings and professional duty. "It's not your job to make it right. It's your job to stop anyone who tries to make a shady deal."

"Shady deal? Shady deal! I'd be willing to deal with anybody to make sure those kids got a fighting chance, but the administrator won't budge!"

Now wasn't the time to mention the number of people Lucky had put behind bars for that same reason. Regardless of motivation, law was law, and not open to negotiation. "You take your chances when you're not careful—you may get the right stuff, you may get poison. It's a crapshoot. The administrator knows that and made a decision."

Thumpa, thumpa reverberated through the living room. "Jeez, Lucky! Are your neighbors always that loud?"

"Pretty much." If Walter hadn't warned him repeatedly about keeping a low profile while undercover, Lucky would have taken the .38 out of his closet and emptied the chamber into the neighbor's stereo. "Have you eaten?"

"Not hungry. Can we go to bed? I've had a rough day and need some sleep, if we can manage to sleep through Armageddon-fest next door. But fair warning, all I want to do is sleep."

Lucky turned off the living room light, locked his door, and beat on the wall while shouting, "Would you quiet down already!" through paper-thin walls. If anything, the folks next door cranked the music louder. One little whiff of pot smoke and he'd have a warrant in hand within the hour. *Hmm...now there's an idea.* The shit they'd cooked earlier *might* have smelled a little... herbal.

"Lucky? You coming?" Bo shouted from the bedroom.

"Not tonight," Lucky mumbled, the throbbing tempo drowning his words.

He undressed and crawled into bed. Bo latched on, digging his fingers into Lucky's shoulders. After a few minutes the grip gradually lessoned and Bo's breathing evened out.

Lucky lay staring at the ceiling. If he knew where to find them, he'd gladly steal all the drugs Bo needed.

At 5:53 A.M. Lucky pulled into the parking lot of an apartment complex worlds away from his. "This is where you live?" Too fucking early for even criminals to be up had to be the reason the car tires survived the night.

"For now." Bo uttered his first words since he'd gotten into the car. "Listen. You could stay with me if you wanted."

Lucky peered up at the pristine complex, guaranteed to have a working elevator, though the buildings consisted of only three floors. "Nobody'll notice you slumming, but they'd sure as hell peek out their windows at the pimpmobile parked here overnight, or at me hanging around." And probably call the cops. "It's too risky." Otherwise, Lucky would have already moved in.

"I don't like staying here and you staying there." Bo opened the car door and stepped out.

"I'm not staying there. Some minimum wage worker is."

"Wanna come up for coffee... or something?" Big brown eyes pleaded.

If Lucky went up to Bo's apartment, he might never leave again. Though he didn't like being at someone else's place, when it came down to a choice between his temporary digs and Bo's, he'd go where Bo was, no contest. It took every bit of his strength to say, "I reckon I'll have to take a rain check." They stared at each other a long moment through the open door.

"Well, if you're sure. I'll see you at work."

"Bo?"

"Yeah?"

"It's just a job. Remember that." Lucky left Bo standing on the sidewalk before he lost his good judgment and took the man up on his offer.

Damn, I'd have taken him up on his offer if I'd guessed that'd be the last time he'd make it. Lucky stared at the message on his phone. *"Working late, can't come over."*

He sat in his apartment, with only Walter's voice for company, should he be desperate enough for conversation to call his boss. The ever-present bass beat rattled the window. If he planned on sleeping, he'd need a good, strong sedative. Or Bo.

Maybe a drive might help. Lucky zipped up his leather jacket, pulled on a ball cap, and stepped out his door. A palmetto bug the size of a mouse skittered from under his neighbor's door and raced across the landing. Lucky raised his foot. He lowered it back down gently and let the insect slink away. Poor bastard had been through enough already if he'd escaped apartment 7B.

The ugliest Malibu this side of Hell sat in the parking lot. Damn, still there. A foray into the glove compartment produced the attachment for his iPod—his salvation from the tasteless shit his neighbors pulsed 24/7. The strains of Pachelbel's Canon soothed his soul.

The traffic on Clemson Boulevard didn't fade with the sunset, and Lucky soon remembered why he hated Clemson Boulevard—no matter how he timed it, he got stuck at every single red light. Start, roll forward a few feet, stop, until he reached the turnoff for the hospital. At that hour of night the building seemed even more imposing, lights in most windows, and a spotlight aimed on a big purple hippo in the front yard.

He edged around the building to the employee parking lot. There sat Bo's high-class SUV. Lucky rolled his gaze upward.

Administrative offices were located on the top floor. Which one was Bo's? Only a dim light shone in one window, not providing enough illumination for someone working. Could someone be up there with the lights off? Bo's new boss certainly hadn't been beaten by any ugly sticks, and with his high-dollar shirts and salon-styled hair, he might even impress somebody who didn't recognize him for the snake in the grass that he was. Evie or Eva or whatever the hell her name was called Bo's boss straight, but Danvers wouldn't be the first man to be on the down low.

And not spotting Danvers's BMW didn't mean he wasn't around somewhere. Something about the man set Lucky's asshole alert to pinging, and he'd be willing to bet more than a few skeletons hung in the bastard's closet. *Takes an asshole to know an asshole?* Lucky's conscience chided. Lucky hated his damn conscience. He'd gotten along without it for years, drugging it into a stupor, and now it decided to prance back into his life uninvited and take over. Fucking conscience. Who needed one?

A snippet of a conversation came back to him, Bo confessing a weakness for prescription drugs. Somewhere in the confines of the hospital, was Bo in need of a good ass-kicking? God, Lucky hoped not. He dug his cell phone out of his pocket. It'd be easy, a few short words, ask a direct question. Bo would answer, and they'd be done with the matter—if Bo told the truth. Instead, Lucky texted: *"What u want 4 supper?"* Their old code for *"Are you tempted?"*

If Bo and Mr. Supermodel Danvers were in a clinch somewhere, no way in hell would Bo answer. Lucky breathed easier when his phone chimed a few seconds later. A message displayed: *"U 2morrow nite."*

Lucky returned to his apartment reassured, even managing to sleep a few hours through the neighbor's all-night jam session, thanks to a pair of drug store earplugs.

"Are you coming over tonight?" The sigh and long pause confirmed Lucky's date with his right hand for stress-relief tonight. He squeezed his cell phone between his shoulder and ear while spreading peanut butter on a slice of bread.

"I'm exhausted." Bo sounded plain worn out. "I'm going back to the apartment, maybe throw together a salad or something, and go to bed. I sent you an e-mail with the names of a few vendors from our 'do not talk to' list."

Four days spent working at Rosario, and four days without sex. "You sure? I'll come over if you want."

"No, that's okay," Bo answered a bit too quickly. "It's late, and you need your rest."

Did Bo think for a moment he fooled anyone? Neither of them slept for shit without the other. Lucky'd heard of relationships based on sex, but his and Bo's "sleeping together" took a literal turn.

Unless something had suddenly changed for Bo, he wasn't sleeping any better alone than Lucky managed. What could he possibly be doing at the center that kept him drained? Lucky didn't buy his excuses for one minute. An accomplished liar himself, reading through a novice like Bo didn't take much skill. If Bo couldn't deal with the pressure of the assignment, Lucky'd have him pulled and back in Atlanta.

"Tomorrow night, I promise." Bo yawned through, "Good night."

Resigned to another night of his own company, Lucky munched his sandwich and busied himself researching the legitimate wholesalers whose products arrived regularly at the center. Other than an FDA warning letter dated five years previously for a matter now corrected, they appeared squeaky clean.

Next, he checked the businesses Bo e-mailed from the center's "do not talk to" list, peeling back layers to find owners, employees, or anything else attention-getting. One entity lost its license to operate in New Jersey for selling counterfeit contraceptives. The owner wasted no time setting up shop in Kentucky, under a new business name. Lucky fired off an e-mail to his department's legal team, asking them to check the laws of New Jersey and Kentucky. Some states conducted thorough background checks, others lacked the necessary resources—a fact unscrupulous businesses took advantage of. Lucky would lay money on the new Kentucky shop closing soon.

Restless thoughts circled 'round and 'round, always returning to Bo. He snatched up his jacket and headed out the door.

One of the advantages—the only advantage, in Lucky's mind—of traffic creeping down Clemson Boulevard was the opportunity the snail's pace provided to become acquainted with the area. He'd spotted an Italian restaurant a few days ago, and took the opportunity to stop by. Bo needed to eat more than a few lettuce leaves and cucumber slices. If his favorite eggplant parmesan didn't tempt him, nothing would.

A half hour later a to-go tray scented the Malibu's interior with spices and tomato sauce. Lucky made his way to Bo's apartment building. Fuck. He hadn't a clue which apartment Bo lived in. A few clicks on his work phone gave him his answer. He waited, expecting Bo to show up at any minute. Fifteen minutes went by, then thirty. Giving up after an hour, Lucky drove to the hospital. Bo's SUV sat in the parking lot. No lights shown from the building's top floor. Well damn. In a choice between Lucky or whatever'd caught Bo's attention inside the children's center, Lucky'd lost out. He gave up and went home.

"Here," he said, shoving Bo's meal into the hands of the guy sitting outside the apartment's main entrance. Instead of his own apartment, he approached his neighbor's.

It took several minutes of pounding to get their attention over the raucous music blaring. A man opened the door, wearing blue jeans and a stained wife-beater shirt that might once upon a time have been white.

"Yeah, what you want?" A cigarette hung from his lips and he glared at Lucky with bloodshot eyes. How the hell did the asshole stand the music blasting with a rather obvious hangover? His breath reeked of day-old Jack Daniels.

"I'm asking you nicely to turn your music down."

"I ain't gotta listen to you. I pay rent. I can do whatever the fuck I want." He slammed the door in Lucky's face. A moment later the volume shot up to painful levels.

If not for the need to keep his cover, Lucky would be featured on the front page of the newspaper the following day, facing some serious assault charges. Instead, he marched back downstairs, where shirtless guy sat in his usual chair, licking tomato sauce from his fingers.

"You got any idea where the breaker box is?"

"Man, whatever you up to, I ain't..."

Lucky hunched down, putting them eye-to-eye. "I fed you, and I'm not in the mood for any more shit. Now, can you show me where the breaker box is?" Lucky let the guy see every bit of the homicidal asshole living inside of him.

"Yeah, man. Calm down. I know where it is." He stood and dug possibly the world's largest keychain from the pocket of the too-big jeans hanging nearly off his ass. "Follow me."

"You're the super?"

"Shh...don't tell anybody, or folks might ask me to actually do something around here." He gave Lucky a conspiratorial grin.

Lucky ducked his head in a "lead on" gesture.

The guy led him down to the basement and tried a few keys before opening the door to an unfinished concrete block room filled with mops, buckets, ladders, and other tools of a building superintendent's trade.

On the far wall a gray panel door beckoned. Lucky flipped it open. "Are the breakers by apartment or floor?"

"Apartment. I'm taking it you want a good night's sleep?"

Lucky nodded. The guy reached out and flipped a switch. The evening grew much quieter.

"Thanks, man." Lucky dug a twenty out of his pocket.

"Don't mention it."

After a brief side trip to the Malibu, Lucky returned upstairs, plugged his iPod into the cheap stereo he'd found in the place, and turned up the volume to full blast. Not a peep came from next door. Lucky scrolled to his "Crazy" playlist, as in "Songs to Drive Coworkers Crazy," and hit the "play" button on his favorite form of torture.

Positioning himself as close to his neighbor's wall as humanly possible, he screeched loud and off-key, and not necessarily in tune, with Billy Ray Cyrus's crooning.

CHAPTER TEN

The next morning Lucky *accidentally* bumped into Bo in the clinic's coffee shop. Stalking? Who, him? "Hey, tomorrow's Saturday and Walter wants me back in Atlanta. You coming? I figured with us being this close to the state line, we can drive back up tomorrow night and stay near Cherokee. Maybe ride around in the mountains a bit, or go to the casino. The mountain laurels are blooming up there, too, right?" Cherokee, far enough from home not to risk being seen.

"I'm sorry, but I have to work. Maybe some other time," Bo replied.

What? As bad as Bo harped about learning more about each other, he intended to pass up a golden opportunity? "Why do you have to work? I thought you hospital executive types got weekends off."

Bo gusted out the longest breath Lucky'd ever heard. "With the drug shortage crisis, I'm up to my eyeballs, calling every damned manufacturer in the country. Most of the pharmacy staff are pulling overtime, too." He stared into his tea, fingers clinched so tightly around the cup that the cardboard started to crumple. Huh? Bo didn't lie often, at least not about important things. Until lately. "Maybe next time."

"Well, how about tonight? You said you'd come over."

"Sorry, Lucky. I truly am, but I have work to do."

After another night alone, Lucky headed back to Atlanta to complete a few reports and relinquish the microphone he'd kept from his last assignment. Damn it. Keith had to go running to Walter, didn't he? Lucky'd intended to stay the weekend at his own home, but found himself halfway back to Anderson before realizing he'd missed his turn for the grocery store.

At nine o'clock on a Saturday night, Bo couldn't possibly be working, yet his Acura sat in its normal spot outside of Rosario. Damn. What was up with him? He didn't call Lucky all weekend, and Lucky found the Acura in the parking lot on Sunday at seven A.M., noon, and six P.M. Did Bo ever go home? Lucky debated calling Walter, but what would he say? "Bo's really involved in his work"? Still, the sinking in the pit of his stomach remained.

On Monday morning, Ava said, "I'm liking Eric a whole lot better than Danvers. That man does what it takes to get the job done."

Eric? Oh, they meant Bo, or rather, Eric Scott, the new assistant buyer.

"And, honey, he got an ass on him!" Martin exclaimed, tracing his hands around an imaginary hiney.

Lucky attempted to sear the man with laser vision. It didn't work.

Ava shot Martin a dirty look. "Don't you be talking 'bout my boy, now. He don't mind rolling up his sleeves, unlike some other people I could name."

What the hell was she talking about?

He barely made it to his apartment before texting: *"U R coming over 2 nite. No excuses."* If Bo didn't have a real good reason for staying at the hospital night after night, an intervention loomed. Ava might have given him a good report, but Bo's office sat on the fourth floor. What was he doing in the pharmacy?

For once the neighbors were fairly quiet. However, if they started their normal shit tonight, Lucky might have to kill them, or whip out the badge he kept carefully hidden in his closet, along with the golf shirt and ball cap emblazoned with the SNB logo.

A few moments later his cell phone chimed with an answer from Bo. *"K. Catching cab."* Not an overwhelming response, but Lucky would take it.

He shoved dirty dishes into the dishwasher, scooped clothes off the floor and tossed them into the closet, and put a pot of water on the stove to make Bo a cup of green tea. A knock counterpointed the steady *ba-boom, ba-boom* starting up from the next apartment. Fucking hell! Why couldn't the assholes be decent neighbors for one damned night? Lucky opened the door to find Bo slumped against the wall, shirt wrinkled and hair in an every-follicle-for-itself state of disarray.

"You look like warmed over shit." Lucky held the door open, suspicions about a drug relapse igniting anew.

Bo managed a half-hearted smile. "Yeah, it's good to see you, too." He staggered into the apartment and collapsed onto Lucky's couch. "God, am I ever tired."

"Tired? What do you do every day? Sit behind a desk and talk on the phone?" Catty, yes, but after days of being ignored, Lucky wasn't in the mood to play nice.

"I've been scrambling since daybreak, tracking down dead-end leads for someone who might supply us with some drugs."

Lucky put a finger to his lips. "Shh... keep your voice down. You'll get my crackhead neighbors excited shouting the 'D' word."

Bo pinned Lucky a glassy-eyed glare. "I don't care who's living over there, the scary's on this side of the wall. As I was saying, I've been following leads, trying to locate *pharmaceuticals* for the hospital." He gave Lucky a "happy now?" face.

"What kind of leads? Any of interest?"

Bo dropped his head back to rest on padded upholstery. "We've been approached by seventeen different wholesalers today, not on the list I gave you, who've offered us stock at ridiculous prices. The first question they ask is what meds we're having trouble getting so they can go snatch them up and sell them to us for enormous markups, the bastards. It's against company policy to tell them anything.

"Graham called another meeting with the department heads for tomorrow. We're putting in one more plea to let us consider a gray market broker. We're pretty fucking desperate."

"Graham?" And *we're?*

"Mr. Danvers, the head buyer."

Lucky had a file on Graham Danvers, such as it was. Squeaky clean with a nauseating disposition toward humanitarian awards. Apparently, he invested a good bit of time and money in local charities. Ava didn't seem to like him. The highly vocal pharmacy tech just became Lucky's new best friend. "Bo, remember what I told you about getting personally involved with suspects? You've got to remain objective."

Bo shot to his feet. "Damn it, Lucky! Graham isn't a suspect! He's a pharmacy buyer, for crying out loud. Do you have to be suspicious of everybody?"

He had to ask? "Yes, I do. It's in my job description."

"Your job description is the same as mine. I read it, I signed it. There's nothing in there about mandatory trust issues." Bo added under his breath, "Or about being an asshole."

"Hey, maybe you got a new revision. Take Keith, for example. 'Asshole' was definitely in his."

Bo pinched the bridge of his nose between his thumb and forefinger. "Lucky, I work with Graham, and trust me, he's on the up and up."

"Oh my God! You haven't told him why you're there, have you?" Shoving Bo back toward Atlanta seemed more and more likely.

Arms folded across his chest, Bo glowered, the stance and expression reminding Lucky of himself. "Do you actually believe I'm an idiot?"

Lucky opened his mouth to reply but Bo cut him off. "Don't answer that. But remember, I graduated head of my class at pharmacy school and served my country in Afghanistan. I'm not a moron and I'd appreciate it if you didn't treat me like one."

After a moment Lucky ventured again, "Did you?"

"Did I what?"

"Tell him why you're there."

Throwing his hands up in the air, Bo stomped across the living room. "No, you suspicious son of a bitch, I didn't. But I also believe you're out of your mind if you consider the man a suspect." He flopped back down on the couch with a huff.

Lucky remained standing, leaning against the bar separating the poor excuse for a kitchen from the poor excuse for a living room. He studied his partner, cataloguing the telltale signs of burnout. Tired? Check. Moody? Check. Less sociable? Double check. Some folks weren't cut out for handling the type of shit the Southeastern Narcotics Bureau dealt with, and from day one Lucky had suspected Bo wouldn't make it. Of course, he'd said the same about Keith and anyone else who'd stayed long enough for Lucky to learn their names.

"Are you hungry?" Lucky asked, though at the moment he didn't have much in the way of vegetarian cuisine handy, unless he counted the makings for peanut butter and jelly sandwiches.

"No." Bo stared out the window at the brick wall of the next building.

"Can I fix you some green tea?"

A weak, "That'd be nice," barely reached Lucky's ears.

Moseying into the kitchen and going through the motions of tea preparation allowed Lucky time to mull things over. He recognized the listlessness, the lack of greeting when he opened the door. Even to himself, he and Bo appeared to be merely coworkers right now, nothing more. Losing Bo as a lover hurt like hell, for he alone came close to understanding what made Lucky tick. Or, lacking understanding, accepted Lucky's quirks as part and parcel, never trying to change what made Lucky "Lucky." Bo only nudged and manipulated for the greater good, like weaning him off caffeine so he slept better. Oh, and the whole, "Tell me about yourself, Lucky" thing. Maybe Bo should have been a shrink instead of a pharmacist.

Plain and simple, the man couldn't handle the job, though Lucky couldn't imagine very many people dealing with sick kids and remaining unchanged. Before when the pressure reached critical levels, Bo sought comfort in alprazolam. Had he resorted to self-medicating again?

Watching a man he'd come to care about slowly slide back into the nightmare of addiction, and a possible jail sentence, was more than Lucky could bear. He'd do his damnedest, talk to Bo in a better moment, and only if he couldn't break through would he fill Walter in.

Not tonight. If Bo allowed him to, tonight Lucky would hold him, love him one last time before doing what he had to do. Because if Lucky's hunch proved right, Bo might never forgive him.

His chest tightened, momentarily cutting off his air. No way in hell could he throw Bo under the bus. But what could he do? He couldn't simply turn a blind eye and hope the man came around on his own, could he? No, he couldn't, but as long as Bo didn't jeopardize their assignment, he'd protect his partner however possible—if Bo allowed someone else to take care of him for a change. Afterward, when they got back to Atlanta, into therapy he'd go.

Damn it! Moisture sprang to Lucky's eyes and he blinked it back. He added sweetener to Bo's tea, stirring and then taking the cup into the living room to face the cold hard truth.

Bo wore a more neutral expression. "I didn't come here to fight," he said. "I sent you my reports today, and don't have much other news to share. I came here to see you."

He took the cup from Lucky's hand, gave a brief nod of thanks, and took a few quick sips. After setting the cup on the coffee table, he extended a hand to Lucky. "Let's go to bed."

Lucky led the way to the tiny room he slept in each night, to the double bed he found far too empty. He turned on the bedside lamp.

Bo made short work of his white button-down shirt while stepping out of a pair of loafers. Lucky joined in to remove a rather stubborn belt and slide his pants down and off.

Unwilling to risk a mood-dampening chewing out by Bo, Lucky hung the shirt from a doorknob, and folded the pants and placed them on the dresser. He watched as Bo peeled a T-shirt over his head, his sleek runner's build thinner and less muscular than Lucky remembered. Or maybe he misremembered. They hadn't seen much of each other in the past month, being on separate assignments.

While Bo reclined on the bed, Lucky shimmied out of his own T-shirt and jeans.

"I've missed you," Bo said, holding his arms out. Lucky slid into them, plundering Bo's mouth. Faint traces of familiar cologne mingled with the distinct taste of green tea. Home. Lucky's heart clenched. What would he do without this?

He traced his hands up Bo's sides, skating roughened fingers across smooth skin. Gasps and twitches and sharply drawn breaths guided him on his quest to bring pleasure. Lucky shrugged off the yoke of worry and lost himself in Bo's long moan when he caressed the point where leg and thigh joined. The scent of the man, the solid rightness of Bo in his bed, overwhelmed Lucky's plans to make their evening all about Bo. His cock rose to nestle against his lover's sparsely furred thigh.

The world outside faded away, leaving only the here and now. He trailed kisses down Bo's throat, stopping to savor the steady throb of Bo's pulse quivering against his lips. What went on in the man's mind? At what point had the two of them begun slipping apart?

He couldn't think about that now, and shimmied down Bo's body to take hardened flesh into his mouth. If this were his only way to connect to Bo, he'd give it all he had. He sucked Bo down, way down, and slid upward again, tracing a bulging vein up the underside of Bo's cock with his tongue.

Bo began to struggle—Lucky held fast. Bo pushed him off. "No. Not like this." He rummaged through the bedside table, finding the supplies Lucky had stashed there in hopes of future need. Their gazes met. Something haunted hid within the depths of Bo's sable-eyed regard, gone before fully registered.

Supplies in hand, he wasted no time turning Lucky on his back and unrolling a condom down his length. *Oho! So this is how it's going to be!*

Bo slicked two fingers and crawled on top, locking their lips together like their lives depended on the connection. Grunts, moans, and rocking motions hinted at Bo preparing himself.

He pushed back and Lucky groaned, sinking inch by inch into welcoming flesh. "God how I've missed this," Bo murmured.

So have I. Lucky gripped Bo's hips. He gave his brain cells the night off and fell into the slick-slide, thrust-squeeze, pant-whimper rhythm of their coupling.

Bo's moans grew more urgent, his quiet, "Oh God!" a strangled sob. Lucky took a deep breath, splayed his hands on Bo's thighs, and withdrew.

"Wha..."

He cut off Bo's protest with a kiss, flipped him onto his back, and slid back into delicious heat. Face-to-face, with the erotic sensation of hands exploring bare skin, he crashed his mouth against Bo's.

The bed squeaked, Lucky gulped in air, and Bo emitted frantic sounds and not-quite words.

Quivering began deep within. Lucky stopped and scrunched his eyes closed. He clamped down inside, fighting, fighting. Gradually the pressure eased. He grabbed Bo's cock and frantically stroked in time with his renewed thrusts. Waves pulled back to the ocean. His muscles trembled, and he braced his weight on one arm to keep from smashing into Bo. For one brief moment all stilled. No sound, no feeling, no nothing. In one final lunge he let go. The waves crashed down.

"Oh God! Oh God!" Bo chanted.

Lucky's come-slick grip glided more easily. He lost the battle with gravity and weakened limbs, hanging on to Bo for dear life. *Thumpa, thumpa, thumpa* beat in his ears, but not from the apartment next door. He sucked in sweet, sweet air. Bo's muscles tightened, drawing a shuddering aftershock from Lucky. That was... That was... Holy shit.

Lucky waited for Bo's inevitable retreat to the bathroom to clean up. Gentle snores reached his ears. What the fuck? He rose up on his elbow, staring down at Bo's slack face. Asleep. Thirty seconds after coming he fell asleep. Damned if that didn't beat all.

The dark circles under Bo's eyes explained a lot. Poor guy, must be plum tuckered out. Lucky held him a few moments, memorizing the feel of the man in his arms. What he wouldn't give to erase the worries plaguing Bo's mind.

Bladder pressure built. Lucky ignored it, settling on his side and bringing Bo against his chest. His bladder twinged again. Lucky shifted to a more comfortable position. Once more and... *All right already!* The chill of the bedroom provided an unwelcome contrast to the lump of warmth lying in bed. Lucky tossed a wistful gaze over his shoulder while padding to the bathroom.

While washing his hands, he stared at his reflection in the mirror. "You think you got all the damned answers," he snapped. "What now, huh?"

He returned to the bed and wiped Bo down with a damp washcloth. Bo shivered. Lucky tucked him under the covers and settled on the side of the bed.

Something was very, very wrong here. Normally a ball of energy, now Bo resembled an extra for a zombie movie. Lucky lifted one eyelid. Bo let out a *Hnnnn* and jerked away. His pupils didn't appear dilated or contracted, yet he lied about his whereabouts, seemed unconcerned with his appearance, and could spin his moods on a dime. Burnout? Addiction? They shared some of the same symptoms. And how did Bo's combat-induced PTSD figure into the equation? Lucky snorted. Hell, if he'd been through half of what Bo had, he'd depend on chemicals too. *You're not helping here, Lucky.* Yeah, right.

On the one hand, he owed it to Bo to do everything in his power to help him. On the other hand, although he'd satisfied his legal obligation to Walter, paying back a moral debt meant he couldn't keep secrets. His assignment, his career, and newfound self-worth all screamed at him to do the right thing. But what was the right thing? How in the hell could he ask, "Hey, you getting stoned?" without earning more "suspicious asshole" points.

Whatever the solution, it wasn't likely to magically appear in the next few minutes. Lucky turned off the light and settled in beside Bo, clinging to his lover, for however long he kept the title.

CHAPTER ELEVEN

Thwack! What the fuck? *Thwack!* A hand smacked against Lucky's head. He grabbed Bo's arm before he got swatted again. "Bo! Bo! Wake up!"

Bo bolted upright. He blinked, eyes vacant until he woke enough to focus. "Oh my God! What time is it?"

Lucky aimed a blurry gaze at the clock. "Four thirty. Go back to sleep. We've got plenty of time."

"No, we don't!" Bo flipped on the light and jumped out of bed. He scrambled into his clothes, mismatching the buttons on his shirt.

"What are you talking about?" Lucky rubbed the side of his head. "You don't have to be at work until nine. I can take you later, or you can call a cab."

"You don't understand! I have to be in the pharmacy before six." Bo hopped up and down, wriggling into his pants.

Lucky shot to his feet. "You're right, I don't understand, and you're not leaving this room until I do." He dodged around Bo to block the exit. Stark naked and only five foot six against Bo's six feet, he probably didn't appear intimidating, but come hell or high water, Bo wasn't leaving until he'd explained a few things.

"The drugs, Lucky! I gotta go get the drugs ready."

Lucky caught Bo's arm, hauling him back to the bed. "Sit!" He aimed a glare and a finger.

"I don't have time…"

"I said, sit, damn it!"

Bo sat. "Don't talk to me like a dog. And my name isn't Damn It!"

Lucky wasn't about to waste time with petty bickering. "For days now you've been staying late at the hospital, even

94

lying—lying to *me*—about where you were. Now if you've had some kind of relapse, or are in some kind of trouble, I want to help you. But first, you gotta come clean. Why do you need to go to the pharmacy? Your office isn't anywhere near there."

"But I *am* a pharmacist."

This was too important to let Bo off with a half-assed excuse. "Not anymore. You work for Walter Smith, and you do whatever the hell he tells you to keep from breaking whatever the hell agreement you've got going with him."

"I'm not violating my probation."

Lucky gripped Bo's shoulders, holding him still when he tried to rise. "Then tell me what's going on. Have you given in to temptation?"

Bo shrugged Lucky's hands away. "Is that what you think? That I'd take medicine from those kids who so badly need it? Do you think I'd stoop that low?"

Stubbornly holding his ground, Lucky shot back, "Addiction blurs the lines between good people and bad behavior. While I don't want to believe you'd do such a thing—"

They stared each other down. Bo glanced away first, bravado deflating under the force of a harsh exhale. He dragged his fingers through his already disheveled hair. "No, I wouldn't, but I understand why you might think so. I guess I should have told you already, but I thought you might try to stop me, tell me it's not my fight."

Lucky tensed. He wasn't going to like what came next, he'd lay money on it. "What's not your fight?"

Bo collapsed in on himself, sitting stoop-shouldered on the bed. "You realize how short the center is on meds, right?"

"Yes."

"And the hospital refuses to let us buy from the gray market?"

"Yes." That wasn't news.

"We... a few other pharmacists and I, have been working after hours, scrounging to get enough doses to go around. If we can't get prefills, we buy liquid if we can and load the syringes in-house. We've filled capsules. As a last resort we snatch up raw materials and compound the drugs ourselves. We're tired, Lucky, every last one of us, but if we stop, patients will die." He stared at his twisted-together fingers where they lay in his lap.

"You'd take the gray market goods." It wasn't a question.

"In a flat minute. We're desperate."

Lucky hated to ask, but the words came unbidden from his mouth. "Is Danvers part of your little after-hours party?"

"No. He's home with his wife and kids."

Hmm... apparently Danvers's humanitarian streak only existed to get him noticed, and didn't extend to good works committed with no promise of glory.

Lucky grasped Bo's chin, raising it until their eyes met. Bo Schollenberger was perhaps the best man Lucky had ever met, and far too good for the likes of an ex-con. But if Lucky weren't around to save this man from himself, the world would chew him up and spit him out.

Suffering abuse at the hands of someone honor-bound to protect you changed a man. Walking down the street expecting gunfire from every civilian changed a man. Watching friends die changed a man. After dealing with all that, Bo was no weakling, and somewhere underneath that gentle exterior lurked a recovering warrior. With a little time and healing, the hard-edged Marine would return to kick ass and take names. Until that day came, Lucky was asshole enough for them both.

With the best of intentions, he opened his mouth to deliver a good, harsh dose of reality check, but in the end, with mournful eyes begging him for something he couldn't figure out, he replied, "What can I do to help?"

Lucky dropped Bo off at his apartment to shower and head to work. Throughout the day he considered the problem, wracking his brain to find a solution. Who was he kidding? If a smart guy like Bo couldn't figure it out, Lucky didn't stand a hope in hell. Given a few days to work out logistics, he'd gladly steal a whole truck of whatever Bo needed and deliver it to the center door. Ha! That'd earn him a black mark on his next annual review.

He scanned his way into the pharmacy.

"Hallelujah!" Ava exclaimed, eyeing the sealed totes on Lucky's cart. "Eric! Get over here. Christmas done come early, baby. You gotta sign for these controls."

"Christmas? It's only a third of what we need." Bo avoided Lucky's eyes while checking in the inventory and carting the drugs to the pharmacy's restricted access area. So that's how it worked. Martin signed in regular inventory, while buyers checked in the good stuff. Damn. The first "good stuff" shipment in a week? For a hospital this size?

Bo steadied himself against the cart while signing for the shipment. How far did he intend to push himself before he buckled? After he returned the empty totes, Lucky pushed the cart into the hallway.

Bo slipped past, shoulder skimming Lucky's. "Another meeting," he whispered in passing. He stopped outside the conference room, briefly meeting Lucky's eyes before opening the door and disappearing into the room.

"Inside the heart of this whole damned mess," Lucky huffed. "Hell of a place to be." He entered the elevator and punched the basement button.

The door slid open, a woman stepped on, and Lucky stepped off, noticing too late the big red "3" on a garishly painted wall. A giraffe jumped rope while a lion pushed a cub in a swing on the hallway mural.

He turned too quickly to press the down arrow and nearly rammed his cart into a wheelchair. A little girl stared up at him, all big blue eyes and bald head. Standing, she wouldn't have reached Lucky's waist. An equally bald Barbie doll lay on the floor. The girl reached over the chair arm, fingers not quite long enough to grab hold.

"I'll get it." Lucky squatted down to retrieve the doll. When he glanced up to return the toy, adoring eyes stared at him, dimples showing in each cheek when the girl smiled.

"Thank you, mister. You're new, aren't you? My name's Stephanie, but everybody calls me Steph. What's yours?"

"Reg..." Lucky started to say. Gazing into the sweet face of an angel, he couldn't bring himself to lie. "Folks call me Lucky."

"Lucky?" The girl giggled. "That's not a man's name, that's my kitty's name!"

Sammy probably waited downstairs with more packages, wondering where he'd gotten off to. Lucky couldn't care less. "Oh yeah? What kind of cat you got?" No matter how the girl answered, Mrs. Griggs likely had one just like it.

"A tuxedo kitty. He's black and white and sleeps on my bed when I'm home."

Kneeling beside a wheelchair in a children's ward at a cancer center, Lucky lost his heart. This sweet little girl likely went through hell and back on a regular basis, and yet she smiled at a stranger.

"How do you like my doll? My brother cut her hair off." Steph didn't sound a bit upset. Lucky had done the same to one of Charlotte's dolls once, and she hadn't been nearly as approving. "He said she was my doll, she should look like me." The girl stroked her fingers over Barbie's smooth head.

At a loss for what to say, Lucky tried, "Sounds like a good brother."

"Oh he is! Know what my Aunt Karen did?"

He feigned surprise. "No! What?"

"She let her hair grow down to her butt." She whispered, "Mom says butt's a bad word. Daddy says it's okay as long as I don't say it in front of Nana. Anyway, Aunt Karen went and got all her hair chopped off! They're gonna make a wig for me." Her dimples appeared impossibly deep.

What the hell could he say to that? "That's good."

He stared at a girl he'd just met, picturing a younger version of his sister. An uncomfortable pressure grew in his chest. The elevator chimed and Lucky rose. "I gotta get back to work now." The door opened. Lucky stood and watched the doors close. He'd catch the next one.

"Come back and see me, okay?"

"Sure, Steph." When the doors opened again Lucky stepped onto the elevator. His heart pounded a frantic beat, and his breath wouldn't come. "Dear Lord in Heaven," he prayed for the first time in recent memory. "If you're up there, please save that little girl." He wiped at his eyes. Damn, what kind of cleaner did they use that stung so badly?

That evening he called Walter. "Boss, you've told me time and again how we're not supposed to get personally involved, but we need some help here." He rattled off items from Bo's shopping list, providing a few contacts from his old lawless days who'd been lawful enough at the time to escape prosecution.

"I see you've been talking to Bo. He sent in a list this morning. I'll tell you the same thing I told him, Lucky. We're not in the pharmaceutical brokering business. There's a nationwide crisis going on. Hopefully, our efforts to put an end to the gray market will help. Beyond that, there's not much we can do." Walter paused before asking, "Is everything all right? It's not like you to show an interest in anything besides finishing up your case."

No, it wasn't. It had to be Bo's influence. "Mellowing in my old age, I guess." Lucky rubbed his fingers against his temple. The neighbor's stereo sent a throbbing pulse through his head. He gripped his cell phone to keep from hurling it against the wall. Fuckers wouldn't even hear it hit.

Walter might have sighed. The music was too damned loud to tell. "If something comes up, I'll keep you informed."

Lucky hung up the phone and tossed it to the couch. What the fuck had he gotten himself into? He paced. He flumped down on the couch. He jumped up and paced some more. Nervous energy pulsed harder than the neighbor's music. He dragged the coffee table into the kitchen and shoved the couch against the wall, leaving a few feet of empty space.

Ewww... That was some nasty-ass carpet, most likely trodden on by palmetto bugs or worse things. Towels. Lots of towels. It took four to give Lucky enough room to work. He sucked in a deep breath and squatted, dropped down for a pushup, then sprang to his feet, arms in the air. "One!"

He dropped again, keeping time with the *thud, thud, thud* from next door. The pounding threw his count off. He set his goal for lasting through the song. At least the tuneless shit might be good for something.

After roughly five minutes of burpees, he rolled into a side plank position, free hand to the back of his head. He raised his lower knee to upper elbow, repeating the process until he faltered. He took a five minute break and rolled to the other side, continuing until unable to lift his leg any more.

Worn out but still frustrated, he grabbed his apartment key, locked his door, and sprinted to the stairwell. Up, down, up, down, he jogged down seven flights and back again ten times, mindful only of his breathing, nothing more.

The sun had set before Lucky returned to his apartment. How late did Bo plan to work, and did the man bother to eat while pulling overtime? "Gotta watch out for my partner," Lucky told the empty room.

After a quick shower, he donned a pair of jeans and a T-shirt and slipped on his shoes before heading for the nearest pizza place.

Thirty minutes later Lucky dropped off two large Tony's Pizza boxes at the main desk, pretending to be a delivery boy. In a hospital this size, he wasn't likely to be recognized. "One veggie and one pepperoni, for the pharmacy," he said. He didn't explain he'd gotten an extra pizza for Bo's coworkers only because of a buy one get one free sale. But hell, do-gooders had to eat too, right?

He returned home and spent the next few hours on his computer, checking for whatever Walter might have found. No matter how many times he looked, no messages appeared on his cell phone. A few minutes before he crawled into bed, his phone finally chirped. He snatched it off the nightstand to read, *"Thx."*

CHAPTER TWELVE

Another day, after another night spent alone. Lucky schlepped a few pitiful totes up to the pharmacy. One look at Ava and Martin confirmed they'd likely been a part of Bo's drug packing party the night before. Lucky shot a lethal glare at a woman in a white dispensing jacket who appeared far too rested to have been up half the night.

"Shit! Is that all?" Ava moaned. "This won't last half a day."

Good people. They might paint themselves blue and dance naked around bonfires on their off time, for all Lucky cared, but they actually gave a fuck about their jobs. He'd make it a point not to growl the next time Ava smiled at him.

At lunchtime Lucky joined the throng in the cafeteria, hoping to catch sight of Bo. The man couldn't keep pushing himself like this. Lucky made it halfway through the lunch line before realizing he'd made selections with Bo in mind and not for himself—vegetable soup ("No, sir, there's no meat in there"), a Granny Smith apple, and a deviled egg sandwich on wheat bread.

Nearly every chair held a uniformed worker of some kind, but Lucky managed to find a two-seater table out of the way. He stared down at his plate. Had Bo bothered to eat today? A shadow fell over his table. "I hate to bother you, but there doesn't seem to be anywhere else to sit. Mind if I join you?"

The smile on Bo's face didn't reach his eyes. *Uh-oh. What now?*

"Sure, if you don't mind sittin' with a basement dweller."

Something flashed across Bo's face that Lucky couldn't quite identify. Embarrassment, maybe? For Lucky being a basement dweller?

101

"You should try the coleslaw," Bo suggested. "Pretty tasty." Like Lucky guessed, Bo had chosen the vegetable soup and egg salad sandwich. He kept up a running monologue of inane banter, merely picking at his food. Lucky moved the apple from his plate to Bo's.

The more Bo said, the faster he talked, and the faster his leg bounced. At last he excused himself and took off for the door, barely pausing long enough to deposit his tray and garbage in the bins provided. What? He didn't recycle? He must be pretty tired, or shook up.

Lucky finished his meal and stood to leave when he noticed the folded sheet of paper where Bo's glass had been. He ran a napkin over the table, sliding the note under his lunch tray. On his way out the door, he parted company with the tray and slipped the note into his pocket.

He ducked into a convenient bathroom and parked himself in a stall to read Bo's message. *The hospital administrator refuses to buy from the gray market, but Danvers isn't going to listen. He gave me this number to call. They didn't ask what I needed, they told me, and rattled off a list of everything we're short of. They even had meds we haven't been able to get in weeks. How the fuck did they find out?* He'd given a number with a local area code.

"Danvers" not "Graham." So, Bo felt the need to add a little distance, did he? Was he losing faith in his boss? The bathroom door opened and closed. No telling who'd just entered. Instead of calling Walter, Lucky texted: *"It's going down."*

Tired of spinning his wheels and ready for some action, when Lucky arrived back at the seventh floor armpit of Hell he lived in, he donned tennis shoes and running shorts. The evenings were getting warmer this close to May, and with no particular destination in mind, he ran.

He blanked his mind, focusing on nothing more than the steady in/out of his breathing, heavy pulse of blood through his body, and his rhythmic footfalls pushing him on.

A man and his body, no background noise. No work, no Walter, no future, no past. Only now. No wonder Bo loved running.

Gradually rational thought returned and Lucky slowed, rolling over the events of the past few days in his mind, always coming back to Danvers. A humanitarian, news articles said, though they'd not mentioned a wife or kids. Normally Lucky's intel served him better. Maybe they were divorced. But no, Bo said Danvers didn't voluntarily work overtime because of a wife and kids waiting at home.

If the hospital and the patients meant as much to the overpaid asshole as he pretended, wouldn't he do every legitimate thing in his power to help in this time of crisis, like working overtime, before turning to questionable sources?

In, out, Lucky breathed. *In, out.* Why did Danvers suddenly buck the hospital and decide on his own to deal with a possibly shady vendor? And of hundreds of gray market wholesalers out there, why give Bo a single number, when Bo got paid to shop around and find the best deal? Surely with an underling at his disposal, Danvers hadn't actually gone through the trouble of negotiations himself, had he?

Danvers's recommendation gave Lucky a name, someone unknown to the SNB database. Again, what was up with the shoddy intel? While they'd taken on this exercise to ferret out newcomers to the game, Lucky hadn't expected any surprises.

Who the hell was Primero Care? What was Danvers's connection? Not many wholesalers, legit or otherwise, managed to fly under the SNB radar for long.

He returned to his apartment, sweaty and out of breath. Shirtless Guy sat by the door, flipping through a motorcycle magazine. "Hey, G-man," he said, not bothering to take his eyes off his magazine. "Your boss is here. I let him into your apartment."

"G-man? My boss?" Lucky swallowed hard. Had the super been snooping in his apartment?

"Don't go getting paranoid," the guy said. "I don't reckon nobody's pegged you but me."

Lucky glanced right and left to assure no one else listened in. "What makes you say that?"

"Number one, you the only one living here not to hit me up for drugs. Number two, that guy comes by from time to time?

103

He throws off Fed vibes like sonar. You need to tell Junior to back off on the gung-ho a bit.

Bo? Gung-ho? Really? "And you are?"

Shirtless Guy stood, gaining IQ points by the second. "I'm just a man who watches the world. But don't worry. I like having you around. This used to be a nice neighborhood when my granddaddy bought the place. Your kind keeps the crime down." He turned and ambled around the building.

What the fuck? Lucky checked the parking lot, but didn't notice Walter's distinctive black Range Rover. Probably didn't want his tires stolen.

He clattered up the stairs, giving Walter plenty of warning, since the neighbors seemed to be observing some kind of moment of silence. Maybe they'd blown out their stereo and run out to buy a new one. His door was unlocked, his boss sprawled on his couch. "Crack central, how may I help you?" Lucky asked.

Walter swept his hand out, indicating a line of vials on the coffee table. "I brought my own, thanks. We didn't get much on Primero Care. They're a startup, apparently less than a year old." He sat up, resting his elbows on a pair of meaty thighs roughly the size of tree trunks. "They're licensed as a pharmacy, but there's no record of them dispensing any medicines. They appear to be selling one hundred percent of their purchases to other entities. Sit." Walter unrolled a flowchart across his lap.

"Hold on a sec." Lucky dashed into the kitchen for a towel and bottle of water. "Need anything?"

"No, thank you."

Lucky dropped down beside Walter, downing his bottled water in one go. He mopped at his sweaty hair with the towel. "Now, what did you want to show me?

Walter pointed at the diagram in his lap. "In a perfect world, the manufacturer," he jabbed a finger at the first point on the chart, "sells product to the wholesale distributor, here." He moved his finger to the next rectangle. "The wholesaler sells to hospitals and pharmacies." The third rectangle came into play. "However," Walter slipped the diagram behind a much more complex markup, "based on product and lot numbers provided by Bo, in this case, the wholesaler purchased stock from the manufacturer, selling it to another wholesaler for a phenomenal profit. The new purchaser sold it to another wholesaler." Names and numbers filled the page. "The last wholesaler passed control to Primero Care, who offered the products to Rosario Children's Center."

Lucky whistled, staring at the vials on the table with renewed appreciation. The diagram showed mind-boggling prices. While "casual sales" took place between wholesalers on a regular basis, he'd never seen this magnitude. "You mean to tell me folks are willing to pay six hundred bucks for one dose of a med that the manufacturer sold for seven measly dollars?" Damn! The gray market had certainly expanded after Lucky and Victor's downfall. Some of the figures on Walter's chart didn't seem possible. Perhaps Lucky had been a bit hasty in going legit.

Walter held a vial up to the light. "This represents the difference between life and death to a leukemia patient. I had to pull strings to get these little beauties."

Lucky stared at Walter's chart, mentally calculating excursion times between wholesalers. "With so many changes of hands, how long have the drugs been traveling? Are they safe?"

"Start to finish, five days, from what we've learned."

"Five days? That's it?" Sometimes it took a month or more for Lucky and Victor to move a shipment.

"Some buyers never took physical possession, simply requesting the current owner to drop-ship to the next point on the chart."

"What you want me to do with these?" Lucky waved his hand toward the vials.

"Give them to Bo. Tomorrow you'll receive your first shipment of fluorouracil from Primero. Mind you, we're still walking a line. Other than violate state laws against pharmacies reselling more than five percent of its stock to another entity, Primero has done nothing legally wrong. Until the pending legislation passes, the other companies are perfectly within their rights to buy and sell."

"Even if people suffer?"

"That's why we want them out of business." Walter, so laid-back Lucky occasionally accused him of moving in reverse, growled, "We intend to make an example of them. Right now they might appear heroes, swooping in and saving the day. In reality, they're vultures, and we're going to stop them. These vials are from the same manufacturer and same lot as you're scheduled to receive tomorrow. I want Bo to swap these for some of the received goods. We need to analyze them."

"Analyze? If they're suspect, why not seize the shipment?"

"And risk cancer patients' treatments on mere suspicion? Remember, this is a lawful transaction."

"Oh." Damn. While Lucky'd learned respect for the law over the years, sometimes he didn't truly understand the nuances. If he couldn't stop Primero, he could slow down the flow of money into their greedy hands by taking out their accomplice. "Have you found anything on Danvers?"

"Not yet, but we're still searching. Do you have information you haven't yet shared?" Walter raised a bushy gray brow.

"Just a gut feeling. Being around vermin for much of my life taught me to smell the rats."

"I'd pit your intuition against most documented research any day. I'll have the team focus more on Danvers. Anything else?"

Lucky studied his mentor, the open face, the leaned-forward, I'm-all-ears stance. *Now I know how a traitor feels.* He took a few deep breaths to gather his courage. "I'm worried about Bo. He's getting too close."

Walter offered a sad little smile. "That's what he does, Lucky. You scratch the surface, you dig and you dig until your reach the heart of the matter. Bo starts inside the heart."

"Inside the heart." Lucky'd said the same thing himself.

"You don't give up easily," Walter continued, "but you've got a keen sense of when to pull back and wait rather than go charging in. Bo will learn from you. Do you have any idea how much inside information he's getting from the disgruntled pharmacists he's working with after hours?"

Oh good. The boss knew. Lucky didn't have to tell him.

Walter patted Lucky's shoulder with a heavy hand. "Now,

Keith will be back any minute to get me, and I'm due in Atlanta by morning. Keep up the good work."

Lucky lay on the couch a long time after Walter left. He and Bo worked well together. They made a good team. Damn it, he hated when Walter was right.

"Fluorouracil! Do you have any idea how much these are worth?" Bo ran his hand lovingly over the vials.

"A lot more than they should be. You need to switch those off with tomorrow's shipment. Then I'm heading back to Atlanta with the goods." *Thumpa, thumpa* pounded in the background, the wanna-be disco next door back in full swing. Damn it.

"You're leaving?"

"Are you kidding? I can't wait to get out of here. To date, we've been able to track down most of the suppliers you've given us. The others are only a matter of time."

Bo paused, more questions in his eyes than what he finally voiced. "That's it?"

"What's it?"

"We close them down? What happens to the people who need those drugs?"

"That's not our problem."

"Not our problem?"

Lucky should have gone up in a puff of smoke under Bo's glare. "Once we close down a few shady dealers, it's only a matter of time before the law goes into effect, making gray markets illegal. After the shysters are gone, the legitimate supply chain will start working again." He quoted the department's official stance. No need telling Bo that he'd already asked Walter for help for Rosario.

"Damn it, Lucky! Are you always this cold?"

"What?"

"Don't you give a damn about anything?"

Where the fuck did that come from? "Of course I do!"

"What if it was one of your nephews lying in a bed at the center? Would you be so quick to dust off your hands and walk away?"

"Bo…" Lucky sucked in a deep breath. He held out a hand.

Bo backed away. "I've got what I came for. I'm leaving now." He pulled out his cell phone and yelled Lucky's address over the neighbor's chaos. "I'll be back tomorrow with the samples," he said after hanging up his call, and left without saying goodbye.

At two in the morning Lucky lay staring at the ceiling, imagining one of Charlotte's boys lying in a bed at Rosario. He pictured Stephanie, her big eyes and bright smile, despite fighting a battle with cancer. A weight bore down on his chest. He wanted to punish the people who valued Ben Franklins over Stephanies. He wanted to fix the broken system that allowed such opportunists to flourish.

"Lucky," he groused to himself. "You're getting too fucking close."

"Here ya go!" Lucky offloaded the last package from his cart in the gift shop.

A customer approached the counter, carrying a few magazines and a box with a smiling baby on the cover. "Will you gift wrap this for me, please?"

"Can you wait a minute?" the middle-aged clerk asked Lucky. "I'll be a few minutes. I need to check these in before I sign."

Lucky grunted what he hoped sounded like an "Okay."

Instead of hurrying about her chore, the clerk asked about the customer's family, job, and a million other things. Apparently, the owner of the shiny platinum credit card was a personal friend with lots of gossip to share.

Lucky bit down on several choice words he'd like to say. He'd love to vent his spleen on the molasses-slow clerk. He'd never been known to idle well, and he rambled through the store, inspecting an item here and there to keep himself occupied. Why the hell would anyone pay those kind of prices when the same stuff was sold elsewhere for a lot less?

He rounded a corner and halted. Green eyes caught his attention first, followed by whiskers and yellow fur. Lucky stepped closer, the stuffed cat reminding him of one of his landlady's.

Through a mass of gold, he spotted a splash of black, buried beneath yellow. He dug out a black-and-white cat, wearing a black bow tie and a top hat. What had Stephanie called her cat? A tuxedo kitty?

Some unseen force guided Lucky's hand, first to caress the toy's softness, then to carry it with him to the counter.

He held out the forms for the clerk to sign, paid for the cat, and slunk away, ignoring the woman's, "Oh, do you have children, Mr. Picklesimer?"

The cat stared at him all the way down the hall. "Whatcha looking at?" he asked the stuffed toy while on the elevator. Leaving his cart by the door, he dashed down to the nurses' station. Was he a complete idiot? Other than her first name being Stephanie, he didn't even know the child he'd spoken to. What if she'd left the hospital?

He stood by the desk, waiting for the attendant to notice him. "Got supplies for us today, Reggie?" she asked.

"No. I...um..." He held up the cat. *Don't you dare tease me.*

Her face lit up. "Oh, how cute! Who is that for?"

Now came the complicated part. "Steph. I mean, Stephanie. She didn't tell me her last name."

"Big blue eyes, carries a bald Barbie, could talk the hind legs off a mule?"

Lucky chuckled. "Sounds like her."

"That'd be Stephanie Owens." The nurse's smile fell. "Poor little thing. Seems like she's been here forever." After a moment she added, "She's going to love this. Who should I say brought it?" She checked the blank card on the cat's collar.

"Lucky."

"Lucky? Who's Lucky?"

Lucky felt his face flame. "Ummm... her cat. She said he sleeps on her bed when she's at home. I thought she might like another cat to sleep with while she's here."

"Well aren't you an angel?"

Angel? Lucky'd been accused of being many things before—angel wasn't one of them.

Another nurse wandered by. "Brenda! Guess what this nice man did—" Lucky hightailed it down the hall. The last thing he needed was their misguided praise.

CHAPTER THIRTEEN

The next day Lucky made three trips to the pharmacy to lug up a single delivery. Maybe now Bo would no longer be mistaken for the walking dead. Neither would Ava and Martin.

He stepped off the elevator with his empty cart, Ava's happy squeals still ringing in his ears, and he swore Martin hadn't hugged him in gratitude but rather to grope his ass.

"Oh my God, I can't believe it." Sammy came running out of the clerk's office. "They let Danvers go! Fired him! Canned him! I heard from a guy in security. They're walking him out now."

What? "Why?"

"He pissed off the wrong people. Apparently, he bought drugs from someone the big wheels told him not to, and now he's going down." Sammy rubbed his hands together, a grin creasing his pudgy cheeks. "'Bout time if you ask me, strutting 'round here like he owns the place 'cause he married money."

"Oh shit!" With Danvers gone, Bo became the hospital's buyer, a position that just might kill him.

"'Oh shit' is right," the normally silent receiving clerk exclaimed. "Tomorrow's going to be hell."

"What do you mean?" Lucky asked.

"You'll find out tomorrow."

"You gonna be okay?" Lucky lay back in his bed, Bo cradled to his chest. He idly ran his fingers up and down his lover's back. The closed bedroom door helped muffle the chaos filtering through the living room from the next apartment, but not much. If it weren't for the threat of blowing Bo's cover, he'd say the hell with it and move to the nice part of town, pimp-mobile and all.

111

"I reckon. The hospital administrator stopped by today to make sure I was up to the job."

"Are you?"

"I suppose I should be pissed off at your lack of faith in me, but the truth is, I honestly don't know. I'm in over my head. Sure, I helped place orders at some of the pharmacies I worked for, but nowhere near the scale of Rosario's purchase orders."

"What'd the admin say?"

"We held a conference call with Walter, who agreed I'd continue on as buyer while Rosario finds someone else. Danvers had only been there less than a year, and from what I heard, he'd started trying to bring in Primero a week after he started."

A red flag waved. "That's odd. Walter believed Primero to be a new kid on the block."

Bo shrugged, shoulder bumping against Lucky's. "Even though he makes good money, I don't understand how Danvers affords the lifestyle he keeps bragging about. He's got a five bedroom weekend house on Lake Hartwell, owns a condo on Edisto Island, has pictures of a yacht on his desk, and lives in a gated community. He spent a month in Europe last year with his family."

"Sammy down in receiving said something about marrying money. His wife must be rich."

"Maybe." Bo yawned. "I may not be able to afford a condo, but summer's coming. What say after we wrap up here we go away somewhere? We don't have to go hiking if you don't want to. Pick a place. I still owe you a getaway. Do you like the beach?"

"I love the beach. Only, don't you have to check in with Walter when you go anywhere? I did."

Bo wriggled, pulling a few of Lucky's chest hairs in the process. Lucky, too satisfied to complain, merely shifted a bit. "I have to give two weeks' notice whenever I plan to leave the state. And Walter doesn't ask too many questions."

The door stood open. Lucky walked through. "What're the terms of your deal with Walter, if you don't mind me asking?"

Bo rolled his head back to stare Lucky in the eyes. "Why would I mind? You have a right to know."

"I do?"

"You're my partner, aren't you?"

Lucky started to mouth off an automatic protest before clueing in that Bo might mean simply a work type partner. "Yeah, I guess I am."

The corner of Bo's mouth lifted enough to form the fascinating dimple in his cheek. "I'm on two years' probation, yet I don't really feel like it. I kept my pharmacist license, draw a paycheck, pay my own rent, and do pretty much what I want. On the down side, I get drug tested regularly and keep Walter up to date on my whereabouts. Pretty good trade if you ask me. I can't leave the country, though, in case you'd like to see Mexico."

Sheesh. He got off easy. Good thing he'd only gotten probation. Lucky'd been given a ten year sentence for his crimes and not even his own name on his lease. "Have you thought about what to do after your time is up?" Two years wasn't very long, with nearly a year already gone.

"Yes, I have. Probation or no, I realize I have a drug problem. I'm still a part of the Pharmacist Recovery Network."

They hadn't talked much about Bo's counseling sessions. Every so often Lucky ate supper alone, Bo coming over later if his session wasn't too rough. Sometimes he liked to get away by himself afterward. Lucky simply waited until Bo came back. He'd always come back—so far. "Why? You're not doing anything wrong, are you?" Yeah, and not too long ago, he'd been ready himself to accuse Bo of a relapse.

"No, and I want to keep it that way. I don't have a bad job with Walter, and the two of you keeping an eye on me gives me added incentive to stay on the straight and narrow."

"What are you saying?"

"That when my time is up, if Walter asks me, I might stay on. Will that be a problem?"

In light of Bo's plans, the remaining year might prove to be a very long time after all. What if someone at work made an issue about them? While Lucky made no secret of his orientation, he didn't wave a rainbow flag at work either. Most of the department already considered him an evil to be avoided. However, it seemed everyone liked Bo. Would they sneer at him behind his back if his being gay became common knowledge? Lucky would hate to aggravate Walter by ripping off the heads of bigoted assholes.

Lucky deserved to be shunned, he'd earned the right. Bo didn't.

Crash! came from next door. Bo jumped up, whipping his head toward the sound. "I have a lovely, *quiet* apartment across town. We could go there, let your neighbors party to their heart's content."

There was that. Only, Lucky wasn't about to let some asshole with a loud stereo win. "I'm comfortable. Don't wanna move."

"That music's blasting more than eighty-five decibels. We might wind up with hearing loss."

Lucky wrapped an arm around Bo's shoulders, dragging him back down. "The noise keeps the bugs out. They don't like it either." He turned off the bedside lamp and fell asleep quickly despite the ruckus.

Bo woke him up before sunrise for a ride back to his place, the only time of day Lucky could count on the neighbors settling down. Before leaving, he turned his stereo to full volume, setting his iPod to play Kenny Chesney's "She Thinks My Tractor's Sexy" on continuous loop. It being Saturday, Lucky hoped they'd planned to sleep in.

"Remind me never to piss you off," Bo told him.

After dropping Bo off at his apartment, Lucky pulled into the parking lot at the center, to be greeted by an angry woman carrying a hand-lettered sign. "We want our hero back!"

Lucky pushed his way through a crowd of picketers. At least two news vans sat parked on the hospital lawn. "What the hell's going on?" he asked one of the more rational-looking banner-wavers.

"Danvers did what he had to do to get drugs for these sick kids. The hospital fired him. It isn't right."

Lucky wanted to ask, "And it's right for your insurance company to pay six hundred bucks for something that should cost seven?" but, under Bo's influence, he'd learned to pick his battles.

"That new guy, he won't do one damned thing," sign-woman whined. "I'll bet he's the one got Danvers fired, wanting his job."

"There he is!" Banner-waver cried. So much for being rational.

Bo, probably unaware of the impending ambush, stepped out of his SUV into a swirling shit storm. Several protesters spotted him and surged in his direction. Lucky shouted, "Hey! There's Danvers!" and pointed toward the front of the building. Grabbing Bo, he hauled ass toward the receiving door, dragging his lover along with him.

"What the fuck's going on, Lucky?"

Lucky pulled Bo into a store room. "They're out for your blood. They believe you had something to do with Danvers getting sacked. Whatever happened in the boardroom yesterday promoted him to martyr. The situation is out of our control, I'm calling in the big guns.

"Get me those samples and disappear into your office. Stay there until I come for you." Lucky pulled the door closed and swept Bo into his arms. "I know I don't make it easy at times, but you gotta trust me on this."

Bo nodded, straightening to his full height. For a moment Lucky pictured him in a Marine uniform. Damned impressive vision. PTSD might have cost the man some confidence, but with jaw clenched and gaze as hard as steel, the soul of a warrior lurked beneath the surface. He escorted Bo as far as the elevator, not encountering a soul. A two-person crew ran receiving on weekends. Chances were they didn't want to cross the picket lines.

It took a good stiff arm, a few threats, and bit of growling, but Lucky made it back to the Malibu. He called Walter en route to his apartment. "Walter, it's gone to shit. I'm taking drastic measures."

"We're on our way."

Lucky stormed past Shirtless Guy, taking the steps two at a time up to his apartment. *Ba-boom, ba-boom* thumped through the walls, drowning out his country music revenge. He ripped off his T-shirt and reached into the back of the closet for his equivalent of a superhero's costume—a navy blue golf shirt emblazoned with "SNB." He adjusted the matching cap in front of the bathroom mirror. A pissed-off man he barely recognized stared back at him, one mean-looking motherfucker. During his years with the bureau he'd seldom worn his uniform, pushing the limits of the office dress code and letting others believe he hated the trappings of his job. His love for a few sewn scraps of cotton was a secret he'd take with him to his grave. To the rest of the department, the issued clothing merely marked them as the good guys when on assignment. Lucky's navy blues were a badge of honor he'd earned the hard way. And when he put them on, he fucking meant business.

A holster and .38 completed the outfit, the gun's weight against his side a comforting presence. Lucky lived to buck the system on most matters, but when it came to firearms, he'd take tradition over newer, faster, shinier. Restricted from firearms during his sentence, the gun, more so than the badge, marked him as a full-fledged member of Walter Smith's team.

He ran his fingers over the symbol of his status with the SNB. Even if he hadn't favored a Smith and Wesson, he'd carry the gun anyway.

The felon Lucky Lucklighter died, birthing agent Simon "Lucky" Harrison. An oddly wrapped package greeted Simon his first day on the job. He'd torn off the garish paper to discover the .38. No card declared "From Walter Smith." Lucky didn't need one.

Before heading downstairs, he paused to beat on his neighbor's door.

The same guy as before answered. "I done told you, asshole—" He stopped, eyes trained on Lucky's scowl and rolling upward to the emblem on Lucky's hat, then down to the gun.

"And I'm telling you. If I ever catch your music up loud again, I'm coming back with a search warrant and some friends."

"Go right ahead. You won't find nothing."

Lucky studied the nervous tick above the guy's eye, how he drummed his fingers against the doorframe. Oh yeah, somewhere in apartment 7B lay a drug dog's "Attaboy" waiting to happen. "Who you trying to convince? Me or you?" He winked and sauntered away. He added "anonymous tip to Anderson PD" to his to-do list.

While the SNB may not be as familiar to some folks as the FBI or DEA, an emblem, kickass attitude, and a badge opened a lot of doors, or rather, parted a lot of demonstrators. No one stopped Lucky on his way across the center's parking lot, through the supply department, and up to the top floor. Of course, the Smith and Wesson strapped to his side probably helped.

He found the assistant buyer's office with no trouble.

"Lucky, thank God!" Bo exclaimed from his desk. His hair stood at odd angles, his fingers no doubt having run through the messy strands the entire morning. Bo eyed Lucky up and down. His mouth dropped open. "I've forgotten how bad-assed you look decked out." At the office in Atlanta, Lucky normally dressed casually, and Bo dressed up. Bo added with a bit of a leer, "I think I like it."

Lucky acknowledged the compliment with a slight nod, and too much warmth creeping though his insides. "I felt the need to take things up a notch. Can you get in Danvers's office?"

"Yes."

"Good, take me there." He followed Bo down two doors, to an office far more opulent than Bo's. Lucky practically smelled money oozing from the room. A laptop computer sat on the desk. He'd leave any electronics for Keith and his techie buddies back in Atlanta.

He told Bo, "Get back to work, do what you do. I'm gonna have myself a little look-see until the cavalry arrives."

Bo hesitated. "Lucky?"

"Yeah?"

"I'm sorry I called you cold."

Oh. That. "You only told the truth."

"But I didn't have to say it out loud. That's rude." Bo let a hint of a smile leak through his worry, and slipped out of the door before Lucky managed a comeback.

"All alone in a roomful of secrets." Now to root them out. Lucky started with the file cabinets, containing the hospital's licenses, and those for vendor licenses. All up to date, no restrictions. Oops. They'd better get Danvers's name removed as manager-in-charge.

He checked the desk, extracting an envelope from Primero Care. His pulse quickened as he pulled out a glossy green brochure. The first ten pages listed available drugs, "prices available upon request." *Uh-huh. Sure they're legit.* He skimmed the offerings and whistled. Most of the items from the current FDA shorted list resided in Primero's warehouse, or so they claimed. Page after page of hard to find drugs, all available for immediate shipment—at the right price. The last page contained a letter, signed by Olivia Cunningham, CEO.

He located a phone listing on Danvers's desk and dialed Bo's extension.

"Find something?" Bo asked.

"Who are you dealing with at Primero Care?"

"A salesman named Rick, why?"

"Have you ever heard of a woman named Olivia Cunningham?"

"Sure. That's Danvers's wife."

The cabinet doors stood open, a pair of rookies Lucky barely recognized loading down boxes to take to Atlanta. If so much as a Post-it note contained the name "Primero Care" it counted as evidence.

Keith sat at the desk, pecking away at Danvers's laptop. Why the fuck bring the asshole to Lucky and Bo's party? Walter could easily have taken the computer back to Atlanta.

Walter motioned for Lucky to follow him into the hallway. Together they traipsed back to Bo's office.

Walter claimed a chair across from Bo. "You have the samples?"

Bo tapped a bulging envelope on the desk.

"The pedigrees?"

He handed Walter a stack of papers. Lucky moved in to peer over his shoulder at the documents that tracked each leg of the product's journey between manufacturer and current owner. He whistled. "Damn! Those drugs have been around the block more times than I have."

"Why the hell can't the manufacturer simply sell to the hospital?" Bo groused.

"Because they'd need a whole different set of licenses, following a whole different set of laws. Even keeping their sales to wholesalers may require several licenses per state," Lucky replied.

"Well then, why do wholesalers sell to these cutthroat bastards?"

Walter fielded the question. "Wholesalers take orders, check for valid licenses, and send the product. They have no way of predicting what their customers intend to do with the goods."

Bo's frown turned into a scowl. "And there's nothing we can do?"

"There's legislation in place that, once passed, will discourage the price gouging, but if there's money to be made there'll always be devious individuals to take advantage of the situation. That's where we come in." Walter grinned his most feral. He might present himself as a teddy bear when it suited his purposes, inside beat the heart of a grizzly.

"What now?" Bo slumped in his chair.

"Now, we process what we've found and find out who's being naughty and nice. Bo, I'm afraid the gray market sharks may up the stakes to take advantage of the feeding frenzy, and they might see you as easy pickings." Walter turned his no-nonsense gaze on Lucky. "Given the situation with the picketers, we need to maintain a presence here. Lucky, conduct whatever investigations you feel are necessary." The side of his mouth lifted, engaging a smirk that'd be right at home on the face of a late night movie villain. "I'm sure you'll have no trouble gaining the staff's cooperation. Keep in mind the nature of this hospital, however. If you discover suspicious product, contact Bo to have it quarantined for testing immediately."

Walter rose to his feet, clutching the documents. "Your cover remains in place, Bo. You're the hospital buyer, cooperating with the SNB. You can deal openly with Lucky. Once the lab analyzes the samples you provided, we'll send copies of the results. If it were up to me, we'd impound the lot. Unfortunately, we currently have no legal basis to take drastic measures." He rounded the desk and dropped a massive paw to Bo's shoulder. "Keep up the good work."

Samples and paperwork in hand, Walter headed for the door, crooking a finger at Lucky. "Walk me to the elevator, please."

With a curt nod to Bo, and eye contact meant to offer reassurance, Lucky followed his boss. Halfway down the hall Lucky asked, "What's up?"

"Danvers's termination set off a chain reaction. Parents, not understanding the situation, have begun to remove their children to send elsewhere, believing Rosario is denying patients proper care. An emergency meeting was called. The hospital board stands by its decision not to purchase from untrustworthy sources. Too many of the drugs they use require special handling. If they cannot guarantee the safety of their medications, they won't use them. Which brings me to our next problem."

"Don't we have enough problems as it is?"

Walter barked a humorless laugh. "It seems Keith uncovered evidence from Danvers's computer. Apparently, Danver's has been trying for some time to allow purchasing from Primero Care."

"Yeah, Bo said as much. And all this time he tried to fool people into believing he cared about the kids. No one I've talked to here liked him much."

They stopped by the elevator and Walter pushed the down arrow. "You didn't trust Danvers?"

"No, I didn't. But I've been told I don't trust anybody."

The elevator doors opened and Walter stepped inside. "And you're usually right. You've made it abundantly clear that you prefer working alone, but I need you to keep an eye on Bo."

"Keep an eye on Bo? Why?" Lucky's heart paid his throat a quick visit.

"The situation is volatile and emotions are running high. The hospital has received death threats."

"Death threats!" The door closed in his face before Lucky got the chance to insist Walter take Bo back to Atlanta.

CHAPTER FOURTEEN

Lucky spent his day tracking down the paper trail, checking licenses, laying groundwork, and forwarding his reports to the Atlanta office. How he hated faxing, filing, and copying evidence. Apparently, Danvers fed Primero information about what drugs were needed, and through a series of bogus wholesalers, every last one owned by members of the Cunningham family, set about earning a tidy fortune through collusion.

Except for Primero selling too much stock to wholesalers, Lucky couldn't find any solid legal reasons to shut them down either, and he kept searching long after Walter began hinting at defeat. Danvers's employment record showed he'd been fired from his last job for poor performance. Good thing the bastard had a rich wife, though if Lucky had his way, he'd send the lot of them to the poor house.

Occasionally he checked in on Bo. Each time, Bo offered a brief, if strained, smile, holding a phone receiver to his ear with his shoulder, while steadily tapping away on his laptop. Other times, he checked the parking lot, to find the protest going strong. Didn't these folk have jobs to go to? Oh right. The weekend. Damn it.

At noon he brought Bo a sandwich. It still sat on his desk, untouched, at four o'clock.

With the day winding down and no new evidence to show for the hours of work they'd put in, Lucky found an empty conference room and phoned Walter. "We're done here. I've pulled anything of interest, Keith's got the laptop, and the hospital's interviewing for a replacement buyer. They need to step up their game. How'd the samples come out?"

"Based on preliminary testing, they matched product specifications. Though the center paid through the nose, they did get what they paid for. You and Bo finish up and report to the office Monday morning. I'll return early tomorrow for a wrap-up meeting with the hospital administrator. Keith's there until tomorrow afternoon."

"Sounds good," Lucky lied.

With the boss pulling the plug, maybe Lucky'd get to spend more time with Bo. He trotted down the hall to share the happy news. "Guess what? You're outta here tonight."

Bo gazed up from a stack of papers on his desk, a desk more resembling Lucky's disorganized mess than Bo's tidy one back in Atlanta. "What? We can't! There's still tons to do. I've got to..."

"Bo, look at me."

A pair of big brown eyes stared up at Lucky, indignation sizzling from their depths. Bo held his tongue.

"That's better. Now, you've got to understand that your job is catching criminals. This"—he waved a hand to indicate the center—"is not your job. Take it from me and past experience, as long as Walter lets the center use you, they will."

"But...but... What about the kids?"

"What about them?" With his words Lucky struck a match. He watched it fall on gasoline.

"You really are a heartless asshole, aren't you?" Bo jumped up, sending the chair crashing to the floor. "You mean to tell me you honestly don't care if these kids get their medicine or not?"

Ouch. "I care, believe me I do. But this situation isn't only here. Across the country hospitals are struggling. Do you think you're the only one spending the day on the telephone, calling salesmen, wholesalers, and even the manufacturers, asking when they'll have product to ship? And do you think they'll actually tell you that for every order they get out the door there's three more they won't? We can't fix the problem. There're plenty of folks with a lot more experience working on it, and if they can't find an answer, what the hell makes you think we can?"

All emotion fled Bo's face, along with the color. It returned in abundance, a flash fire of red chasing away his paleness. "Have you ever heard the expression 'crazy people change the world because they're too crazy to believe they can't?'"

Bo's stance brought to mind a certain bull on Lucky's daddy's farm. A red cape wouldn't be enough to hide behind when he charged. "Listen, Bo, you're catching the blame for Danvers being fired, and folks are mad enough to get violent. You're not safe here. Why do you want to stay?"

"You wouldn't understand."

"Try me." Death threats. Idiots had issued death threats. Lucky would drag the man kicking and screaming if he had to, but Bo was getting his ass out of danger one way or another.

"I joined the Marines, and went to school to be a pharmacist, to do some good in the world. I don't want to pass through life taking, living day to day. I want to make a difference."

Lucky clenched his teeth. Just because he didn't run around with his heart on his sleeve, donating all his hard-earned pay to "Save the Pickled Herrings" or whatever, didn't mean he didn't care. "Are you saying that's what I do? Take? I'm not ashamed of it," he said, though deep inside Bo's words cut him to the core. "'Cause let me tell you, if you don't take, you don't get. No one hands you anything in life. Nothing worth keeping anyway."

"Do you have to be so damned hard all the time?" There it was, the little defiant chin lift, to match the sparks flaring in Bo's eyes. "If you've got somewhere else to go, go there. I've got work to do, and I don't like you very much at the moment."

Ah, hell. Lucky'd gone too far. "Bo..."

Bo raised his splayed hand. "I don't want to hear anything you have to say right now. I don't even want to talk to you. Please leave."

Lucky skulked back down to Danvers's office. Maybe Keith would open his mouth and give Lucky a reason to work off his aggravation. Only, Keith wasn't there. The clock on the wall said five o'clock. Damn it, the asshole must've gone back to his hotel, probably a far cry better than Lucky's third-rate apartment.

His cell phone vibrated in his pocket. He fished it out,

heart giving a leap when he read, *"I need u NOW."*

He ran back to Bo's office, skittering to a halt outside the door. A deep breath later, he'd composed himself enough to go inside. Bo sat at the desk, head in his hands. His shoulders shook. Was he... laughing?

Bo raised his head, peeking out between splayed fingers. Misery. Pure, utter misery. "We lost two patients this afternoon. They suspect tainted drugs."

CHAPTER FIFTEEN

The blood in Lucky's veins froze. He gasped for breath. Were Steph's blue eyes now closed in death? A hard swallow didn't dislodge the boulder blocking his throat. "Any... any idea who they are?" he manage to strangle out with his too-thick tongue.

"I don't have names yet, just two boys from the second floor. It's a mess, Lucky. I've already told Walter that I'm staying another day."

Lucky whooshed out an exhale. Not Stephanie, yet two kids died. Two boys. Two poor little tykes who hadn't yet gotten the chance to truly live. How did people stand to work here, going home to their families at night after losing a patient?

"I know you said you weren't talking to me, but if you insist on staying I reckon it'd be better if you slept at my place tonight." No way in hell did Lucky want Bo to be alone.

"No. I need time to think. I'll talk to you tomorrow. I just wanted to tell you face-to-face." He'd made it nearly to the door before Lucky grabbed him. Hesitation. One split-second of backward glance, and Lucky read his open-book lover. Why did the man run when he needed to be held the most?

Bo struggled, but not hard, and not long. He melted into Lucky's arms. Sniffles escaped, Bo's whole body trembling. Lucky held tightly through the tears, rubbing Bo's back and whispering, "It's going to be okay. I've got you. Let it out." Anyone else and he'd be running. He'd never desert Bo.

The sobs gentled to quiet gasps, and Bo slowly withdrew. "I'm sorry. If you don't mind, I have a lot to think about. I need to be alone for a while."

Damp splotches marred Lucky's shirt where Bo's face had been. "Can you drive yourself? At least let me take you home."

Bo nodded. "I'll manage."

Please let me help you. What can't you admit you need me right now? Lucky stepped away from the door. If Bo wanted to leave, Lucky wouldn't stop him. "Call me later, if you need me?"

Again Bo nodded, dropping his gaze.

Lucky drove to his lonely apartment, not even bothering to eat before going to bed. He turned his stereo off, plodded to his room, and collapsed onto the bed. A venomous rap rant from the apartment next door added fitting background music for his stormy mood.

No matter how many times he checked his phone, Bo didn't call or text.

"Lucky, can you come and get me?"

Lucky shot out of bed, cell phone pressed to his ear. "What's wrong?"

Bo snapped, "Nothing!" a bit too quickly. "I just need you to come get me. Please."

Duty called. A shower would wait for later. Lucky grabbed the previous day's clothes and dressed on his way to the door. His heart pounded all the way up Clemson Boulevard to Bo's apartment. "Damn it!" he raged at the fourth light in a row to stop him. A black Toyota cut him off. "Cocksucking, mutha-fucking—" He inched his way forward. Every vehicle in his path sported an invisible X. Even at his most understanding, Walter wouldn't turn a blind eye to a swath of hit and runs. "It's your lucky day," Lucky told the asshole in the Toyota.

Twenty minutes. Twenty minutes to drive six miles. What were those handful of folks doing milling around Bo's SUV? Was Bo lying on the ground or something?

A woman stepped back and bile hit the back of Lucky's throat. Neon orange spray paint spelled "Murderer" along the side of Bo's vehicle. Lucky raised his cell phone and snapped a picture.

From out of nowhere Bo raced to the passenger side of the Malibu and crawled in the moment Lucky parked. He tossed his laptop case in the backseat. "Get me the fuck out of here."

Lucky wasted no time. "You okay?" He rubbernecked between the road and Bo, checking for bruises, blood, or torn clothes.

"No." Bo trembled in the passenger seat, arms wrapped tightly around himself.

"Want me to take you to Atlanta?" Lucky wanted to stop the car, take Bo into his arms, and promise to make everything better. Then he'd track down the bastards who'd spray painted Bo's SUV and kick the living shit out of them.

"No. We need to finish this."

A few minutes of hand-squeezing peace ended at the hospital. Protesters screamed, banners waving. A news crew shoved microphones in Bo and Lucky's faces. Lucky, hat pulled down to minimize exposure, growled and moved on, while Bo, remaining in character, paused long enough to mumble the occasional "No comment." What a cluster fuck.

"Mr. Scott, is it true that counterfeit drugs killed two patients at this facility?"

Lucky grabbed Bo's arm and ran.

Lucky settled Bo on a couch in his office with a cup of chamomile tea from the cafeteria. Bo ignored the tea and stared out into space. Lucky placed the tea on a low table and sank to his knees by the couch.

"Bo, talk to me." He tapped his palm against Bo's cheek. No response. After glancing over his shoulder out of long habit to ensure no witnesses, he pulled Bo to his chest. Bo resisted for a moment, and then settled in with a sigh. He didn't cry, he didn't scream, he merely shook so badly Lucky feared he might fly apart.

Bo needed to go back to Atlanta. Yesterday. "Are you okay?"

Silence, save for the distant *clop, clop* of high heels down the hallway outside. After a while, Bo whispered, "No. I may never be okay again."

Lucky placed a kiss on the top of Bo's head. "That's fine. I've been 'not okay' for years. It's not too bad once you get used to it. Now what's going on? I can't imagine how people got the notion you had anything to do with those patients dying."

"I got the call late last night. The ki...patients died of renal failure."

Until yesterday Lucky had managed to convince himself the patients at the center checked in sick and checked out well. Rational? No. Effective in helping Lucky live with himself? Yes. As his nursing aide sister would say, *Dream on, buddy.* "I hate to say this, but aren't they used to losing patients once in a while?" *Here it comes, go on, say it, I'm cold.*

"Yes, but not to kidney failure. The patients in question weren't critical, had shown no signs of kidney problems prior to a day or two ago."

"You're the pharmacist. Got any idea what could cause them to suddenly develop bad kidneys?"

"Yes. It happened a long time ago, but I read about a similar incident while in school and pray I'm wrong. We need a list of the medications they took, and any current stock should be checked for diethylene glycol."

"What's that?"

"A substance pretty close to anti-freeze."

"Anti-freeze!" Back home neighboring farmers used to lace deer hides with anti-freeze and leave them out for coyotes. A couple of the barn cats got a hold of one. It hadn't been pretty. But for a child to go through the same thing? "You think someone deliberately poisoned those kids?"

"Glycerin is an inactive ingredient in a lot of liquid medications." Bo lapsed into "textbook mode." "In the past some shady manufacturers used diethylene glycol because it's cheaper than glycerin. Back in 2007, over three hundred fifty people died in Panama from tainted cough syrup, and in the nineties wineries used it to make wine sweeter. They wound up killing several customers."

"Oh shit."

"Yeah. We need to act now, or there'll be more deaths."

"I gotta make a phone call." Bo's flexed his fingers around Lucky's arm. Lucky settled back. Old habits died hard, his need for secrecy, but he wouldn't say anything to Walter that Bo couldn't hear. He texted his boss the pictures of Bo's SUV, then made a call. Walter picked up on the first ring.

"Lucky, what's going on?" Edginess laced Walter's Boston twang.

"Two kids died yesterday of kidney failure, and apparently rumor's gotten out about bad drugs. Someone decided to pin it on Bo."

"Crap."

Crap? From Walter? Not reassuring. "Yeah. Bo wants the drugs those kids took tested for diethylene glycol. How much access do I have here?"

"Whatever you need."

"Bo's in danger. I want him outta here."

"We're recalling him immediately."

"No!" Bo yelled. "They don't have a buyer now. We can't leave them."

"Put me on speaker," Walter demanded.

Lucky clicked the button on his phone. Walter's voice carried from the tiny device. "Bo? Is there any reason you have to be physically on site?"

Bo chewed at his bottom lip. "No."

"Good. I want you uncompromised. We may need you to get information from Danvers. Work with Lucky today. Get the information and samples we need. Quarantine any suspicious product."

"Tell the woman who hands out cars that Bo's isn't going to make the auction," Lucky said as he scooted farther back on the couch. Bo sat with his knees drawn up to his chest, rocking.

"Understood. Keith is returning to Atlanta this afternoon. Bo, I want you with him. And Lucky?"

"Yes, boss?"

"Do what you do. I should be there shortly. We'll talk strategy when I'm on site."

The quietly spoken words might sound like mere encouragement to anyone else. Lucky took them for permission. "Don't I always?"

"Good. It's time to summon the locals, who'll likely bring Danvers and the Cunninghams in for questioning. Let's make sure they have the right questions to ask."

Lucky ended the call. "We have work to do," he told Bo. "You gonna make it?"

A look of grim determination settled over Bo's face. "I don't have a choice. Mind loaning me some of your son-of-a-bitch? I have a feeling I'm gonna need it."

"I told Martin there was more to you than you let on," Ava groused, printing out a prescription history of one of the victims. It didn't surprise Lucky a bit to find her and Martin both in the pharmacy on a Sunday. "I couldn't quite figure out why a man with as much spunk as you let Sammy run you over. I bet he shit his pants when you flashed your badge at him."

"No, actually I haven't talked to him lately." Although Lucky would love to watch the kid's reaction.

Ava leaned down a few inches to murmur into Lucky's ear, "Maybe you should. Anything shady going on 'round here, he'll be right smack dab in the middle of it, mark my words."

She handed Lucky a few printed pages. "This is everything. If you need anything else, let me know." She dabbed at the corner of her eye with a well-used tissue. "Those poor li'l babies."

Lucky raised his hand and hovered it over her back. Should he pat her? One pat or two? How hard? Martin approached. Lucky gave Ava a quick tap and beat a hasty retreat.

He took the lists back to the office designated as command central. Bo sat behind the desk, peering into his laptop. Keith wasn't there. Probably still in Danvers's office, the closest the asshole would ever get to a corner office of his own. "Here ya go," Lucky said, handing Bo the printouts.

Bo tapped a few keys on his laptop, ran a finger down a printed page, then tapped a few more times. "That's strange."

"What's strange?"

"The shipment we got from Primero contained fluorouracil. Neither of these patients had orders for fluorouracil. And it gets worse."

"How can it get worse?" Lucky stared at the printout,

recognizing a few drug names, mostly the narcotics. *Hello, chloral hydrate, my old friend.*

"They're listed as receiving a med that only prolongs life, since their chemo drugs are unavailable."

"I don't understand."

"Both patients were being treated for leukemia, but paclitaxel, the drug they were originally prescribed, is on the indefinite back-order list. The doctors switched them to something more readily available, but not nearly as effective."

"You mean to tell me they weren't receiving what would help them?"

Bo shrugged. "The doctors did all they could with what they had on hand. But, and this is the strange part, judging by their charts, both patients showed improvement. We need to talk to their doctor, or better yet, the pharmacy staff. These can't be complete lists. Both kids had the same doctor. You find Dr. Stanley Grayson, I'm going to check up on his other patients."

Lucky left Bo in the office to report in to Walter. Sammy met him outside the door. "Reggie! Oh my God, man. Am I ever glad to see you!"

Huh? Those were words Lucky didn't hear often.

"I'm kinda busy right now..."

"No, man. I need to talk to you." Eyes a few shades lighter than Bo's begged Lucky. Damn but he was a sucker for imploring brown eyes.

"Make it quick."

"Are you really an undercover narc?"

Narc. How Lucky had once hated that name when he'd been on the other side of the law. "Something like that."

Sammy nodded, staring at the floor. "I need you to meet me in the parking lot after five."

Whoop! Whoop! Alarms rang through Lucky's brain. "Why?"

"I didn't know, man. I swear I didn't!" He staggered, slapping a hand against the wall to steady himself. "I gotta make a run tonight, and I need you to go with me. Whatever you do, don't tell Dr. Grayson."

Lucky watched Sammy slink down the hall. Didn't that

beat all? An episode of his favorite soap opera couldn't beat the drama at Rosario Children's Center.

He dialed Walter's number, stopping midway when Keith poked his head out of Danvers's office door. "Oh, there you are. Saves me the trouble of hunting you down." Keith clamped his mouth shut. A muscle twitched in his jaw. Anger, not insults? Nope, wasn't Lucky who'd pissed in the man's corn flakes—this time.

For Walter, Lucky put up with Keith. He'd never dare tell the man, but for Walter, he'd do pretty much anything, like he'd do for Charlotte—or Bo. Damn it! He needed to quit adding names to his "I'd do for" list. Still, one glimpse of those big soulful eyes had him wanting to do the damnedest things. Like be nice. Lucky didn't do nice. Keith's muddy brown peepers didn't have nearly the same effect.

"What is it?"

"Come with me." Keith spun on his heel and stalked back into the office to punch a few keys on the laptop.

Lucky aborted his call and sank down into an executive chair probably worth more than his car. He stared at strings of numbers and dates, eventually making sense of the data. He closed his eyes and fisted his hands. A punching bag, the ugly couch in his apartment—Danvers. Anything to hit. Keith in a pinch. Not that Keith's discovery deserved punishing, but this might be an emergency.

A knock sounded a moment before the door opened. Walter filled the doorframe.

"Every time the pharmacy turned in an inventory sheet, that son of a bitch e-mailed the information straight to Primero Care," Lucky told him. "They knew exactly what Rosario needed, and set about getting it."

Walter hurried across the floor to peer over Lucky's shoulder. "I want hard copies printed, and the entire contents of this computer transferred to our server."

Keith nodded, oozing smugness.

Lucky let Keith slide for the moment, too busy wanting to find Danvers and beat him to a bloody pulp on principle. And the worst part? The part sticking in Lucky's craw? Danvers hadn't done one fucking thing to break the law. He deserved to be fired and a whole lot more, but so far he'd not done anything to merit jail time.

"He's being interviewed by the Feds. Maybe they'll find more than we did. If not, the asshole walks." Though Lucky hated to admit it, and the words didn't come easy, he quietly added, "You did good, Keith. Walter, I need to talk to you."

He rose and stalked from the office, not wanting to look back and find a smirk on Keith's face or he might be tempted to physically remove it. It'd be a whole lot easier to like the guy if he weren't such an asshole.

Walter followed Lucky into the hall. "Boss, we got a worse problem here than Danvers. We need to set up interviews with the pharmacy personnel and nursing staff without tipping off a Dr. Grayson."

"What do you suspect?"

"Bo believes the victims may have received drugs from a source other than the pharmacy."

"While administrators frown on the practice," Walter said, stroking a hand over his chin, "it's not unheard of for a doctor to order medications. However, some states are enacting laws preventing them from dispensing prescriptions directly. It allows addicts to doctor shop."

Doctor shopping, the latest drug craze. Even Bo'd gotten in on the act at one time, going from doctor to doctor, making up symptoms to get scripts for narcotics and filling them at different drug stores to avoid notice. Thanks to a new national system, more states were coming on line, requiring pharmacies to report prescriptions to a common database, making such practices easier to catch. Still, patients slipped through the cracks.

"Set up the appointments and include the hospital administrator. I want you there, too, Lucky. Since the drug shortage began two years ago, seventy-nine facilities have been found to be importing from shady sources. Some were counterfeits."

Counterfeits. A little of this and a little of that, cooked up in a vat and sold for the real McCoy. It might cure you. It might kill you. Lay down your money and spin the wheel. "There's a guy from receiving, says he has a delivery to pick up and wants me to go with him after hours."

"Go. But you'll have company."

Lucky back-burnered his "I work alone." Whoever'd coined the phrase "Where angels fear to tread" must have meant a drug trafficker's lair.

CHAPTER SIXTEEN

Lucky sat in a conference room with the center's administrator, the Director of Pharmacy, Walter, Keith, Bo, and one visibly shaking nurse. Bo sat in a corner, taking notes.

"Dr. Grayson is such a good doctor. Everyone loves him. He's devoted to his patients," the nurse said, dabbing away tears with a tissue.

"Did you notice anything unusual about the two patients in question?" Walter asked, in full "I'm your favorite uncle, you can tell me anything" mode.

"Well, with their preferred treatment unavailable, the meds we gave made them comfortable, kept them stable until we could find the injectable chemo they needed. When they started to improve, we nurses thought it was a miracle."

"Did Dr. Grayson ever see patients without a nurse present?"

"Like I said, he loved his patients. Sometimes he'd visit, just to chat with them or play video games."

Lucky glanced sharply to the left to find Bo looking back. Bo dipped his chin in a barely perceptible nod. Interesting.

Walter turned to speak to the hospital administrator. "I want Grayson's office searched for samples. Keith? Go with him."

The nurse twisted the tissue in her hands. "Am I in trouble?" Tears shimmered in her eyes, spilling over her lashes and leaving mascara-darkened streaks down her face. "Was Dr. Grayson doing something wrong?"

"No one's being accused of anything," Walter assured her, pushing a box of tissues across the table. Lucky added a mental "yet" to Walter's assurances.

The interview continued, Walter asking innocuous questions easily answered by the woman's personnel file. "How long have you worked at Rosario?" and "Where did you work before?"

No one but Lucky seemed to notice Walter's sneaky glances at the door, or the way he flexed his fingers when he talked. Stalling for time. Lucky helped him out. "How long have you known Dr. Grayson?"

The administrator returned and placed two vials before Walter. "I found these in a cabinet in Grayson's office." Even from a distance of a few feet, Lucky recognized the name "paclitaxel." He snatched up a vial for closer inspection. Whoever designed the phony label knew their stuff, but the number listed for National Drug Code didn't match any sequence he'd ever encountered with US goods. If he had to guess, he'd bet on the vials originating in China. He accessed the Internet via his cell phone and keyed in the number. No match. Not good.

"Do you recognize this substance?" Walter held a clear glass container up for the nurse to see. His thumb dwarfed the tiny bottle. Lucky would hate to play poker with the man, for Walter Smith never gave away anything, but this time, Lucky couldn't help noticing the lips set in a thin line, the tightening of his jaw. Mount Walter fast approached eruption.

"Oh my God! Where did he get those? We haven't been able to get our hands on this stuff in weeks!" The nurse stared wide-eyed at the tiny bottle.

Bo scribbled away. When he'd finished, Walter said, "That will be all. Thanks, you've been a big help."

The nurse managed a wavering half-smile. "Can I go now?"

"Yes, you may. Please don't discuss our conversation with anyone."

"I won't." She dashed out the door.

Walter turned toward the administrator. "I'll need the names of every patient who could possibly be receiving this medication. These won't be going back into stock."

The hospital staff filed out, leaving Walter, Bo, and Lucky. "Grayson is on vacation, I'm told," Walter began, rubbing the bridge of his nose under his glasses. "Just as well. I have a feeling he'd hamper, if not hurt our investigation." He waved one of the vials in the air. "Bo, I assume it's safe to say that his visits with his patients allowed Grayson time to administer this."

"Yes." Bo plucked the vial from Walter's fingers. "Some chemos have to be administered slowly. An hour would be plenty of time. I'm guessing while the patient played Angry Birds."

"Why would the bastard poison his own patients?" Lucky asked.

"He wasn't trying to poison them," Bo replied. "He was trying to save them, even though paclitaxel is an off-label prescription for leukemia. With other chemos in short supply, he used what he could get, even if he had to go out on a limb to get it."

"You're taking up for him?" Sometimes Bo baffled the hell out of Lucky.

"No, I'm not taking up for him." Bo slammed his free hand down on the conference room table. "You asked a question, I answered. For two weeks now I've watched this hospital struggle, rationing drugs and doing its dead-level best to treat its patients. What would you do if someone you loved was sick, couldn't get better without meds, and no matter where you went, no pharmacy had them? What would you do, huh? Then you find ad after ad on the Internet, promising exactly what you need. Would you take a chance? Would you, to save their life, especially knowing that, if you do nothing, they'll die?"

"Bo, calm down." Walter placed a hand on Bo's shoulder. "We're not here to decide motives. We're here because these are here." He indicated the vials. "We need to find out where they came from, and more importantly, we need to have them analyzed. I'm assuming Keith is rounding up any stock as we speak. I'll take them with me to the lab. Bo, the car we issued you has been collected. I'd like you to return to Atlanta this afternoon with Keith. Anything else the hospital needs can be handled from the office."

"What about Lucky?" Bo held the vial in a white-knuckled grip.

"He has one more task to finish." Walter gave Lucky a raised-brow glare.

"Yes, sir." Lucky checked his watch. By the time he immersed himself ass deep in alligators, Bo should be pulling his suitcase out of the back of Keith's car in the parking garage of the SNB.

"Gentlemen, while we're still officially on the job, due to the nature of this case, the FDA is assuming control. Any evidence you've collected please forward as soon as possible."

Damn. When the bad guys went down, Lucky wanted to be the one swinging the bat.

Lucky arrived at Sammy's Toyota ten minutes early, allowing enough time to slip a tracker under the front fender unobserved. He fussed with the St. Christopher medallion hanging from his neck, one of Keith's less obvious listening devices. No telling where the evening would lead. He texted a picture of the car and tag to Walter.

Across the parking lot Keith's Hyundai Sonata pulled away, two distinct shapes inside. Lucky replayed his and Bo's last few conversations. What would he find when he returned to Atlanta? Had Bo had enough, or would he cool down once he'd seen the big picture? Time enough for worry later. Right now Lucky had a job to do.

Sammy trotted out the door at exactly five P.M. He nodded once to Lucky and unlocked the vehicle. It took a few moments for him to arrange himself under the steering wheel.

"What's this about?" Lucky crawled into the passenger seat. He hated the passenger seat. While other people might have passed a test and earned driving privileges, if Lucky ruled the Department of Motor Vehicles, half the assholes behind wheels would find themselves walking.

"What's your real name?" Sammy asked, ignoring Lucky's question.

"Does it matter?"

Sammy shrugged. "What am I supposed to call you?"

"Simon will do." Best to keep conversation to a minimum unless it included a confession, since every word out of either one of their mouths would be recorded. With Keith heading back to Atlanta, no telling who monitored Lucky's transmission. "Where are we going?"

"You gotta wait 'til we get there." Sammy didn't say much while navigating through traffic and out to I-85, a well-known corridor to drug traffickers. Lucky'd spent his time on that long stretch of blacktop.

They headed north, Sammy alternately biting his lip, drumming his fingers against the steering wheel, or running his free hand through his close-cropped hair. After a while he finally spoke. "I didn't think I was doing anything wrong. In fact, he told me I was doing the center a favor."

The words interrupted Lucky's private fantasies of spotlights, a chair-bound suspect, and *We have ways...* "Who told you?"

"Grayson."

Sammy mumbled low enough to worry Lucky about him not being heard by the right people. He added, a bit louder than Sammy, "Grayson? As in Dr. Stanley Grayson?"

"That'd be him. He didn't like Danvers much. Said he was more concerned with himself than the kids." Sammy pulled off the interstate a few miles north of the North Carolina state line, turning down a two-lane county road. "Dr. Grayson took matters into his own hands."

They pulled up at a run-down brick building that might once have been a mill. Many such relics dotted the southern landscape, a testament to a bygone era. Grass pushed through broken asphalt, and kudzu climbed up one wall, nearly obscuring the aging brick from view. When they rounded the building, a white Chevy van came into view by the loading docks.

Sammy pulled in, parking a few car lengths away. "Wait right here."

It took every ounce of Lucky's normally nonexistent self-control not to follow Sammy. He strained his ears, hearing only birds chirping and the occasional roar of vehicles passing on I-85. As discreetly as possible, he snapped a few pictures of the van, the loading docks, and the van's tag. He texted them all to Walter, then made a call.

"Boss," he murmured quietly, "I'm gonna need a car around exit 100. As quick as you can get one there. And get the local boys to pull over the car I sent pictures of earlier. Search it, and get the contents to the lab ASAP."

Waiting proved sheer agony, but also allowed time for Walter to put Lucky's requests into action. Sammy reappeared, carrying an unmarked case in his hands. Without a word, he secured the box in the backseat. "That case is worth more than my house and car combined," he said, angling back under the wheel.

"Grayson sends you here?"

"Yup." Sammy kept his eyes straight ahead, navigating the neglected parking lot out to the two-lane road.

"How many times?"

"Ten, so far."

Ten? And no one noticed? "Always one box?"

"Sometimes more. I never thought nothing of it. He's a doctor, right? He wouldn't do anything shady. But when those kids died..." Sammy braked at a stop sign, turning toward Lucky. "Since I'm helping you, you won't arrest me, will you? I mean, I'm innocent, a flunky."

Lucky ignored the question. He needed more information before he could make any kind of educated guesses as to what might happen to Sammy. "How much did he pay you?"

"What?"

"How much are you making for this?"

"Not much. A hundred bucks a trip, to pay for my gas and time."

"Can you prove it?"

"Hey! It's not like he writes me checks or nothing."

And that, boy and girls, is how gullible people wind up doing others' dirty work. "I'm guessing what's in the box isn't legal. You're hauling it across state lines. That makes you a drug trafficker."

"What?" The color fled Sammy's face. He gunned up the ramp to I-85, hands trembling on the wheel. The car tires jolted off the pavement. Sammy jerked the steering wheel hard and fishtailed. Lucky grabbed the "oh shit!" handle. He wanted out of the car. Now.

The kid got the car under control and kept to the slow lane, bracing both hands on the wheel when an eighteen-wheeler in a hurry blew past. "I'm helping you. That's supposed to get me immunity, right?"

Ah, the saps of the world. Always in plentiful supply. "I'll put in a good word for you with the boss."

Sammy jumped at the *rrrrrrr* and flashing lights shortly after they'd crossed the state line. "Crap!" He stared up into the rearview mirror. "It's the cops! What'll I do?"

And about fucking time too. "Pull over."

"What? But..."

"Pull over. This is where I get out."

Lucky checked the side mirror. The vehicle bearing the distinct markings of a South Carolina State Trooper's car, and an unmarked Ford, pulled up behind them. "Tell 'em the truth. You're in this neck deep. You can swim or drown, it's up to you. But a word to the wise. When questioned by a man named Walter Smith, you'd better tell him everything you know."

He left Sammy sputtering and casually got out, nodding his head at the approaching troopers on his way to the unmarked vehicle.

"Where to?" a plainclothesman asked when Lucky crawled inside the car. A plainclothesman who didn't look old enough to vote.

"Take us north." Lucky bit off the "junior" he wanted to add. For some reason, young 'uns didn't like being reminded of their youth any more than Lucky wanted reminding of his age. Thirty-six wasn't old, damn it!

"Yessir, Agent Harrison." The guy pulled out on the highway, cutting through the grass median to head north. "I can't tell you how excited I am to be helping—"

"Can it, I'm wearing a wire." Ah, the sweet sound of silence. Lucky called Walter, wishing to high heavens for a good old cup of Starbucks. "What ya got for me, boss?"

Walter's smug tones oozed over the phone. "Very good work. The van belongs to a Luther Calhoun of Charlotte. I'm sending Art to the area to watch the man's house. I take it you're following the van?"

"I will. But first, I want a peek inside the mill."

"I'm en route. I'll be present when they question Samuel Haskins."

"Samuel who?"

"The shipping supervisor at Rosario. Better known as Sammy, I believe."

"Oh. Him." Samuel L. Haskens. The L stood for "Leonard." Graduated from T.L Hannah high school. One speeding ticket on his record. Lived with his mother and sister in a trailer park. No need to let on about the background check. Next thing you know the boss would think Lucky cared about his job or something. "Has Grayson been brought in?"

"Not yet, but he will be, once located." Walter's voice took on a scary note, reminding Lucky of his reputation as a real terror during his time with the DEA, not that Lucky'd dealt with him personally back then—thank heavens.

Lucky hung up the phone and directed the driver back to the abandoned mill. He mentally chanted, *Pull the fuck over and let me drive,* like a mantra. Having been on the receiving end of too many lectures from Walter on professional courtesy kept him from mouthing off. He settled for, "Find a place to pull over, and keep your eyes open for a white van. Got a flashlight?"

They parked on a logging road a quarter mile from the mill. The guy dug into a pile of gear on the backseat and pulled out a government issue flashlight. "I got this one," he said, before digging some more and extracting a huge Q-Beam, like Lucky's daddy used to use for illegal spotlighting during deer season. Lucky took the Q-Beam, which likely outshone the flashlight four to one.

"Now we're talking. If I'm not back in thirty, you holler good and loud." Lucky tucked his wallet into the glove compartment, taking only his badge, gun, work cell phone, and the flashlight. He hiked through a dense stand of trees to reach the building's loading docks. The van still sat parked outside.

Two men stepped out of an open loading bay. One stopped to lower the metal door behind him. A few minutes later they drove away. Lucky made a quick circuit around the building before venturing up the stairs to the docks. A padlock secured the loading door. He found the other entrances similarly secured. While no lock stopped Lucky for long, he didn't want to leave evidence that'd he'd been there.

Giving up on an easy entry, he slithered up the gnarled kudzu vine, wider around than his wrist in some places. It would have been one hell of a lot easier to climb with tennis shoes, instead of the lace-up business shoes mandated for the uniform, and once or twice he clung to the vine to keep from falling. He peered through a broken window on the third floor. With the sun shining on the other side of the building, and an overhanging roof and the kudzu providing shade, the space appeared dark, even hours before sunset.

He wriggled through the window. His feet connected with the floor, he slipped and *Wham!* He landed flat on his back, breath whooshing out. *Screek, screek, screek!* Lucky rolled to his feet, snapping the borrowed Q-Beam on and aiming it at the ceiling. Wings fanned up a breeze as two dozen or more upside down bodies screeched in protest.

Bats! He wrinkled his nose in disgust at the bat shit now smeared on his arms and pants. What a fucking smell. Using the wall for handholds, he picked his way across the slippery wooden floorboards, breathing a sigh of relief once he'd cleared the exit.

Down rickety stairs he climbed, clutching a rusted iron railing. Outside the sun shone, but the mostly boarded up windows let in little light. What had the place looked like in its heyday, back when textile mills provided the lifeblood for sleepy little towns? His grandfather had once worked in a similar place. Lucky shuddered. How in the hell had the man worked indoors eight hours at a time, doing the same ole, same ole, day in, day out?

Thick grime spoke of long disuse, until he reached the bottom level. A ray of sunlight shone through a crack in the wall, dust particles dancing in the beam. The scent of decay hung heavy in the air, along with grease and oil smells from years ago.

At the base of the stairs he found an office, old metal desk overturned and graffiti spattering the walls. A file cabinet stood empty and open. He tiptoed down the hall on plank flooring, gritting his teeth at the creak and grind of rotting wood. The kudzu vine grew on the far left, with the loading docks around the back. That meant... This way! He turned left at the next hallway. "What th—" He shrank back, biting off a shout. A rat scuttled out of the way of his Q-Beam's glow.

"You leave me alone, I'll return the favor," he muttered under his breath. Eerie, creepy silence. No traffic noises, no voices, no electrical hum of machinery. Prickles rose on Lucky's arms. Walter in lecture mode; the honks, beeps, and squealing brakes of downtown Atlanta at rush hour; hell, even his neighbor's never-ending rap music beat the total absence of sound.

After passing a men's bathroom and what might have once been an employee break area, he stepped out into a cavernous room with soaring ceilings and unboarded windows. A bird took wing, flitting among the rafters overhead.

Wood and metal racks that probably once held raw cotton or finished fabric appeared cleaned and somewhat patched, the floor less filthy than the rest of the building. Cases upon cases sat piled in a corner. Lucky set the Q-Beam down and ripped the top from one of the cartons. Roughly two dozen glass vials stared back at him. He held one up to the light. Unless he missed his guess, the vial matched the one he'd held in his hand in the conference room at Rosario.

He reached into his pocket for his cell phone to call Walter while slipping two vials into the waistband of his pants.

A man's voice snarled, "Hold it right there."

CHAPTER SEVENTEEN

Lucky froze, hands out in front of him. He listened for breathing, footsteps, or any other clue of how many assholes he'd let slip up on him, but his heart beat loudly enough to drown out everything else. *Stupid, stupid, stupid!* He glanced at his wristwatch. He'd told the plainclothesman thirty minutes. He needed to stall ten more before help arrived. Without an earpiece, Lucky's escort wouldn't pick up his signal, and who knew how close Walter might be?

"Before you get any ideas about the cavalry coming, we dealt with the lookout you posted up the dirt road." The rumbling growl plunged a lead weight into Lucky's belly. Maybe he'd need more than ten minutes, after all. Lucky hoped like hell "dealt" meant temporary. The voice emanated from directly behind him, a shuffling sounded to his left. Two of them, at least. Probably a third guarding the cop.

The shuffling grew closer. Lucky waited, betting his experience against theirs. Surely they weren't idiot enough not to try to take his gun from him.

"Nice looking gun you got there. Take it off, nice and slow."

Never had Lucky wished so hard to be surrounded by idiots. He eased the .38 out of its holster and reached down to place the firearm on the box in front of him. Adding a little more motion than necessary, he attempted a peek over his shoulder.

"Uh, uh, uh. Keep facing the wall. What we look like don't matter to you."

If they didn't want him to be able to identify them, then his chances improved for making it out of here alive. If they planned a bullet in his brain, who cared if he saw them? Maybe the kid in the unmarked car might make it home for supper too.

"Good. Now put your hands on top of your head."

Though a dozen cocky retorts fought to escape his mouth, with God knew what aimed at his back, Lucky complied.

The shuffling grew closer and a pair of none-too-gentle hands patted him down. Fingers wiping against his back followed a muffled "Eww..." Maybe the bat shit would discourage any frisking. No such luck. The hands returned, spending more time than necessary near his crotch, in his opinion. With any luck they'd bypass the vials.

Of course, in his past experience, the crotch made a good hiding spot simply because of others' reluctance to go there. More than once he'd cramped his cock with a bottle or two of smuggled goods down the front of a pair of briefs.

"Touch my prick again and I'm gonna charge you fifty bucks," he snapped. If he went down, he'd be swinging.

Instead of stopping, the hand frisking him locked down on his dick—hard.

"Hey!" he bellowed.

"That's enough!" the man behind him shouted. The groper backed off and snatched the gun off the box, without finding the vials tucked into the top of Lucky's pants. The faceless thug made off with Lucky's badge and cell phone.

A female voice asked, "What's SNB? I ain't never heard of them before."

A woman? Fondled by a woman? Oh the horrors!

"Southeastern Narcotics Bureau," the man behind Lucky explained. "A bunch of useless wannabes if you ask me. Whatcha sniffing round here for, SNB man? We're not dealing with narcotics. This isn't your concern."

Lucky debated how much to say. Volunteer too much and they might run. Then again, he needed them off-kilter. He decided on the truth. "Kids died because of you." He bobbed his head toward the boxes. "Those cartons contain pure poison."

The woman gasped. "You told me—"

"Shut up, Annie. He's lying to get us to do something stupid." Oh goodie, a name.

"Back the truck up," the leader ordered. "Mr. SNB here is the first ant at the picnic. More are coming, I guarantee. We'll be long gone before they arrive. You three get the cases loaded and be ready to go when I get back."

Ah, four of them. And maybe another with the cop. "And what do you plan to do with me?" Lucky asked. *Boss, you'd better be listening.*

"Drop you off somewhere it'll take you awhile to get back from. Nice and easy now, pick up the flashlight and leave the way you came. Show me where you got in." Pointing out se-curity weaknesses—Lucky's strong suit. Only now, he wasn't being paid for the hard-learned lesson.

Shit. Not the bats again, with their wide-open, screech-ing maws, their flapping wings, their... *Oh, yes, the bats!* And Lucky alone against a single man. The sun shining through the boarded up windows had dimmed, sunset ap-proaching. What time did bats normally get up? Time for a wakeup call.

Lucky dragged his heels, slowing his progress to leave his boss an "I went this way" trail through the dust. Together he and his unwanted escort wandered down the hallway, the man's footsteps heavy behind Lucky's. A big man. His voice already gave away his height, coming from in back and above Lucky. Lucky clutched the iron railing on the way up the stairs, leaving plenty of fingerprints. Once he'd have carefully avoided leaving evidence. Not now.

Behind him his captor wheezed. Hmmm... grunts and groans sounded promising. Lucky wasn't even winded. An out of shape man couldn't match Lucky for speed or agility.

"Kids really did die," he taunted the soon-to-be-convicted drug trafficker.

"Annie doesn't need to hear that. She can be one of those bleeding heart liberals on occasion. Can't get her to under-stand we're simply the middlemen. We buy and sell. It's not our problem what's in it. Damned nurses probably gave 'em too much."

For this man's conviction, Lucky would gladly wear a suit to court. Eventually they came to the room where Lucky'd sneaked in. He took a deep breath, flung open the dilapidated door, and aimed the Q-Beam at the ceiling.

Screech, screech, screech! Flapping wings fanned the breezed, bats diving and soaring. Lucky threw himself to floor, ignoring the squish of bat shit. He kicked with all his might, toppling his captor. The guy fell to his knees with a heavy *thud.* The gun clattered to a landing a few feet away. Whirling and on his feet in an instant, Lucky lunged for the weapon. The plus-sized felon gave him a glassy-eyed stare and keeled over... right on the gun. Sprawled on his back like a turtle. Damn! When did Shamu the Killer Whale learn to walk on two feet? Walter had nothing on this guy.

Lucky stooped beside the man and jammed two fingers into his neck. He counted out the pulse-beats, watched the rise and fall of a massive chest. The guy must have fainted. He grabbed a handful of shoulder and hip, like he'd been taught for first responder training, and heaved. The plus-sized felon rolled an inch and flopped back.

A truck engine rumbled in the area of the docks. Lucky jerked upright. Should he stay here with his former captor, already down for the count, or go after the others? He patted his belt loops. Why the fucking hell hadn't he brought cuffs?

"Hey! You up there?" someone shouted up the stairs.

No time to think. Lucky tossed the Q-Beam out the window and then hurled himself through. He grabbed at the kudzu vine with one hand.

His hand closed on open air. Molten lava shot through his arm, the vine gouging a deep gash. Leaves and tendrils ripped at his skin as he grasped desperately for a handhold. Lucky juddered down the vine, snapping branches slowing his fall. *Wham!* He hit the ground—hard. Fire exploded in his left ankle, and a dagger jabbed through his left hand. Holy great mother of God! He shoved his palm into his mouth to stifle a scream.

Shit, shit, shit, shit, shit! He moaned and rolled on the ground, clutching his injuries. If anyone came, they'd have him. Gradually the flames faded to glowing coals. Lucky ground his teeth together, huffing through his nose.

He poked at his wrist with a fingertip. Bruised, maybe, but not too bad. Thank God he hadn't reinjured it. With a bit more caution he assessed his leg, running his hand down his ankle to his foot. "Oh my God!" White hot pokers jammed into his foot clear up to his knee. Blackness gathered at the edge of his vision, and he tucked his head low, fighting for consciousness. Broken, for sure. His belly gurgled, giving a five second warning. He turned to the side, guts heaving.

Fuck! Could his life get any damned worse? He breathed slowly, clearing his head. His leg throbbed. *Don't think about it. Put it out of your mind. Think about getting your sorry ass out of here.* Five minutes! Five minutes he'd wasted. Why hadn't they captured him by now?

How long would it take them to find their fallen leader? Had Lucky already used up his precious head start? Grabbing the vine, he managed to pull himself upright, clenching his teeth when he moved his ankle. Damn it! That hurt!

Teeth gritted, he hobbled away from the mill, grasping handholds on the rough brick walls. He wouldn't get far, but maybe far enough to buy him some time.

Setting off in the direction he'd left the cop, Lucky hopped one-footed from tree to tree, and chanced a backward glance. An eight-wheeled tandem truck sat backed up to the loading dock. An occasional echo reverberated through the trailer, the bams and slams of cargo being loaded.

Latching onto trees to help pull himself along, Lucky shambled through the woods. Damn! He shot an angry glare at the sapling that dared catch on his injured leg. He'd been roughed up enough in the past to recognize a broken ankle, and possibly the foot, too, the bones grinding if he put his weight down. Another wave of nausea burned his throat. Nope, not going there. He spat a mouthful of bile and kept on moving.

His knee wobbled. Two steps later he stumbled, the knee giving way. A handy tree stopped his fall. He took more weight on his arm, swinging from low-hanging limbs. If Keith somehow managed to film this...

"I hear him! He's over that way."

Oh shit! Lucky crab-scuttled, using his good hand, an elbow, and his unbroken leg. He dived for a heavy thicket of huckleberry bushes and dragged himself beneath their sheltering branches. His leg pulsed a steady beat, matching the heartbeat in his ears. Breathing slowly in and out through his mouth, he waited, heart sinking as running footsteps grew closer and closer. Where the hell was Walter?

Step by step he tracked his would-be assailant. "Make it easy on both of us, mister. Come on out." Lucky recognized the voice of the woman called Annie, the one who'd been shocked by the kids' death. She might listen to reason.

"Right now you're looking at some pretty serious charges," he ventured. "The decisions you make in the next few minutes will affect the rest of your life."

The footsteps stopped. "How many kids died?"

"Two, last I heard."

"I never meant to hurt anybody. This is strictly business," she said, sounding more like her accomplice now.

"Then why don't you make a business deal with me? Why don't you walk back down to the mill, pretend you didn't find me, and I'll disappear."

More rustling sounded in the bushes directly behind him.

Voice more assured now, the woman replied, "I'm sorry but I can't."

Movement to the left. Lucky whirled to meet a tree branch face first.

CHAPTER EIGHTEEN

The earth shook. Lucky awoke in the middle of an earthquake. His leg jarred and he bit back a moan. A pounding head competed with the pulsating bite in his foot.

No, not earthquake. Truck. *I'm inside the truck.* Cold metal kissed his cheek, and every jolt and bump vibrated through his body as the vehicle chugged slowly up an incline. They weren't on blacktop, and based on the screeching of what had to be tree limbs scraping the top and side of the truck, they were in the woods somewhere.

The guy at the mill had planned to "Drop you off somewhere it'll take you awhile to get back from." Well, at least they didn't seem hell-bent to put a bullet in him. Lucky could work with that.

Full dark created zero visibility, and he strained his ears for hints he might not be alone. After a while of fruitless listening, he coughed, revealing his wakefulness. No one told him to be still, or whatever the hell might have been on their minds.

Nursing the headache from hell, he pushed aside cartons and inched toward the back of the truck. Too bad they held cancer drugs and not pain relievers. What he wouldn't give for a couple of ibuprofen right now. He ran his fingers gently over a lump on his head. His fingers didn't come away sticky. He'd count that as a little victory—his hard head against a good hard whack. Of course, folks accused him of being hardheaded on a regular basis.

He could try to escape, or wait to find out where the truck took him. Something prodded his hip and he reached into his waistband, grasping one of the vials he'd taken from the mill. Damn. He still had it.

152

The truck slowed, gears grinding. The incline grew steeper. They must be in the mountains now. He'd spotted the distant peaks from the mill, and he might still be within two hours of where he'd last called Walter. Or he might be in Bumfuck, Egypt by now. He reached for his pendant. Fuck. Not there. Either he'd dropped it or the assholes took it. Didn't matter, though. More than likely he'd lost signal a long time ago.

He rose up on one knee, probing around the door. The metal panel wouldn't budge. Locked. Lucky sank to the floor, waiting for the inevitable.

Had the man back at the mill recovered? He didn't bring to mind any two-bit criminal of Lucky's acquaintance, and Annie sounded more like a housewife than a felon. Of course, criminals came in all sizes, shapes, and colors, from white collar banker types to bad B-movie villains. While in prison Lucky had met the sweetest young man, always smiling, always happy, yet he'd chopped his wife up and tossed pieces out the window along I-26 on his way to work one morning. You couldn't tell about some folks.

If Lucky's captors were after money only, and would do anything to get it, they wouldn't have qualms about pulling the trigger when they'd had the chance, would they?

Trying to solve the mystery of the soccer parent drug traffickers took too much energy. Where was Bo now? Did he make it back to Atlanta? Did he know Lucky was gone? Did he care?

Lucky lay back down, cradling his pounding head on one arm. How he'd love to be home, lying in bed. He imagined the smooth slide of skin against skin, Bo's breathy little moans when Lucky worked the toy inside of him. So much he didn't know about the man, so much more to discover.

What would it be like to have Bo in his bed every night, wake up to hot coffee and freshly cooked breakfast every morning? His empty stomach rumbled. How he'd love some grilled portabellas right now, or even an omelet with lots of cheese. It wasn't the food or the coffee he really wanted, but the caring. The way Bo did things for him without expecting anything in return. And that damned dimple whenever the man smiled. Lord, The Dimple. Even in agony, Lucky smiled.

A hot cup of coffee would be nice. And maybe a warm bath followed by a massage. Whatever, he just wanted Bo. Bo, to dole out ibuprofen and tuck him into bed. Now to get out of this mess and get the hell back to the man. He'd worry about whether or not Bo wanted him to come back later. One thing at a time.

The bumping and grinding slowed to a halt. Two doors slammed. "You get him out," Annie said. "Here's as good a place as any."

Lucky suddenly saw the sense in Bo's "protection" birthday present. The weight and row of spines along the dragon's back would make the heavy-as-lead ornament one hell of a weapon. Pow! Right between the eyes!

A scrape and a click and the door popped open. A flashlight's beam swept through the trailer. Lucky scrunched his eyes closed, feigning unconsciousness. A hand latched onto his injured leg. Holy fuck! Blazing agony shot up Lucky's leg. He roared.

"Easy now," Annie scolded. "We don't want him hurt, just lost for a few days." Her voice grew closer. Through the flashlight's glare, and black-around-the-edges vision, Lucky caught a glimpse of a blonde-haired head peeking through the door.

"You okay?" she asked.

"Broke my leg." Lucky moaned, pouring on the drama to win sympathy points.

"Oh." She turned to someone hidden in shadow. "Be careful with his leg."

The hand latched onto his good ankle, pulling him out of the trailer and setting him upright. He hissed through clenched teeth when his foot hit the ground.

"Look, I'm sorry about this." Annie shoved a bottle of water at him. "This is all I have. This section of trail is closed down so no hikers will find you. With any luck, you'd make it to the main road in a day or two, if you were able to walk. Ted might shoot me for this, but is there anyone we can call? No way in hell are you going far with a broken leg, and I'm not leaving you out here to die."

He immediately thought of Bo and reconsidered. "Have someone call the SNB office. They'll take care of it."

"No." The man holding Lucky spoke up for the first time. "They'll trace us. If we're gonna call, it's gotta be a private number, someone they won't be watching."

"In that case, why don't you call a buddy of mine?" He gave them Bo's personal cell phone number. "What about the cop? The one who came with me."

"Ted took him somewhere else," Annie replied, retreating into the darkness with her accomplice. Two slams left Lucky all alone in the dark.

He stood in the middle of a rutted dirt road, watching the headlights fade as the truck backed down the track. Eventually the engine roar faded, and he rested against a tree trunk, with only the chirping crickets and mournful whippoorwills for company. A hooting owl added its voice on occasion. He checked his waistband, shifting the vial to his pocket for safe-keeping. Did he dare to hope they'd actually call Bo?

After a while the darkness faded and his eyes adjusted to moonlight. Overhead a million stars twinkled, and he breathed in crisp mountain air. Even in late spring, this high up the night grew cool. Lucky rubbed his arms. Damn, what he wouldn't give to have his jacket. Reaching for a darker shape among the shadows, he grasped onto an overhanging branch, using handy limbs to drag himself along. He banged himself against a few trees along the way, tripped over roots and thick underbrush, but step by painful step, he staggered down the road.

Traces of pink edged the horizon, and Lucky sat beneath a tree, watching the sunrise. When was the last time he'd been up early, with nothing to do other than watch the stars fade and the darkness overhead lighten to blue?

He recalled lying on the hill overlooking the family farm, talking to his sister, sharing his dreams. Once, all he'd wanted from the future amounted to watching the world go by through the windshield of an eighteen-wheeler. Did he even have dreams anymore? For ten years he'd focused solely on completing his sentence and getting his life back, first in prison, and then as one of Walter Smith's experiments in gaining inside knowledge of drug trafficking from an actual trafficker. Last year Walter had handed Lucky a second chance on a silver platter. What did he intend to do with it?

Bo's face appeared in his mind. How did a man get to be Bo's age, going through all the shit he'd gone through, and still manage to be a nice guy?

Compared to an abusive father, losing friends in Afghanistan, and fighting against a prescription pill habit, Lucky's problems seemed light. And yet Lucky was the inconsiderate asshole, and Bo was all, "Can I get you anything?"

The pieces fell together about Bo's compulsive neatness. For a kid growing up with no stability, maybe he'd learned to control the things he could, like ensuring he never had to hunt for anything, or like Lucky did too often, give up hunting and simply buying more. But wait, Bo grew up poor, too, barely having enough to eat. His obsessions began to make sense.

Bo needed structure and stability and Lucky didn't have the foggiest clue how to be what the man needed.

Has he asked you to change? his inner voice asked. "No," Lucky replied. "But he will. It's only a matter of time, once he gets tired of my mouth."

Arms folded around his knee, wishing he could fold them around Bo, Lucky finally dozed.

He awoke stiff and sore, the sun shining brightly overhead. Stretching out kinked muscles, he took a mental inventory of his hurts. Beat up, scraped up, covered in dried bat shit, he'd probably sunk to a new all-time low, or as his landlady might say, "Another wild night."

I'm getting too old for this shit. Lucky made his unsteady way to his feet. His ankle throbbed, now swollen to twice its normal size. He limped around the area, finding a forked branch lying on the ground. Damn. Too short. Another proved too long. His third choice wasn't perfect but close enough. Tucking the forked portion under his armpit, he experimented with his makeshift crutch. One step, two steps. He wouldn't win any marathons, but it beat the hell out of sitting still.

He swallowed down a few mouthfuls of water and tucked the bottle into his shirt. This far out in the wild he didn't even hear traffic sounds. Lucky set off to find civilization, following the way the truck had brought him in.

The sun beat down, sweat poured down his back, and he winced at a horrible wind-borne stench. He sniffed, and sniffed again closer to his armpit. Oh. It was him. A shower, a tall glass of sweet tea, two ibuprofen, something unhealthy to eat, and a nice long nap—in that order. Not much to ask, right? No wait. First he wanted Bo.

How long would it take for someone to find him? Had Annie called Bo yet? Had the search begun? His stomach grumbled and complained, hunger battling nausea for dominance. Shortly after noon he turned up the water bottle, catching the few last remaining drops on his tongue.

On and on he plodded, his improvised crutch chafing his armpit. The sweet song of flowing water started softly, and he tracked the sound, the melody growing stronger with each step. Silver flashed in the bright sunlight, in a gorge at the bottom of the ridge. Ah-ha! There. Through the trees. Lucky stumbled downhill, finally resorting to sliding down on his ass after he fell the third time and tumbled several yards, snapping his crutch in two. If anyone searched for him, they had to have heard the screams when he hit his leg against a tree.

He sat at the base of a waterfall, sucking in a deep breath before removing his shoe. He'd have to recommend a change of uniform. His black dress shoes might be considered professional, but for field work they sucked. Made his swollen foot hurt like hell, too, when he yanked his shoe off. Lessons from long ago Boy Scout training guided him to a spot where the water rushed over the rocks to drink.

One inch at time, he lowered his battered leg into the water, purple and green mingling with pink and white. Holy fuck! That was cold! The mountain-fed stream chilled his swollen ankle, and the pain faded somewhat. He stuck his head under the fall's spray, gulping in sweet mouthfuls and shivering at the frigid drops.

A rock wobbled beneath him, and the world turned upside down. Grasping helplessly at lichen-slickened rocks, he lost the fight with gravity and plunged into a deep pool. Oh, dear God in Heaven! He came up sputtering and gasping. *Brrr!*

He maneuvered himself onto the bank to keep from being swept downstream, and set about cleaning up the best he could with only a handful of sand for soap and his golf shirt for a washcloth. No telling what'd happened to his hat. Bloody scrapes marred both forearms, and he'd definitely bruised his wrist and a few other areas. A goose egg stood out against his scalp, tender to the touch. The ankle didn't work and electricity shot through his leg when Lucky gently rotated his foot. He screamed, dropping his throbbing limb into the icy current.

Teeth gritted together, he rode out the agony. Holy fuck! Holy fuck!

Slowly the stabbing pain ebbed to steady pulsing. Dried blood and bat shit floated downstream, leaving Lucky cleaner but still miserable.

He crawled over to a flat rock, to let heat seep through his wet pants to his chilled body. He tossed his shirt over a nearby bush to dry. Gradually he relaxed, lulled by birds chirping overhead and wishing, not that he was home, but that he'd taken Bo up on the offer to go hiking together. Right now he'd give anything to see the man.

Insistent buzzing grew louder. Eyes closed, Lucky swatted at his ears to drive back mosquitoes.

Wait a damn minute. Those weren't mosquitoes. They were four-wheelers.

CHAPTER NINETEEN

Lucky struggled upright. "Hey!" He waved his arms above his head. "Hey!"

The four-wheelers' humming drowned him out, and the drivers didn't even slow down on the ridge above his head. He scrambled on hands and knees up the hill, forgetting his shoes and shirt until halfway up. Winded and strength nearly gone, no way in hell was he turning around.

Another four-wheeler passed by, with him too far away to get the driver's attention. At least they appeared to be searching for him, since Annie mentioned this section of the forest closed. Where was he anyway? Caesar's Head State Park? That's where he'd have laid his money on a bet.

He'd left his watch on a rock by the stream, but estimated two hours passed before he managed to claw his way back up to the road. He collapsed on the dirt track, heaving in and out. Was there another way out of here? Surely those four-wheelers had to pass back by again. Fate couldn't be cruel enough to tease him.

The picnic he'd refused to attend, all the times he'd shied away from Bo's apartment, every missed opportunity condemned him. In that moment, Lucky would've gladly strolled into the office hand-in-hand, just to see the man one more time.

"Yeah, baby, like that." Lucky lay on his back, Bo rising and *falling above him. Tight heat squeezed Lucky's cock.*

Bo's leather chaps creaked and groaned as Lucky thrust up into him. Bo reached out, slapping Lucky's cheek.

Lucky grinned. "Oh, you like the rough stuff do you? I learn something new about you every day."

159

Bo grabbed him by the shoulder, giving him a good hard shake.

"Oh my God!" someone shouted. "Are you okay?"

What the hell?

"I found him near the falls. Yeah. It's him." Why was Bo speaking into a two-way radio during sex? Why did he sound far away? And why did Bo sound like someone else?

More buzzing. Lucky swatted at a pair of hands attempting to lift his eyelids. "Go 'way. Sleepy."

Something swatted back. "Lucky? Can you hear me? Damn it, Lucky! Talk to me."

Lucky's snapped his eyes open, an upside-down face coming into view. "Bo?" Bo! Lucky tried to grab the man, but flopped back down with an "Oooomph!" *Ow!*

Bo righted himself, scuttling around to look at Lucky full on. His mouth turned up at the corners, then down again. Then twitched, like he couldn't make up his mind whether to laugh or cry. "Lucky, thank God!" He crouched closer, arms outstretched, but stopped short. Another man stood off to the side, shouting out coordinates into a squawking radio—the voice Lucky'd heard earlier. "I want so bad to hug you right now," Bo murmured.

"I stink."

"I don't care."

"I hurt."

"Where's a good spot to hold?"

Lucky raised his right hand. Bo grasped on and squeezed. Even with a witness, Lucky wouldn't have turned down a hug if he weren't so disgusting. And sore. At least it looked like he might not be alone when he got back to Atlanta.

"I worried you were dead," Bo said. "We all did, until I got a call. How bad are you hurt?"

So Annie came through, huh? Even felons kept their promises sometimes. Through a mouthful of stale cotton, Lucky choked out, "Left ankle and foot are broken. A few cuts and scrapes. Maybe a concussion."

The other rider approached and dropped down beside Lucky and Bo. "Do you mind if I examine you?"

I'd rather be examined by Bo, Lucky nearly said, but beggars couldn't be choosers. "I reckon," he replied, only after Bo prodded him.

"Simon, this is Russell, a certified first responder. Russell, meet Simon."

Russell nodded and grunted, roving his eyes and hands over Lucky's body. He paused to study Lucky's scraped forearms before moving down to the injured leg. Lucky winced when the guy pressed a hand against his side, adding bruised ribs to his mental inventory of hurts. "Sorry, 'bout that," Russell said.

"Exactly what happened?" Bo asked.

Lucky shrugged as far as his awkward position let him. "How much did Walter tell you? I'm too tired to rehash old news."

"A kid from receiving wanted to show you something. He took you to an abandoned building and picked up a case containing what looks like the same vials from the center. They're being tested. That's about it."

"Sammy met some folks at the old mill. They left, I went to have myself a little look-see and got ambushed by the local PTO." Russell lifted his foot. "Yahhh!" Dear Lord God! That fucking hurt!

"Sorry!"

Lucky tightened his grip on Bo's hand, using pain as an excuse for contact.

Bo lifted Lucky's head, resting it on his thigh. "Better?"

"Yeah." Not much warmth soaked through Bo's riding attire, but Lucky breathed deep of cologne, sweat, and man. The pain in his foot lessened from "motherfuck!" to "sumbitch!"

"Now, what were you saying about PTO? As in parent-teacher organization?"

Bo sweeping cool fingers across Lucky's brow chased back the headache. "Beats anything I ever stumbled into before. If I had to guess, I'd swear they were regular folk, not drug dealers. I know they come in all shapes and sizes, and can't be profiled, but they didn't want to hurt me and the woman seemed truly upset when I told them kids died."

"Didn't want to hurt you? Have you seen yourself?"

A blush required too much effort. "I'll tell you 'bout that later. Anyhow, they dumped me here to keep me out of the way while they made a break for it. Did Walter find out anything more about the van owner's connection?"

"I haven't talked to him since this morning. If he did he didn't mention it to me."

Another four-wheeler pulled up. "You boys find him?"

Russell called out, "Yeah. We got it," rising to approach the new arrival.

Ignoring the man now quietly murmuring with Russell a few feet away, Lucky told Bo, "Not that I'm not happy as hell to see you, but what're you doin' here? I though you went back to Atlanta."

"Walter recalled us as backup when your escort didn't report in. You know I'm a hiker, right? Well, I'm signed up with Appalachian Search and Rescue. When I got a phone call, I alerted Walter and the group. Since I had a location, a few of us started with the road. We've got several groups on foot with bloodhounds." He jerked his head toward the man. "Russell found you and called us in."

The four-wheeler pulled away and Russell darted to his own to retrieve a first aid kit. Bag in hand, he returned to hunker down on the ground. "What do you need?" he asked.

Lucky wanted to say, *For you to leave me alone with Bo for a minute,* but he held his tongue.

"Got any water?" he asked instead.

"I do." Bo unclipped a tube from his shoulder and lowered the end to Lucky's mouth. "Bite and suck." The other end of the tube disappeared into Bo's backpack.

I'd rather suck something else, Lucky bit back, his heart not quite in his intended kidding. Tired. So tired. He allowed Bo to raise his shoulders while chomping the end of the tube and taking a tentative suck. The sweet taste of water flooded his mouth.

Bo laid him back down, but after a moment he motioned for the tube and Bo handed it over. Water never tasted so good.

Bo busied himself with the first aid kit, cleaning a nasty cut on Lucky's forearm, while the first responder wrapped his foot. "I'm splinting to keep it stable, for anything else you'll need the pros. I might do more harm than good."

Together Bo and Russell managed to wrangle Lucky into a spare jacket and onto the back of Bo's four-wheeler for a jolting, shuddery trek down the mountain. Wrapped tightly around Bo, squeezing when the bumps shook his leg, Lucky might've enjoyed the ride under different circumstances.

Russell shot ahead, out of sight, and Bo stopped his vehicle. He twisted around on the seat to face Lucky. "Are you all right? Do you need to rest a minute? The ride's gotta be killing you. I..." He killed the engine and slammed his mouth down hard on Lucky's, delivering a kiss that bordered on violence. The whole time he kept his fingers moving over Lucky's head, neck, shoulders, as though he feared Lucky might suddenly vanish.

Lucky *Mmmmphhhhed* through the pain of cracked lips.

When Bo finally let go, he said, "I thought I'd lost you. Don't you ever scare me like that again!"

Gazes locked, Lucky told the honest to God truth. "I work for Walter." Not the SNB, but Walter. "I can't promise you I won't be late to dinner sometimes, and you won't know where I am. And I can't promise that one day you won't be called upon to pack my desk up, 'cause I won't be back."

Neither said anything for a few moments, they sat staring into each other's eyes.

"You may have to do the same for me some day," Bo whispered. He started up the four-wheeler before Lucky could answer.

A million scenarios played out in Lucky's head—a pharmacy hold-up, a crash during a high-speed chase, a gun-toting junkie resisting arrest—all ending with a very dead Bo. It wouldn't always be tearful parents with picket signs. A painful ankle couldn't compete with the jolt through Lucky's heart. Why the hell did he have to bring up the very real prospect of dying in the line of duty? Until that moment, Lucky'd believed only he was at risk.

He held a little tighter as they approached the flashing lights of an ambulance.

***

Flat on his back—again—and no Bo hovering above to make it worth his while. Lucky gazed down at his poor, abused leg, now covered by a light blue cast. His toes peeked out the very end. Huge neon letters declared, "Keith was here!" along with a smaller, more subdued, "Get well soon—Walter." No "Bo was here," mainly because Bo hadn't been there, not that Lucky knew of. Of course, Lucky hadn't been there all the time either, having spent much of the first day in la-la land, courtesy of drugs that apparently weren't in short supply. Nope, not at all. Press the nurse call button, yell "Ow!" and get a shot. Pretty efficient system. And all he had to do was break his ankle bad enough to need a pin. And surgery.

Walter sat at Lucky's bedside. They really had to stop meeting like this. "Glad I don't have to attend another one of your funerals. I must say I like you much better among the living." While normally a visit from Walter wasn't cause for celebration, Lucky welcomed the Starbucks cup firmly clinched in the big man's paw. "You have more lives than the average tabby cat."

Lucky held up a finger in a "wait a minute" gesture. He swigged down half the cup of coffee, rescuing the brew from the horrible fate of getting cold. "Actually, I got off pretty light."

"Yes, and Bo's been telling some rather thrilling tales of how you broke your foot, each one more fantastic than the last."

He had? Maybe he had come by. Several flower arrangements sat on a table near the bed, shorter vases in front, taller in the back, bows all facing forward. Yup, he'd been by.

"Mind filling me in on the truth, to keep me from worrying about the alien encounter rumor? I must say, some of your coworkers are quite gullible, and Bo's very gifted at pulling their legs."

Lucky damped down pride. After all, Walter had entrusted him with Bo's training, right? The rookie learned from a master. "Any story he's telling is bound to be better than the truth. I wallowed around in bat shit and jumped out of a window."

Without blinking an eye, Walter replied, "While I've always encouraged hobbies, Lucky, I'd rather hoped you'd take up golfing. Are you serious, or did I lose the betting pool?"

"To tell the truth, I wish I was lying. But I saw a chance to get away, created a diversion with a bunch of bats, and dove for the window, counting on a kudzu vine to break my fall. I missed." Damned short-assed arms. Not that he'd tell Bo.

Walter sat stony-faced for a moment before throwing his head back in laughter. His entire body shook, and he raised a finger to his eye, wiping away a tear. "I'm sorry, Lucky, I don't actually find that funny. Well, yes I do, but it's amazingly close to a story Bo told about magic beans and a castle in the clouds."

Lucky rolled his eyes. Walter's sense of humor would be the death of him someday. "Well, I did meet a giant, bigger than you even."

"We tracked the van. The owner hasn't been seen in days, according to his neighbors. We still have no leads on the woman. Have you thought of anything else useful?"

"Only that she seemed upset when I told her kids died. That doesn't mean anything. You'd get the same reaction from my sister. What have you found out on the vials?"

"The label is of Chinese origin, though no manufacturer is listed, which makes tracing back to the source difficult."

Fuck. Lucky'd been afraid of that. "In the meantime they're still cranking out poison."

"I'm afraid so. The lab results came back for paclitaxel, a chemotherapy drug, which matches the label. Normally the raw drug is bound to a variety of delivery agents, in most cases, ethanol or albumin."

"But not in this case."

"No. I'm usually thrilled when a team member guesses correctly. I'll make an exception this time. According to the label, the product contains glycerin. According to the lab, it contains diethylene glycol."

"Shit." While he trusted Bo, Lucky'd hoped the man had been wrong this time.

"I'm inclined to agree with you, Lucky. However, that's not the worst of it."

"No?" He didn't want to know, he really didn't.

Walter told him anyway. "Two more patients died."

CHAPTER TWENTY

Bo poked his head in the door promptly at three o'clock. "You ready to go?"

Lucky sat in a wheelchair, casted foot propped up in front of him. He wore a slipper on the other, and a T-shirt and pajama pants, courtesy of Walter's missus. Crap, he could pass for Mrs. Griggs' long-lost brother. "While I appreciate you coming to get me, shouldn't you be at work?"

"Actually, Walter asked me to make sure you got home."

"He did?" *Okay, Walter, why not just come out and say you know about us?*

"Yes, he did. Now mind if we get a move on? I'm double-parked out front. Let me go get some help." Bo disappeared out the door, and returned a few minutes later with a hospital orderly. The orderly pushed Lucky while Bo wheeled a cart loaded with flowers, a goodie bag from the hospital, a pair of crutches, and Lucky's shoes. With any luck a thoughtful nurse had burned his clothing.

They rode down the elevator, Lucky's heart constricting when they stopped on the third floor to pick up a passenger, before realizing, *different hospital.* He started with "Dear God," and silently stumbled over a prayer for Stephanie. He ended with "Amen."

At the front door Bo abandoned the cart. "I gotta go get the truck."

Lucky scowled. "You said you were double-parked."

"We'd still be arguing up in your room if I hadn't lit a fire under you."

Damn. Bo really was getting better at lying.

Bo brought his Durango around. A little pushing, pulling, and a few muttered oaths later saw Lucky strapped into the

166

passenger seat. Bo tucked Lucky's bag, shoes, flowers, and crutches in the backseat.

"Made any progress on the case?" Three damned days Lucky had been out of the loop, three damned days too many.

"Not much. Mostly I've been working with the Feds. Walter wants you to stay out of the office until next week."

"I'm going back tomorrow." Lucky had questions. The office had answers.

"I brought your laptop. Can't you work from home?"

Home. Lying down, doing nothing, too much time to think? Or office, neck deep in paperwork, but access to details of their case? "I'll give it some thought."

They arrived at Lucky's duplex. Bo bounded around the hood to open the passenger door.

"Oh! A gentleman!" Mrs. Griggs gushed. A solid black cat sprawled across her lap and a gray and black kitten licked a paw beside her on the swing. Two more felines lay at her feet. What did she plan on doing, collecting every cat in the neighborhood?

"Hey, Mrs. Griggs!" Bo called, waving at the woman wearing a bathrobe at four o'clock in the afternoon. To Lucky he said, "Give me your keys."

"What?"

"You heard me. Give me your keys."

"Why?"

Bo extended his hand. "Now, please. Unless you'd like to haul everything in by yourself."

Lucky handed over his keys. Bo settled him on crutches before trotting to the front door, arms loaded. He returned two more times, for the remaining flowers and a grocery sack, all while Lucky worked on getting the crutches to move the way he wanted them to.

Bo appeared at his elbow the moment he reached the front steps. "I'm not helpless," Lucky barked, immediately wishing he hadn't. One crutch hurt his underarm where he'd rubbed it raw in the woods with his improvised tree branch support.

"I'm not helping you. I'm helping the neighborhood by getting your ill ass inside the house, so you won't be their problem anymore."

Once inside, Lucky aimed his lopsided gait toward the couch. Bo steered him toward the bedroom. "I'm not bed-ridden," Lucky snarled.

"You need your rest," Bo replied, applying a bit more pressure to the guiding hand on Lucky's back.

"I'm not dying." He'd already lost too much time lying in the hospital. And, damn it, he had work to do. The trail grew colder with each passing minute.

"You should take it easy."

"I've been taking it easy!" Lucky splayed his crutches, digging in and holding his position. The only way he'd agree to a bed is if Bo intended to join him, and being seen as an invalid didn't bode well for wild reunion sex.

Bo grinned. "I won't blow you if you're sitting on the couch."

Damn, but Bo fought dirty. "Lead on."

The Dimple appeared in Bo's cheek. "I figured you'd see things my way." He made a great show of settling Lucky on the bed. "Why don't you take a nap while I fix supper?"

"Um... I believe you promised me a blow job."

"Food first, dessert later."

"I'm not helpless."

"Not saying you are. Now here, lift up your arms so I can get this shirt off you."

"You're kidding, right?"

"Do I look like I'm kidding?" Bo tapped Lucky's arm. "Up."

"Jeez, man! Beat up on the invalid, why don't you?" Lucky scowled, but raised his arms when Bo out-scowled him. The shirt slipped over his head. Hmm... not too bad. He held up his foot. "Slipper?"

Plop! The slipper hit the floor. "Pants?"

A bit of maneuvering, a few false starts, and much grunting and groaning later, they'd worked the thin cotton pants over Lucky's cast.

Lucky waggled his brows. "Boxers?"

Bo's pushed him down on the bed. "Nice try. You rest, I'll make food." He brushed his lips against Lucky's forehead and retreated.

"A blow job might help me sleep!" Lucky shouted through the closed door. He twiddled his thumbs. He glowered at his cast. He counted the spines on the dragon statue's back where it sat in his nightstand—twenty-seven. Still no Bo. His eyelids drooped. Maybe he'd close them for a minute. Didn't mean he'd suddenly become obedient or anything.

Bo woke him some time later. "Sit up. Time to eat." Something smelled delicious. Lucky glanced from the plate in Bo's hand up to a pointed chin, high cheekbones, The Dimple, and warm regard in a pair of eyes darkened to ebony in the soft glow of the beside lamp. Hmmm... something looked delicious, too, and it wasn't the food.

"What you got there?" Lucky struggled into a sitting position while discreetly adjusting his very interested erection. Was it kinky that Bo's cooking excited him nearly as much as the sight of the man's bubble-butt?

Bo's upper lip curled. "Feel honored. For you I cooked chicken." He spread a towel over Lucky's lap, ignoring the bulge there. "I also dumped the contents of your fridge into the trash. Anything remotely edible wasn't good for you. The rest looked like some high school junior's science project."

Lucky drew back in mock horror. "You threw out Herbie and Fred?"

A wrinkle appeared between Bo's brows. "Who the hell are Herbie and Fred?"

"My plants."

"Oh, the rotten onion and sprouted potato? I planted them in the back yard before we ever left for Anderson."

Lucky stared hard. Sometimes he couldn't tell if Bo was joking or serious. Somewhere over the last few months, Bo had lost some of his innocent demeanor. Was Bo's sass a good thing or a bad thing? The scent of roasted chicken breast distracted him. His mouth watered.

Bo placed a glass of sweet tea on the nightstand and darted from the room, returning a moment later with a glass of water and another plate. He sat in a chair by the bed, placing his water next to Lucky's tea. "Need help?"

With a hostile glare Lucky dared Bo to offer to cut his chicken for him. "Oh!" He chewed a bite, trying to identify the spices used. Damn, that was good. So good he almost didn't mind the steamed broccoli the chicken shared a plate with. Green things belonged in flowerpots or in gardens, not on plates. He saved the broccoli for last.

"If you dare say, 'There's something green on my plate, get it off' again, I'm gonna whap you," Bo said, eyes focused on his own dinner of broccoli, steamed rice, and what might have been tofu, Lucky couldn't say. His mind refused to wrap around someone actually choosing the tasteless cubes over tasty chicken. Or bacon. Damn but he missed real, came-from-a-pig bacon, or "cancer in a handy one-pound package," as Bo called it. Lucky avoided lectures by agreeing. However, he also avoided bacon when Bo wasn't around, on the off chance that someone who'd undergone years of medical training might be right.

After forcing himself to down the broccoli, saving time by not chewing, Lucky loosed a belch worthy of wresting "Best Belch" honors from Charlotte in one of the contests he used to hold with his siblings. "That was good." He clanged his fork down onto his plate.

One side of Bo's mouth turned up. He handed Lucky the TV remote and took the plates out of the room. A few minutes later Lucky heard water running in the kitchen sink. He didn't feel much like watching TV, but he'd missed a few episodes of his favorite soap opera. After a bit of fumbling he pulled up a recorded episode of *South Bend Springs*. Bo returned a few minutes later, easing down on the bed beside him.

"Lila's pregnant again. They did a paternity test." He flashed Lucky a wicked grin.

"If you tell me who the father is, I swear to God I'll—"

"Just for that I won't tell you it's—"

"Bo!" Lucky lunged as much as his cast let him.

The episode ended. Bo hopped from the bed, strolled across the room, and turned off the TV. "You need rest."

"No, I don't. I just took a nap not too long ago."

"Yes, you do."

"No. I. Don't."

"If I blow you will you go to sleep?"

"Maybe."

Bo snorted. "Has it ever occurred to you that you might not be the only one wanting to get reacquainted? And that rest equals healing faster which equals less time until wild monkey sex?"

Lucky tossed the remote to the floor. "TV can wait."

"I thought you'd see it my way."

Lucky shifted, trying to get comfortable. Bo pulled the covers down. "Damn, I missed you," he murmured, running his hands gently over the healing bruises on Lucky's body.

Not as much as I missed you. Lucky had fantasized this very thing, Bo taking care of him, the night he'd spent in the woods. And here he was being an ass about it. *I can't change who I am.*

Bo framed Lucky's face with his hands, lifting Lucky's head and skimming their lips together. He planted a kiss on Lucky's forehead, on each eyelid, nose, and cheeks, bypassing a healing gash and the goose egg knot left by a tree branch. With light nibbles he tickled Lucky's chin. Down Lucky's neck Bo traveled, licking, nibbling, and sucking a path from neck to ear. He ran his tongue around the shell, briefly darting it inside.

Bo tongued a path downward, reacquainting his mouth with Lucky's chest, seemingly determined to lick every bit of skin at his disposal. Lucky gasped when Bo sealed his lips over Lucky's nipple.

Combing his fingers through Bo's hair, Lucky moaned his appreciation while applying pressure, urging Bo down. His cock strained against the fabric of his boxers, a damp spot forming in the cotton. *There! I need you there!*

Bo sank lower and lower, teasing Lucky by bypassing the goods and running his tongue under the leg of Lucky's boxers, licking as much of Lucky's crotch as possible before the fabric got in the way. He loosed an evil grim and pulled Lucky's balls through the opening in the garment. First one, then the other, he took into his mouth, rolling them with his tongue.

Hip rolling on Lucky's part and tugging on Bo's got his boxers off. Finally! Bo swiped his tongue up Lucky's shaft, coaxing Lucky's rising erection to full life. He whirled around the glans before following a bulging vein to the root with his tongue tip, and proceeded to rain opened-mouthed kisses up and down Lucky's shaft. A little more. Just a little more.

Bo chuckled and withdrew.

Wha...What? No! Not now! Come back! "Tease!" Lucky ground out from between gritted teeth.

"Good things come to those who wait," Bo quoted.

"If you say so." Lucky bucked again. Bo shrank back again.

Fingers pressed firmly at the base of Lucky's balls, Bo began sucking in earnest, taking Lucky into his mouth and gliding up and down.

Oh yeah, baby, that's it! Lucky moaned, twisting wads of blanket in his fists.

Fully clothed still, Bo wriggled against the mattress, humping the bed while he sucked Lucky. Damn that was sexy. Lucky would love to help the guy out, but couldn't bring himself to move. "Oh yeah, just like that." He closed his eyes, letting his head fall back against the headboard.

The pressure began deep within, building, building. Oh fuck! Oh fuck! The pressure exploded, internal spasms pulsing. Electric currents fired though him, curling his toes and tightening his grip on the sheets. He let go into Bo's mouth. Wave after wave after wave of ecstasy rolled over him, around him, through him. "Ahhhh...!" He arched his back off the bed.

Bo latched on to Lucky's hips, holding him down, taking everything Lucky gave. When at last Lucky shuddered one last time and relaxed back on the bed, Bo jumped up and unzipped his fly to free himself. Eyes slightly unfocused and face a mask of twisted concentration, he stroked his length with reckless abandon. He threw his head back, eyes scrunched tightly shut. "Oh fuck," he muttered.

"Thought you'd never ask." Lucky reached out and clutched a firm ass cheek, hauling Bo closer and taking the man's straining erection into his mouth. The scent of male musk rekindled his own spent lust.

Bo thrust frantically into Lucky's mouth. "I'm close! Ah, ah, ah!" He clamped his fingers down on Lucky's shoulders, as spurt after spurt fell on Lucky's tongue.

Once he stopped trembling, Bo crawled over Lucky and

collapsed onto the bed, breathless and glassy-eyed. "Damn."

Lucky couldn't have said it better himself.

Trailing his fingertips lightly through the hair on Lucky's chest, Bo placed a kiss on one shoulder. "You have no idea how much I missed you," he said.

In the woods. Alone. Fearing he'd never see Bo again, all came roaring back on Lucky. The remorse, the things he wished he'd said but hadn't. He struggled for the words to convey all he needed to, but they wouldn't come. He only managed, "Yeah, I missed you too," and wrapped an arm around Bo's shoulders. Clinging in near desperation, he willed Bo to understand, to feel, to somehow *know* what Lucky couldn't say.

Bo snuggled into the embrace, wafting out a contented-sounding sigh. The warm breath grazed Lucky's skin. They lay together, the occasional rumble of a passing car the only sound.

A tentative "Want me to stay?" came out half muffled by Lucky's chest against Bo's face.

"Yes." *Tonight. Always.* Lucky pulled Bo closer, pausing mid pull. *Whoa, where the hell did that come from?*

CHAPTER TWENTY-ONE

Coffee. *Sniff*. Shampoo. *Sniff*. Bo's cologne. A car door slammed outside. Lucky opened one bleary eye. Damn, he'd hoped to be up to at least say goodbye, but maybe this way worked better. Lately he'd been having dangerous thoughts, and last night's *wanting Bo to stay more nights,* or more precisely, every night, quite frankly scared the hell out of him.

He grabbed the crutches propped by the bed and lurched out to the kitchen for a cup of coffee. While his foot and ankle still throbbed occasionally, duty called. A cup sat by the coffeemaker, white crystals in the bottom. Lucky poured a cup of brew, staring out the window at what promised to be a warm day.

It took him longer than normal to get dressed, and he'd never before worn shorts to the office, but he simply couldn't get pants on over the cast. Oh well, "the team" would just have to freaking get over it. He wrestled on his backpack, weighted down with his laptop. Why hadn't he asked Bo to take the darned thing? Was it always this heavy? Oh, yeah. Asking Bo would've meant Bo knowing Lucky's intentions. Which would have led to a fight. Damn it, he was beat up, not at death's door.

It took several minutes to arrange his casted leg on the floorboard of his car. He experimented driving on his own street before daring heavier traffic. Somehow he managed to make it to work without incident.

No one witnessed his staggering journey from car to elevator, and he sagged against the walls on the ride up. Coming in this morning wasn't one of his better ideas.

"Good morning, Mr. Harrison," the perky receptionist greeted him. "Good to have you back." She smiled. At him. People didn't smile at Lucky; they frowned or glowered.

174

Good to have him back? Who was she fucking kidding? Too tired to growl properly, Lucky bobbed his head in the receptionist's direction and set off down the hall toward his cube.

"You're not supposed to be here." Bo glared across the distance separating their two desks.

"I have work to do." Lucky supposed he'd sound more assertive if he weren't struggling to stay upright.

Bo's unrelenting gaze dared Lucky to argue. "I could have brought anything you needed to your house."

Lucky shrugged as best he could, weighted down with a computer bag and awkwardly braced on his crutches. "I'm here now."

"Yes, you are." Bo glanced from Lucky's desk to Lucky and back again. He dragged his fingers through his hair and let out a resigned huff that couldn't quite drown out the "Stubborn asshole," he muttered under his breath. After a moment of obvious indecision, he rounded his desk, grabbed the crutches, and propped them against the wall. Lucky welcomed Bo's steadying hand on his arm.

"Let me catch you up," Bo continued, snaking an arm around Lucky's waist and directing him across the floor. "We searched Dr. Grayson's house and found more of the imported drugs. He's in hiding right now, but not our problem anymore. The Feds are after him."

"Well damn." Lucky'd love to hunt the bastard down himself. A few questions needed answering.

"The funny thing is, we've gone over his financial records. He doesn't appear to have profited from the sale of those drugs."

What? "Then why do it? Why risk getting busted if he didn't stand to gain anything?" Lucky leaned against his desk, allowing Bo to remove the backpack.

"Remember what I told you in the conference room? Doctors take an oath for their patients, Lucky. He's not the only doctor to take desperate measures." Lucky watched Bo set up the laptop, exactly where he normally placed it. "The rest are luckier and get off with a fine and a slap on the wrist 'cause nobody died. Everyone I talked to at Rosario was shocked. They said the man was a saint who'd do anything for his patients.

He even volunteered his off time. I honestly don't believe he's the kind to make a profit off someone else's suffering. And yet Danvers exploited every opportunity. I don't get it."

A lot of things didn't make sense when it came to illicit drugs. Bo would learn in time, as Lucky had. "Reckon we'd find a connection between Grayson and Danvers, if we look hard enough?"

"No telling. I wish we'd gotten to him sooner. The four kids who died were all Grayson's patients."

Lucky swallowed hard. Steph. No, he couldn't ask Bo for fear of what the answer might be. He'd rather not make the man the bearer of bad news. "Any leads yet on his connections?"

"Not yet. No telling where the day might lead, though it's not officially our case anymore."

With Bo's help, Lucky hobbled around his desk, scowling down at an unfamiliar chair. "Where's the Hell Bitch?"

"Keith's out of the office. I switched with him. I figured you'd be stubborn enough to come in this morning, and the last thing you need is to fall over with a broken leg. Your balance might be off because of the cast."

Lucky grumbled, more because he believed Bo expected it than anything else. In truth, he liked having Bo on his side. And if Keith returned unexpectedly and found himself sprawled on the floor, far be it from Lucky not to laugh. The asshole had some humbling coming, in Lucky's opinion. Still, he didn't like the idea of resting his hiney in Keith's ass-print. Hmm... Maybe he'd order tacos for lunch. With a side of beans. "Thanks," he said, easing down into the chair.

Bo nodded in reply. He upended an empty trashcan to prop Lucky's cast on before returning to his own desk. Lucky had no idea what he'd done to deserve the man. Back turned, Bo couldn't see Lucky mouth, "Thanks."

The first thing Lucky did after booting up his laptop was e-mail Walter for a list of the patients who'd died.

He started his morning as he usually did, checking FDA, DEA, and Board of Pharmacy websites for current news, unsurprised to find a blurb about the meds they'd uncovered at the mill. A headline for a local paper read, "US Doctors Buying

Unapproved Drugs." He expected to read about his and Bo's case, but instead found what Walter had alluded to—that nearly eighty medical practices had been caught importing cancer drugs from Turkey, China, and other countries. Had they lost their minds? What made a doctor take such risks?

"Patients are dying. We can't get medicines through normal channels. Of course we're desperate enough to try anything," the article quoted an unnamed physician. Bo'd said pretty much the same thing.

Lucky read the article twice and searched online for similar posts, appalled at the sheer extent of the problem.

"I'm giving my patients a chance," another anonymous source provided. Is that how Grayson saw the situation? Him giving his patients a chance? What kind of world did Lucky live in where doctors risked jail terms to save the folks under their care? What kind of world made such extremes measures necessary?

Lucky compiled a list of clinics and established routes of the mentioned drugs into the US. While some imports proved effective, if unapproved for US use through the FDA, others amounted to colored water, or worse, did more harm than good.

"I've been thinking about Danvers," Bo said, spinning his chair to face Lucky. "I trusted him. I defended him when other people accused him of wrongdoing. I considered him a hero for getting those kids the medicines they needed, even if he broke hospital rules to do it. And all this time he'd been serving his own interests. I'm such a fool."

"You're not a fool, you're just too trusting."

"Same difference." Bo snorted. "I wish I could be more like you and not trust anybody."

Not trust anybody. Lucky reeled. Was that how Bo saw him? Completely untrusting? And Bo wanted to be like him? The man simply wouldn't be the same without his trusting nature. Yes, it got him into trouble sometimes, but Lucky wouldn't wish his suspicious nature on anybody. "Don't say that. It's part of who you are. After a while on this job, you'll learn who you can trust and who you can't."

Bo gave a little half-smile and humorless laugh. "Until then I have you to keep me straight. Remind me to listen to you next time you tell me not to trust someone." He darted a gaze toward the entrance of their cube and wheeled his chair across the floor, closing the gap between them. "You may be stubborn and hard to get along with, but you have a good heart."

"I do not!" Lucky snapped. "Don't even start that rumor."

"Your secret's safe with me." Bo winked. "Although I'm sure Walter's figured it out by now. I'm convinced Walter knows everything."

The words gave Lucky pause. Exactly how much did Walter know, and what did he plan to do with that knowledge?

"Anyway," Bo retreated back to his own desk, "what's going to happen to Danvers now?"

"Not a damned thing."

"What?" Bo nearly toppled over onto the floor, even without the Hell Bitch's help.

"Not a damned thing, Bo. He didn't do anything illegal, just immoral, and he's already paid for being greedy with his job." Damn, how the asshole's double-dealing boiled Lucky's blood. The bastard should lose everything. No telling how many innocent people suffered while he'd shuffled goods back and forth, lining his family's pockets. Lucky would do his damnedest to make sure Primero Care lost their license, but until the anti-gray market bill passed, there wasn't much anyone could do. Sometimes laws protected the innocent, sometimes the guilty. He could dog their heels, however, and arrange extremely regular inspections.

Bo's gaze fell to Lucky's desk. "You don't have any coffee. Let me go get you some."

It suddenly occurred to Lucky that Bo's willingness to do for others actually served as a way to escape scrutiny, have a little private time to collect his thoughts. How many times had he done the same before and Lucky hadn't recognized the distancing technique?

He recalled a park bench in Florida, the first time they kissed, followed by Bo's abrupt departure. And not long ago, Bo's frantic phone call when he'd learned of the first deaths.

He'd delivered his news and taken off, leaving Lucky baffled. More examples came to mind of Bo's sudden disappearances.

The pieces fell into place. Whenever upset, confused, or in need of comfort, Bo ran away instead. Why? Was he afraid of what Lucky might say?

In Lucky's younger days, he'd turned to his family in times of trouble. Having grown up in an abusive household with a father too ready to find fault, Bo probably learned to hide. Damn. Bo admitted to being wrong. Had his father beaten him for being wrong? More than likely. Lucky's own family merely laughed off mistakes or doled out extra chores, but they'd rallied around each other in times of sickness or pain. That is, until most of them turned their backs.

Lucky climbed unsteadily to his feet. Crap! Why did Bo put his crutches so far away? He hopped over to the far wall, checking to ensure no witnesses before tottering down the hall.

He ducked into the kitchen/break area. No Bo, but a fresh pot of coffee brewed, showing he'd probably been there.

Next, he checked the men's room—still no Bo. About to return to his cube or go ask Walter for Bo's whereabouts, he noticed a conference room door slightly ajar. Through the crack he spotted his quarry, staring out over the Atlanta skyline. In the distance stood Stone Mountain. Lucky'd visited there as a kid, awed by the carving of Robert E. Lee, Stonewall Jackson, and Jefferson Davis, heroes of the Confederacy.

Bo hunched his shoulders at the *tap, tap* of Lucky's crutches, not that sneaking up was even possible. Lucky closed the door and crossed the floor at an unsteady gait. He'd never take the simple act of walking for granted again. Balancing on one foot, he set the crutches aside and wrapped his arms around Bo.

Bo relaxed into the embrace, letting out a shuddering breath. "I suck at this kind of work," he said. "I always manage to get taken in by the bad guys. Back in the military, while I may not actually have liked or fully agreed with my commanding officers, they were on the up and up. I accepted their orders without question. In the civilian world, rank doesn't necessarily mean integrity. I need to learn to question everything, like you do."

"You give everyone an equal chance. Me? To me they're guilty, even if they prove otherwise."

Bo sighed. "Aren't we a pair? The man who trusts everyone and the man who trusts no one."

"I trust you."

Bo jerked his head around so fast, amazing he didn't get whiplash. "You do?"

Was that so hard to believe? Well, actually, coming from Lucky, yeah. *I trust him?* Bo, who charged to the rescue when Lucky was lost, who knew all his big ugly secrets, put up with all forms of bullshit and kept coming back. *Yes, I trust him.* When had that happened?

Lucky hadn't let his guard down in a long time, avoided the need too. *If you didn't trust 'em, they couldn't hurt you.*

He nuzzled Bo's neck, breathing in his lover's scent. *Of course you trust him. You love him, don't you?*

Lucky stiffened. Love. Squirmy, uncomfortable feelings moved into his gut. *Yes, I love him, and I trust him.*

And he trusts everybody. Even me.

Lucky's track record for trustworthiness sucked. Now, though, he couldn't love someone and let them down, but—he hadn't let Bo down yet, had he? Not even when that jerkoff tried to run Bo over with a big ass SUV during the Ryerson Pain Clinic bust last winter. Not letting Bo down had nearly gotten Lucky killed, but he hadn't even thought about dying, he'd simply used himself and a highly unfortunate Mazda as a battering ram. And if he'd bought the big one doing it, it would've been okay. Because it was for Bo.

And Bo was here now, bleeding at the heart for innocent kids and tracking Lucky when he'd gone missing. Because— *Damn it, don't go reading too much into what Bo did, he trusted people, he was good to people, he—* But he had to care back, didn't he?

How the hell am I supposed to figure this one out?

Maybe all this crap would sort itself if Lucky could just accept for more than seventeen heart-wrenching seconds that he could love Bo. A guy shouldn't have to stare a rampaging Tahoe in the grill to admit caring, damn it.

If he cared, then he'd want Bo to care too. Nobody cared about Lucky, not even his family. Except for Charlotte. She loved him still, the poor misguided girl. And maybe, for all the ways Bo seemed to have his head screwed on wrong at times, his neck was cricked just right to see what others missed. 'Cause Lucky sure as hell didn't deserve a happy ever after.

Bo did deserve one. *I love this man. And it scares the ever-living hell out of me.*

Instead of saying any one of the many things he should have, Lucky remained quiet, head tucked between Bo's shoulder blades. Bo's heart beat against Lucky's ear, the steady rhythm of his breathing playing a lulling melody. For one moment in time nothing could intrude. Victor and years spent in prison didn't exist, the SNB didn't exist. Nothing mattered but Bo, staring out a window at a sunny day.

The tension bled out of Bo, and he nestled more snugly in Lucky's arms. "I'm okay now. Let's go get your coffee and do what they pay us to." He turned and gave Lucky a quick kiss. "Thanks."

"For what? I didn't do anything."

"Sometimes, being there is enough." Bo slipped from the conference room before Lucky could ask any more questions. He stopped by the kitchen for coffee, leaving Lucky to navigate the halls on his own.

With a weary sigh Lucky dropped down in front of his computer. Oh shit. He'd gotten an answer from Walter. Holding his breath and uttering a silent prayer, he clicked open the e-mail. His heart stopped. "Stephanie Owens" topped the list of victims. Oh dear God, no!

He blinked hard, hoping he'd misread. But no. The name didn't change.

A quick Google search produced a newspaper obituary column. Smiling at him from a full color photo was the little girl he remembered, face framed by auburn curls. In her arms she held a black-and-white cat.

CHAPTER TWENTY- TWO

"Here's your coffee." Bo placed the cup on Lucky's desk. Lucky grunted a reply. A sweet little girl would never smile again, poisoned by a man supposed to help her. He snatched up his crutches. "I gotta go."

"Lucky? Are you all right? Lucky? Lucky!" Bo shouted after him.

Walter chose that moment to step out of his office. "Lucky? You're not supposed to be here."

"I'm not here." Lucky hobbled his way around his boss. "You haven't seen me."

He ignored Bo's and Walter's questions, letting out a pent-up breath when he stepped into the elevator and the door closed behind him.

Ignoring his ringing cell phone, he zigged and zagged through traffic on the way to his house, blinking hard to clear his vision. He slammed on the brakes, hopping and cursing his way up the front walk without acknowledging Mrs. Griggs and the army of cats at her feet. He didn't even bother to bring his phone in with him.

He sagged onto the couch, flinging his crutches down in a rage. Why? Why? Always before he'd kept his distance, not letting his cases get under his skin, why this one?

"Merrrrow?" A cat popped through the front door he'd left standing open. A black-and-white cat. "Mrrrooow?" it asked again. It spotted Lucky and, tail held high, scampered over to the couch and jumped up. Lucky started to yell and stopped himself. One paw on Lucky's side, the feline rose up, touched noses, and rubbed its head under Lucky's chin, purring loudly.

His mother believed in omens and in the dead sending messages from the other side. She'd say that maybe Stephanie sent the cat in payment for the one Lucky had given her, or to tell him she'd be okay. *A bunch of superstitious nonsense, Lucky, get a grip!*

Lucky scooped up the creature and buried his face against the cat, its soft fur muffling his sob. Pressure built in his chest. How could that poor, sweet child be gone? Tears slipped down his nose. He batted them away. Why, why, why, why, why? He clutched the cat, mouth open in a silent scream. Damn it! No! He'd been there. He should've seen! He should have stopped it! Why couldn't Walter have sent them the day he'd completed his last job? Would it have made a difference? What if he tried harder? What if he'd been there investigating the nights Bo worked over, instead of prowling outside, accusing his lover of wrongs? What if, what if, what if?

He wailed, long and hard, like he hadn't since finding out about Victor's suicide. The cat wriggled into a comfortable spot to ride out the storm.

Lucky awoke groggy, sweating where a fur-covered space heater lay against his arm. "What the fuck?" He jumped but the cat merely blinked at him sleepily and lay its head back down. Its throat vibrated against Lucky's skin.

The clock showed 4:55. Bo should be getting off work soon. *Maybe I better go get my phone. I bet he's been calling.* Lucky lugged the cat to the door and let it out, closing the door when it tried to come back in.

A crutch under one arm, he attempted to make coffee the way Bo did, though his never came close to Bo's in the past. A bald head, blue eyes so full of life, and hopeful smile forced its way into his brain. Lucky pushed the image out again. Maybe some other time he'd think about Stephanie. Not right now. His blood pressure rose at the thought of the injustice done her, and the other victims. If he'd been able to use both legs he'd have gone to the gym and beat the shit out of some fool in the boxing ring.

He lifted the dishrag hanging over the kitchen faucet and flung it with all his might. It barely made a sound upon impact with the cabinet door. Next, he lobbed the plastic scrubber Bo used on pots and pans. Geared up and ready to go, he hurled potholders, spoons, anything that wouldn't break. Through the house he stormed, hopping on one foot and using walls for support. He jerked his sock drawer open so hard it sailed free of the dresser, spilling sock balls everywhere. One by one he chucked them against the wall. He hefted a drinking glass, stopping himself before launching it, imagining Bo's, "Why the hell did you break things? Who's gonna clean up this mess?"

On to the bathroom he went. Ah! Soap bars made satisfying missiles. Who knew? He'd advanced to the living room and a stack of magazines when Bo opened the door. "Feeling better?" he asked, eyeing the mess.

Sorrow and destruction stood between them. Bo closed the gap. The safety of his arms, the understanding in his eyes. No words were said. None were needed. As one they moved, Bo wrapping Lucky in his arms. "Oh, Lucky."

He pried Lucky's fingers open, saving a back issue of *Reader's Digest* from an airborne trip across the living room. The magazine hit the floor. Clutching Lucky's face in his hands, Bo held him, brushing their lips together far too gently.

Grabbing the back of Bo's head, Lucky smashed their mouths together, determined to lose himself in the moment and the offered comfort. "I don't want gentle," he ground out between kisses.

Step by step they inched across the living room floor, ending in a tangle of arms and legs on the couch. Lucky rutted against Bo like a demon.

"Lucky, I..." Bo began.

"Don't talk, just do. And do it hard."

A bit of wrangling got them both undressed. Bo's button-down and slacks joined Lucky's T-shirt and shorts on the floor. They pushed and pulled, shoved and wrestled, until Lucky lay naked on his back, cast hanging over the side of the couch.

Bo grasped both of Lucky's wrists, pinning them to the couch with a wild look in his eyes. He froze, and then released his grip.

"No," Lucky insisted. "Don't stop. I like it."

A moment of meaningful eye contact and Bo resumed his dominant pose, grinding his erection against Lucky's. He thrust brutally, near to the point of pain, while Lucky chanted, "Oh God, yeah! Like that! Harder, harder, harder!" Finally he yelled, "I want more! Now!"

"You sure?"

"Yeah, damn it!"

Bo vaulted over the back of the couch, slipping and sliding down the hall to the bedroom and hitting the wall once or twice from the sound of it. He came back in record time, making short work of donning a condom and preparing Lucky. Angling to accommodate the cast, he breached Lucky's opening. "You are so fucking tight!"

Lucky clamped down enough to show Bo what tight really was.

"You're killing me." Bo sounded pretty damned happy to be dying.

Lucky pulled Bo down for a ruthless kiss, thrusting his hips to speed a painfully slow entry. He wanted and he wanted now! No talking, no more foreplay, no thinking. Just primal, instinctual, aggressive, *feeling*. Agony/ecstasy, blurring and blending, carrying Lucky away on an undertow.

The couch creaked and groaned as Bo set up a punishing rhythm. Their bodies slapped together, sweat slickening their skin. Burning, stretching, advance, and retreat. Each thrust rocked Lucky and the couch, giving him all he needed. Each drive of Bo's hips pressed his hard length against that perfect spot inside.

Over and over Bo drove in and withdrew, inciting exquisite pain/pleasure. Lucky hovered on the edge when Bo suddenly wrenched Lucky's hands from the couch, pinning them to the arm and holding Lucky in place with his body.

Lucky lost it, spewing gobs of come without directly touching his cock.

Bo followed a scant moment later, moaning, "Oh God, oh God," into Lucky's ear. He released Lucky's arms and fell. They held tightly to each other, heart rates slowing and breathing returning to normal.

Head resting on Lucky's chest, Bo raised his eyes, connecting their gazes. "You should have told me you liked being held down."

Lucky's brain cells slowly threw off their post-sex stupor. "I usually don't. It's a sometimes kind of thing. Besides, I didn't want it to bother you. Especially after you telling me how you feel about restraints."

Bo rolled his shoulders. "This is me and you talking. It's not something I get into personally, but holding you down was kinda hot." He rose up, skating his lips across Lucky's, barely connecting. "I trust you. You wouldn't hurt me."

Really? Hell, Lucky didn't trust himself that far. Bo rose, holding out a hand to Lucky and helping him upright. "I'll be right back." He pulled the condom off while ambling toward the bathroom. Lucky waited, expecting a lecture about his earlier behavior at the office.

Bo returned with a washcloth, cleaning Lucky up a bit before leaving again. He came back with a glass of iced tea for Lucky and a cup of green tea for himself. He sat next to Lucky, lacing together the fingers of their free hands. "Mind telling me what happened at the office to send you running out like that? You scared poor Walter half to death. He planned to come after you but I convinced him you needed to get home and rest, that you'd overdone things."

"Yeah, I did." Although Bo didn't seem to mind Lucky invading his quiet moments, Lucky wouldn't have been so easy to get along with in reversed circumstances. Well, except for the cat.

"What happened? Can you tell me?"

Can you tell me? Leave it to Bo to open the door yet not try to force Lucky through. If he'd made demands, insisted on Lucky talking, Lucky would have shut down tight. Instead, he offered up the truth. Bo deserved respect. "One day at Rosario I got off the elevator on the wrong floor and met one of the patients."

Bo nodded but said nothing.

"There she was, bald, probably going through seven kinds of hell, but she smiled at me, chatted with a stranger." She appeared in his mind, smiling and proudly showing off her doll. "I mean, even my nephews, and you know how much I love them, can act like spoiled brats, never satisfied with what they have, always wanting more. Yet this sick girl seemed happy."

"What was her name?" Bo whispered.

"Stephanie." Lucky raised his chin, blinking to drive away the burning in his eyes.

"The one who died?"

"Yeah."

"I knew her," Bo said quietly.

"You did? How?"

Bo squirmed, fingers tightening on Lucky's. "Remember all the time I spent working over?"

"Yes."

"I didn't spend all of it in the pharmacy. Sometimes I volunteered in the hospital."

"Volunteered? For what?"

"Whatever they needed me for. Sitting with a child who didn't get many visitors, reading to them. Mostly I read."

"Did you know any of the other kids who died?"

Bo turned, meeting Lucky's gaze. "I knew them all."

CHAPTER TWENTY-THREE

"Lucky? Could you and Bo come into my office, please?" Walter stood before Lucky's desk, a smile spreading across his heavy-jowled face.

Lucky exchanged a puzzled glance with his partner before struggling to his feet. Damn, would he ever be glad to lose the cast. He crutched along behind his boss's broad back and claimed his favorite chair in Walter's office before anyone else could, in case Walter called a department meeting. Bo took the other chair and shoved a trashcan over for Lucky to rest his foot on.

"Although now a federal case and no longer ours, I thought you'd like an update on the Rosario situation." Walter settled himself behind his desk. "And, Lucky, a positive identification from you would be most welcome." He handed Lucky a fax.

At first Lucky didn't get what a missing person's report had to do with him, until he read the name, "Anne Fletcher." The picture was old, but the face and eyes were the same. "That's the woman from the mill. The one the leader called Annie."

"Do you recognize this man?" Walter handed over a professionally printed flier, an advertisement for a chartered plane service. A man who appeared more walrus than human stared back.

"Yeah, we've met. The bigger they are, the harder they fall, especially when bat shit's involved."

Bo kicked Lucky's good leg, shifted his gaze to Walter and back to Lucky. His scowl might curdle milk.

Oh. "Present company excluded, of course."

Walter didn't so much as bat an eye. "I avoid bat shit at all costs. It wouldn't work well with my touch of arthritis."

Lucky studied the flier. "This is the leader, the one who did the talking. Annie mentioned a Ted, but I wasn't sure who she meant at the time. She took my cell phone, badge, and .38." While Lucky didn't mourn the loss of his company phone, and could get another badge, he wanted the .38 back. The gun... meant something.

"His name is Theodore Rasmussen. He and Fletcher own a few small planes, flying into a satellite airport in Charlotte, North Carolina, Fletcher's hometown. Luther Calhoun, the owner of the van, lives near Charlotte and works for them, doing odd jobs mostly. Your friend Sammy from Rosario identified him as the man from whom he received his shipments." Walter handed over a picture that appeared to be a high school graduation photo.

"This man's with 'em too," Lucky said. "Last seen shoving a guy with a broken ankle out into the boonies." Asswipe.

"I suspected as much. His name is Kelly Barnett, an employee of Rasmussen's. He's been questioned, but it seems he now faces kidnapping charges, in addition to everything else." Walter shook his head, fluorescent office lighting reflecting off the gray in his salt-and-pepper hair. "Rasmussen's crew primarily gives air tours, though they act as a courier service on occasion. Guess where they're located?"

"Canada or Mexico?"

"Canada."

"Well, hell. They're bringing in the shit from there?"

"Seems that way. Fletcher's sister reported her missing. She disappeared after you last saw her, and the Charlotte hangar's been shut down tight. This is now the Feds' case. We've done our part until it comes to trial. My guess is that Fletcher, Calhoun, and Rasmussen fled to Canada. The call that tipped Bo off to where they'd dropped you originated from a pay-phone in Idaho."

"And that's it?" Bo bolted from his chair. "Four kids lost their lives! These guys are gonna get away with it, aren't they?"

Walter folded his hands on the desk. "That's all we can do at the moment. Once found, they'll be extradited back to this country to stand trial. Fletcher and Calhoun are US citizens."

What a fucking letdown. Lucky would yell and scream if it would do any good. Instead he merely stood and stumbled out of the office, leaving Bo to rant and rave. What a fucking mess.

He sat at his desk, staring at an ugly gray partition. For years he'd done this job to avoid prison orange. He'd served his time and been released, returning only because Bo asked him to. Bo, who believed Lucky's current stint with the SNB was Walter Smith's doing, but Bo could ask Lucky to jump through flaming hoops and he'd probably give it a try. If Bo only knew how much control he had... Dangerous. For a guy who didn't believe in emotional entanglements, Lucky was edging pretty close to the point of no return.

Bo returned to his desk, still grumbling about, "Letting them get away." He pecked away at his keyboard.

Lucky studied Rasmussen and Fletcher's movements, where they lived, family connections. If they'd bolted to Canada, they might not wander south of the border very far, and they most certainly would avoid anywhere near Rosario, but maybe they'd venture locally. Lucky might have turned a corner a few years back, hunting felons instead of being one, but damned if he'd let this group of fellow traffickers escape scot-free.

He spent the afternoon perusing the records of Grayson's interaction with Rasmussen, barely noticing when Bo dropped a sandwich on his desk.

He'd lost track of time when Bo shook his shoulder. "You want me to come over?"

You want me to come over? Not, *"Your place or mine?"* Inequality existed in their relationship—all Lucky's doing. Why the hell did Bo put up with him?

"Why don't I swing by your place later?"

"What? Really?" Bo smiled like a kid at Christmas.

"Yeah, really. I'll even stop and pick up supper if you want me to."

"No, that's fine. I'll throw something together. Say, seven?"

Lucky glanced at the clock on his computer. Five o'clock. "Works for me."

Bo gave Lucky's neck a quick squeeze before joining the herd stampeding toward the elevator. Once the crowd thinned, Lucky tottered to Walter's office.

"Lucky, come in. What can I do for you?"

"I want to go after Rasmussen."

Walter unleashed a sigh that rocked his entire bulk. "I've told you, the matter is out of our hands. I'm as upset about the situation as you are, but we've done our part. Let others take over now."

"It's too important to leave to chance."

"Yes, it is, and I can assure you, it won't be."

Not good enough. Lucky wanted to watch Rasmussen go down. For Stephanie and the other innocent lives lost. "Is that your last word?"

"That's my last word. Now, how's your leg? Getting better?"

After fifteen minutes of small talk, Lucky retreated back to his desk and typed up a hasty resignation letter. He owed it to a little girl not to give up. Terrible events came of good intentions sometimes, but it didn't change the results. After he found Grayson, he'd go after Rasmussen's crew. And while she'd definitely helped Lucky, he'd make no exception for Fletcher. He set an e-mail to auto-deliver to Walter on Monday morning.

Armed with credit card records, flight plans, and any other information he'd gleaned to help him track his target, he set out on a personal mission. The governments of other countries might get the job done, but Lucky set a timetable. No case of his rode off into the sunset.

Crutches under his arms, he made his way to the parking garage and on to Bo's apartment, stopping for a bottle of wine along the way. He had some making up and planning to do.

191

CHAPTER TWENTY-FOUR

The drive to Bo's took forever, plots and schemes running through Lucky's head. How long this time before he saw the man again? Days? Weeks? Months? One wrong step, and it could be years.

Once more he followed someone else into the building to avoid alerting Bo, though by his estimate he'd arrived three minutes late. Damn. And Bo wasn't the kind to give him any slack either. Maybe he'd whine a bit about how bad his leg hurt.

"You're late," Bo said, opening the apartment door.

"Yup," Lucky agreed, unhooking the bag holding the wine from his crutch and setting it down on the table Bo kept by the door to put keys on. No tantalizing smells drifted from the kitchen.

"I should get you your own key."

Lucky's heart flip-flopped, but he'd worry about Bo's hints about permanence later—no telling what the next few days might bring. He fully intended to sit down over supper, discuss his plans, and hopefully win an ally. A lot hinged on Bo's willingness to get involved. However, the man standing close enough to reach out and touch, wearing nothing but a pair of shorts, hair wet from a shower, changed Lucky's plans.

Where did things stand between them? Lucky couldn't leave without knowing. "We've got some unfinished business." Right now lust won out over good intentions. He latched on to Bo's arm.

Bo's eyes widened. "What unfinished business?" he squeaked.

"This." While Lucky planned to drag Bo across the living room and fling him down onto the couch cushions, he didn't quite make it before a crutch tripped him up and they both fell with a few feet to spare.

192

"Don't try that again until you've healed," Bo groused, untangling Lucky from the crutches and the coffee table.

There went Lucky's he-man dominance display. With Bo's help he dragged himself onto the couch. "Damn broke-ass ankle."

"Did you ever tell anyone how you broke it?"

"Just Walter."

"Good."

Dear Lord! Had Bo always had such an evil smile? Nice! "Why?"

"I've got a betting pool going. Those saps at work bet on anything."

"And?"

"And I stand to win two hundred bucks if you hurt yourself doing something dumb, like jumping out of a window."

"How'd you—"

"Oh my God! You did, didn't you?"

Heat rose in Lucky's face. "Yeah, I did. But you shoulda talked to me before you placed the bet. You might have gotten more for the bat shit angle."

"Bat shit as in crazy?"

Lucky lost the fight to hide a grimace. "'Fraid not."

"Ew!"

"Yup. Now, with my planned seduction so rudely interrupted, you gonna pick up where we left off?"

Bo snorted. "Your planned seduction? By coming on like a Mack truck with no brakes?"

"I thought you liked Mack trucks with no brakes."

"Sometimes. Other times I like—" Bo cupped Lucky's cheek. Shivers raced up Lucky's spine at the heat in Bo's eyes, gone when Bo pressed their lips together. He moaned when Bo's tongue entered his mouth.

The couch reclined without warning. Bo crashed down, body-to-body with Lucky. Lucky might learn to love this couch. He arched up, rubbing his stiffening erection against Bo's thigh through their clothes.

"Still think I'm a heartless asshole?" he had to ask.

Bo withdrew, staring down with the same fiery passion Lucky'd witnessed in the boss's office earlier. "You're an unmitigated, arrogant asshole. But the thing is, you don't hide it. You're what your life made you. You don't apologize, you don't make excuses, you just *are*. And if I find myself up shit creek without a paddle, you're the one man I'd trust to help me get out."

"But I piss you off."

"Of course you piss me off. You take my beliefs and spin them around. I can't tell you how bad it irks me to have to see things from a different angle, when I had them all figured out. Usually, and I stress *usually*, after I've had a chance to give the matter some thought, I see your point. I don't always agree with you, but I get you."

"Are you saying you're willing to put up with me?" Lucky held his breath.

"Put up with you? I wanna be more like you, not let shit get to me. Let it roll off."

Really? That's how Bo saw him? No wonder he'd called Lucky a heartless asshole. "Shit gets to me."

"But it doesn't stop you, you don't even let it show. The harder life pushes, the harder you push back. You've never given up on anything in your life, have you?"

Lucky didn't want to answer the question, too busy absorbing Bo's words. "Well, I—"

"Lucky?"

"Yeah?"

"Are we gonna talk or are we gonna fuck?" Bo brought his mouth down again, gliding his tongue against Lucky's.

He rolled Lucky's shirt up and off. The sweet slide of Bo's flesh against his own stiffened Lucky's cock nearly to the point of painful. He popped the button on his shorts, running a hand between his and Bo's bodies to ease his zipper down and free himself.

He slipped one hand into the back of Bo's shorts, tugging down his own with the other. At last he sat with his shorts and boxers to his knees, Bo stretched out on top of him. A little more shuffling and another wild tilt of the couch had them both naked.

Bo ground down, breath hot in Lucky's ear. "I've been wanting this all day." He traced Lucky's ear with his tongue, stopping to suck the lobe into his mouth.

Lucky splayed his hands across the irresistible swells of Bo's ass, guiding the press of body to body. He loved the feel of his cock sliding against another man's, the guttural moans, the firm muscles flexing beneath his fingertips, the distinctly masculine scent of man-on-man sex. Being with Bo multiplied the pleasure by ten. He snaked one hand down between their bodies and grasped their erections, while stroking his other hand lower on Bo's ass. Brushing his fingers against the pucker surrounding Bo's hole, he explored and caressed, not trying to penetrate.

Bo cradled Lucky's head in his arms, breathy little noises growing in pitch, hips snapping a frantic rhythm. He rammed hard into Lucky's hand and back against the fingers teasing his opening.

While Lucky only intended a warm up, Bo seemed to be speeding ahead of him. Around them the couch squeaked and squawked, Lucky's sweat-damp skin sticking to faux leather.

Pre-come slicked his fingers, sending them sliding over their joined flesh more easily. He pressed a fingertip harder against Bo's opening, too damned caught up to bring it to his mouth for a good wetting. Falling, falling, lost in the slide, push, shove of their bodies, the tingling that heralded things to come. "I'm gonna come!" he growled, rhythm faltering as desperation took over.

Harder and harder Lucky shoved. He gripped them both with one hand, and with the other grabbed Bo's shoulder, back, or wherever his fingers found purchase. Bo's teeth clamped down on his shoulder, sending him sailing over the edge. He stroked his and Bo's cocks at a frantic pace, groaning through completion. With a slippery grasp he continued to stroke until Bo stiffened, crying out.

Sweat and come slicked, Lucky lay with an armload of sated Bo. Once he'd recovered enough breath to speak again he said, "I definitely like this couch."

"You ought to bring a change of clothes over here," Bo said, placing a bowl of cut fruit on the table, along with a platter of cheese cubes, before returning to the kitchen for pita bread, crackers, and hummus. He also brought back a saucer containing deli sliced turkey. How could Lucky not love the man?

Lucky poured them each a glass of wine. "I need to talk to you." Now to ruin his post-sex buzz with business. But they only had a weekend, and a lot to accomplish.

"Oh?" Bo plopped down on the couch, reaching for a strawberry.

"Yeah. Come Monday morning, Walter's getting an e-mail saying I quit."

"You what?" Bo doubled over, coughing. Maybe Lucky should have waited until his mouth wasn't full to tell him. After a few back pats and a bit of gasping, Bo shot him a hostile glare. "Why the hell did you do that for? You're good at what you do, and I thought you liked your job."

Lucky shrugged and gazed anywhere but at Bo. Truth was, he did love his job, and would stack Walter up against any previous bosses. Of course, he'd only had two—a wealthy, opportunistic drug lord and a poor but honest mechanic. A definite pattern there. "Normally I wipe my hands and say 'have at it' when the Feds come in and take a case. Not this time. I... I can't walk away. It galls the hell out of me that no one's gone down, and I can't let it end like this."

Bo's freckles stood out in stark relief against his suddenly pale skin. "What do you plan to do? Lucky, please don't do anything stupid. You just got off probation."

"There's nothing illegal about taking a vacation, is there?" He gave Bo his best innocent expression.

"Innocent isn't a good look for you. Now spit it out. What have you got up your sleeve?"

Lucky grinned, running his eyes up and down his and Bo's naked bodies. "In case you haven't noticed, I'm not wearing sleeves."

"Hardy har har. Stop stalling and spill."

Lucky stopped smiling. "I'm going hunting. And I want you to help me."

***

"This is too easy. And you're sure that's all there is to it?" Their meal forgotten in favor of wine and talking shop, Bo punched a few buttons on Lucky's laptop.

"Pretty much." While Lucky enjoyed breaking the new couch in, pleather, or whatever the hell you called not-leather, wasn't kind to bare skin. He eased a cheek away from the cushion, hoping he didn't stick again. Who knew skin stuck to that shit hurt so damned bad when he tried to get up? "Every other day Grayson's wife gets a call from a cell phone registered to a friend. Even without GPS enabled, it's an easy matter to track back to the source. He's not taking any chances, calling from various tourist attractions. Do you spot the pattern?" Lucky raised his fingertip to the laptop screen. He traced over marked off locations on a map, weaving back and forth and stopping over a star, indicating a major city.

"He's staying here." Bo placed his finger next to Lucky's. "And he's traveling to make his phone calls."

Lucky nodded. "Could be on sight-seeing tours, or might have rented a car, though I haven't been able to track any rental. He might be taking a cab."

"Why haven't the Mexican police gotten him yet?"

"The local cops have their hands too full to track one American. If he faced murder charges, it'd be a different matter, but chances are, he'll get off light. There's no proof he was involved in trafficking, he simply bought a product on faith. Besides, there's precedent, remember? Those other doctors who did the same got off with 'misbranding' or some other minor charge. Grayson's not a killer. He acted to save his patients, or so somebody told me." The resulting deaths gnawed at Lucky, and he planned to set things right. Grayson might get off, but Rasmussen's days were numbered.

"If he's not in serious trouble, what do you want him for? And why's he running if he's not guilty?" Damned if Bo didn't need to work on that annoying sympathy for suspects.

"Grayson has no idea of the possible charges, and he's scared. I need to lure Rasmussen out of hiding, and I'm hoping Grayson can tell me how to find him. Once we have Rasmussen, we can follow the trail back to the manufacturer. It's them that I really want."

"And you don't trust the Chinese authorities to find them?"

"Let's say I'm crazy enough to think they can use my help."

Bo stared into Lucky's eyes. "You're not gonna let this one go, are you?"

"Nope."

"And you're sure about this?"

Lucky didn't let his gaze waver. "I've never been surer of anything."

Bo cocked his head to the side, an "I'm not so sure" expression on his face. "Stubborn ass."

"If you're worried, you don't have to help me. I'll find another way." Lucky took a deep breath before coming as close to a confession as he dared. "I want your support, and for you to understand why I have to do this."

Bo turned away, staring down at his joined fingers. "I understand, and I'll do whatever I can to help. I keep dreaming about those kids."

While nothing could stop Lucky from doing what he believed he must, a load lifted. He planted a kiss on Bo's forehead. "I've got a pretty good idea exactly where Grayson is staying. Once I know for sure I'll pass on the information and you can take it from there."

"I'd go with you, you know."

Tightly pursed lips, chin raised, Bo in full defiant mode. If Lucky ever found himself up shit creek, he'd pick his partner, too, to help him get out. Together they'd drain the motherfucker. "I know you would, but remember, you can't leave the country. And we can't risk your probation."

"But why quit your job? Why not simply tell Walter..."

"I tried. He'll protect his team. What I plan to do he'd never allow. Mexico is way out of our jurisdiction."

"What will you do when it's over?"

"I'll cross that bridge when I get there."

Bo sat quietly for a few moments before reaching over to grasp Lucky's hand. "Will you be leaving?"

Actually, Lucky's current plans pretty much ended at *giving the assholes what they got coming.* "Do you want me to?"

Bo peered up from beneath a fringe of dark lashes. "No. I've kinda got used to having you around. And... I've told you things."

"What things?"

"Things I've never told anybody else."

The blatant honesty was more than Lucky'd earned. He'd always considered himself the least trustworthy man on the planet, and yet Bo had told him about being abused, about the horrors of war, how he hated sleeping alone in a bed because his father used to tie him down at night. And lately, he'd offered not-so-scary stuff, trusting Lucky enough to share his fantasies. Yeah, Lucky'd kinda got used to having Bo around too.

Bo's "You're coming back, right?" shook Lucky out of his thoughts.

"Yeah. There's a rather handsome tomcat I need to get back to."

Bo laughed. "A tomcat? Is that what you picture me as?"

Heh. Bo left himself wide open for a jab. "You?" Lucky shot back, hand pressed to his collarbone. "Why's everything gotta be about you? I was talking about Mrs. Griggs's cat."

"Oh, the one you've been letting in the house?"

Wait. What? "How'd you..."

"Mrs. Griggs told me. Remember the houseplants I found in your refrigerator? Well, I didn't figure you'd take care of them, especially not with us in Anderson, so before we left I called your landlady and asked her to make sure they got watered. She's been keeping me posted. Congratulations. You're the proud papa of a bunch of little spuds."

Lucky found it hard to keep one step ahead with their jokes when Bo took such pains, even weeks of planning, to get the last word in.

The next morning Lucky returned to his house to find the black-and-white feline on his porch. When he opened the door the cat darted inside. Lucky didn't stop him.

He packed his bags. Oh, for two good legs to walk on instead of hopping around on crutches. No help for it now...

"Hey, kitty." Bo stooped in the doorway, scratching the cat under the chin. "What's his name?"

"I dunno. I call him 'Nuisance.'" Under torture Lucky wouldn't admit to calling the critter "Lucky."

"You've called me worse, I'm sure."

Lucky didn't believe he had, but couldn't argue. Likely he'd soon have several choice names for the man, just like Bo's pet name for him seemed to be "Damn it, Lucky!" It beat the hell out of "T-Rex." Of course, Lucky'd been called worse—much worse.

"You ready?" Bo asked.

"As ready as I'll ever be."

Bo placed the cat outside, picked up Lucky's bags, and headed for his Durango while Lucky locked up. They drove in silence to the airport. Lucky'd bought a ticket under his current name of Simon Harrison. Once Walter received the resignation letter, he'd easily guess Lucky's plans. While Walter might not officially approve of such a direct breach of orders, Lucky counted on the man not trying to stop him.

Bo followed Lucky as far as the security line at the Atlanta International Airport, squeezing Lucky's hand while handing over his laptop. "Getting through the security gate is gonna be hell with those crutches." He stepped away, holding Lucky's gaze. "Happy hunting."

Lucky nodded and turned away. To himself he said, "Yeah, I love you too."

CHAPTER TWENTY-FIVE

"Where's a good place to get a drink?" Lucky slid into the backseat of a taxi.

"I take you place all Americans go," replied the driver, whose ID labeled him "Gustavo."

"No. I want don't want a tourist hangout." Lucky summoned a harmless good ole boy smile. "Cab drivers know the best bars. Where would you go?" Thank God the man spoke English. They'd be here all day if Lucky had to summon up his smattering of Spanish.

The driver flashed a grin through the rearview mirror. "I know just the place, my friend."

Twenty minutes later Lucky hit pay dirt, arriving at an out of the way bar surrounded by off-duty cabs. Twenty dollars, US, bought him Gustavo's services for the afternoon as interpreter. Lucky strolled into the building and tossed a picture of Grayson on the bar. "That's my brother-in-law. He done run off on my sister, leaving her with three small kids to feed. Anyone seen him?"

Gustavo translated in rapid-fire Spanish. Several men shook their heads or chattered away. "They haven't seen him," Gustavo replied. Three rounds of drinks loosened a few memories, two men recollecting picking Grayson up from a hotel. One recalled driving him across town, and another swore the on-the-lam doctor was actually a famous American actor, in disguise.

Since no one in the bar appeared to be in any shape to drive, Lucky called another cab, using his drinking buddies' suggestion of where to stay.

A little flirting lured information from a hotel maid, and Lucky didn't even have to buy her a drink. He requested a room on the second floor, overlooking the pool. That night he texted his partner, *"In my sights."* A quick e-mail provided all the information Bo needed to issue an anonymous tip to the Cancun police. The waiting game began.

Sipping orange juice while lounging by the pool, Lucky observed his prey. The hammock rocked gently with his movements. He pulled his hat lower, pretending to study his drink while jabbing a plastic straw into his cast to scratch an itch. Damn, but he wanted the cast off. The garish blue wrapping made him stand out in a crowd. Lucky didn't like standing out in crowds.

On the other side of the pool a man sat on a lounge chair, iPad on his lap. Lucky watched two uniformed officers approach, witnessed the stooped shoulders, the downcast eyes, and extended wrists as Grayson stood and let the authorities lead him away. Lucky texted on his phone, *"1 down, 3 to go."*

For two days Lucky sat tight, waiting for his next move. Walter hadn't called. Those less familiar with Walter might've been nervous. Lucky took the lack of interference as permission to *"Do what you do."*

At last he received an e-mail tagged "Vancouver," most likely traceable back to a public library. A list appeared of pharmaceutical trade magazines and... What the fuck? Rasmussen advertised on Craigslist? A few ads were sent as attachments—copies of Rasmussen's originals.

Bo signed the e-mail, *"What you want for dinner?"*

Lucky hit "reply" and typed in, *"You."*

He spent a few hours crafting a series of carefully worded responses, using Grayson's as guides. He e-mailed his sister.

Charlotte,
You placed a large order for cancer drugs for the Homer Women and Children's hospital in Calgary. Any hits, forward to me.
Love,

He started to sign, "Rich" or "Richie" like he usually did, but ended up leaving the message unsigned. She'd understand who it came from by the e-mail address.

If the bastards wouldn't come to Lucky, he'd go to them. Surely they'd make a short hop from Vancouver to Alberta for a few thousand dollars.

The wheels set into motion, Lucky booked a ticket to the great white north.

Sitting at a desk in his modest hotel room, Lucky fired up his computer, logging into the account he'd set up specifically for his targets. Two advertisements for dating sites, a badly misspelled letter informing him of an unknown relative's lu- crative bequest—requiring him to enter his checking account information—three offers for penis enhancers, and a message he'd been desperately waiting for.

Springbank airport, Tuesday, 2 PM

He forwarded the message to Bo's personal e-mail.

The cloudy skies of Calgary appeared alien after the sunny skies of Mexico. At least the new walking cast, courtesy of a roadside Mexican clinic, made getting from point A to point B easier—made scratching easier, too. Lucky stood by the road at the Springbank airport, located on a flat plain, a few moun- tains visible in the distance. He hunkered down, watching the drama unfold through field glasses.

"That's it, baby. Come to Papa," he urged the Cessna ap- proaching with landing gear out.

The plane came to a halt. Canadian Mounties surrounded the craft and the door opened. Damn, what Lucky wouldn't give for one of Keith's listening devices. After a small eternity, the Mount- ies led two men and a woman out of the plane and to waiting ve- hicles. "This one's for you, Stephanie." He took a picture with his cell phone on highest magnification and sent the image to Bo.

"Whatcha looking at?" his cabbie asked.

"Just watching the planes." Lucky put his phone away and made his way to the cab on a single crutch. "Back to my hotel, please."

The woman turned the car around, returning the way they'd come. "How long you in town for?"

"Not long. My flight leaves early tomorrow." If he could, he'd go to China next, visualizing sending a factory up in flames. But no, he'd never actually resort to arson, no matter how tempting.

"You here on business or pleasure?"

Lucky didn't really feel like talking, but lacked the energy for open hostility. "Both."

"Have you picked up any souvenirs for your family and friends?"

Souvenirs? "No." Maybe his growl would discourage further friendliness. It didn't work.

"There's a really good shop up near your hotel, great selection, great prices." She flashed him a used-car-salesman grin.

"Oh, and while I'm inside you leave the meter running, right?" He already owed her a fortune for the time spent at the airport, ensuring Rasmussen came to justice.

"No. I promise I'll cut the time off."

Lucky glared at her earnest expression reflected in the cab's rearview mirror. "What's in it for you?"

A flush crept up the woman's cheeks. "Nothing, really. My cousin owns the place and I try to advertise when I can. She really does offer the best bargains around."

His next stop being Spokane, after years of not seeing Charlotte and the boys, not showing up empty-handed might go in his favor. "All right."

She pulled up at a small shop designed to look like a rustic cabin. A bell tinkled overhead when they walked in. "Look around," the cabdriver said. "I wanna go say hello to Deb."

Lucky puttered around the shop. What would his nephews like? What said, "Canada" to teenage boys? He picked up two stuffed bears dressed like Mounties—they ought to do. He roamed some more, coming to a stop in front of a display of pendants. Charlotte liked jewelry, didn't she?

His cabbie caught up with him. "Oh, those are nice, and really big sellers too."

"My sister might like one."

"Your sister? Cool! You know these aren't ordinary trinkets, right?"

"What do you mean?" Lucky expected a sales pitch designed to separate him from the Canadian dollars he'd exchanged American bills for.

"These are spirit totems. You should choose one that matches her personality. Now, what's she like?"

Lucky felt a glower settle into place before deciding, *What the hell*, and humoring the woman like he did his landlady. "Her family is very important to her, she's loyal, kind, has a big heart—"

The lady picked up an otter charm, holding it up for Lucky to read the attached card. Despite himself, he cracked a smile. "That's Charlotte, all right. A sea otter."

The woman grinned at him, eyeing his Mountie bears. "Anyone else on your list?"

"Well... " Should he get Bo anything? Okay, not *should he*, but *what should he* get Bo. "There is someone else." The woman would never see him again after dropping him at his hotel, what did Lucky care if she knew about Bo?

"Man or woman?" She traced her finger across the back of a black-and-white orca.

Heat rushed to Lucky's face. "Um..."

The woman threw back her head and laughed. "This is Canada. We don't care who you love up here, as long as you both watch hockey."

"What if neither of us watch hockey?" Oh, damn, he'd as much as said he loved Bo. No way was Lucky ready to admit that out loud, but he'd never see this woman again. This whole "love" thing—he wasn't even clear on how to tell Bo, or even *if* he should tell Bo. He'd been too busy worrying about his jaunt for justice to think much about the future. What now? What would he do for a job? The only thing he'd figured out for certain was that he still wanted to wake up to an armful of warm Bo.

The ice around saying the three life-changing words, even inside his own head, melted with the warmth of knowing they were true. Lucky studied the ornaments. "I'm not sure about getting *him* a necklace."

"It's not a necklace, it's a spirit totem! They offer power, teaching, protection, wisdom. All the good stuff."

Protection? Lucky eyed a charm the size of his thumb. The pendants sure beat the toe-breaker good luck charm Bo got for him. Protection came in portable sizes, huh? "Which one do you suggest?"

"Remember, if you want the magic to work you have to match the totem to the person. What's he like?"

Lucky scratched his fingers against his scalp. "Kinda hard to say."

"How does he make you feel?"

A blaze raged up Lucky's face all the way to the tips of his ears. Good question. How *did* Bo make him feel? God, but Lucky hated feelings, hated having to figure them out even more. He pictured the man who'd gotten under his skin. The mountains, without Bo. The longing, the regret. Then, at home, Bo fussing over him. Bo, warm and sleepy in Lucky's bed. Peace.

"No matter what's going on, no matter how bad things get, when I'm around him, everything seems better. He takes care of people, never putting himself first. He doesn't let life get him down. Oh, and he's a little too trusting at times."

The woman reached to a top shelf and lifted down a pewter bird with jeweled eyes. "The hummingbird." She turned the attached card for Lucky to see.

He read the legend, no doubt created a year ago to sell trinkets to tourists. "Joy, loyalty, beauty in living, quiet courage." Yep, that was Bo all right. "I'll take it." Even if only a lure for tourist dollars, if Bo believed in charms, it'd be worth the price. After paying for his purchases, Lucky limped his way back to the cab and texted Bo. *"Done! 1 more stop & I'll b home."* Funny how when he keyed in "home" it wasn't his duplex, but Bo who came to mind.

***

The house hadn't changed much since Charlotte moved in thirteen years ago. Instead of a neglected, tumble-down dwelling beyond his single-mom-of-two sister's ability to maintain, like he'd expected, Lucky found a well-kept cottage with neatly-trimmed grass, surrounded by beds of red, orange, and yellow flowersthat hadn't been there before. Looked like Charlotte took good care of the place. Still, something twisted in his guts. He'd once promised to always look after her. He'd failed and she didn't appear to need him. Which bothered him more?

He sat in a diner sipping coffee and studying the house across the road. A late model Ford Focus sat in the driveway. After a while a woman emerged, digging into her pocketbook while trotting down the steps. She wore her light brown hair pulled back in a bun, and had dressed casually in jeans and a T-shirt.

Damn, but she'd aged, and lost weight too. But wait, she was now past thirty. How damn long had it been since Lucky had seen her face-to-face? A fist closed around his heart. *I did this. I'm the reason I can't run out there, take her in my arms and never let go. Sis, I'm sorry I fucked up. So, so sorry I can't be the brother you deserve me to be.* The fist squeezed.

She stopped at the car, eyes trained straight at the diner. Lucky flinched and ducked behind a menu. Had she spotted him? Did she somehow know her brother was near? The house door opened and she turned, speaking to the two boys trailing behind. One stood a few inches taller than Charlotte, the other a few inches shorter. Both had their mother's light brown hair, the younger boy's more of a dirty blond, like Lucky's. The older boy grinned, taking the keys from Charlotte's hand. Todd was driving now? Lucky did a mental calculation. Damn, more time had passed than he'd thought. Maybe the boys were old enough to entrust with Uncle Rich's secret, but he wouldn't want to burden them. Chances were, they still spoke with Grandma and Grandpa on occasion, and wouldn't understand why they had to pretend Uncle Rich was dead.

Lucky blew out a heavy breath. Maybe coming here hadn't been such a good idea after all. The family climbed in the car and drove away. He picked up his coffee cup and swallowed down the dregs. How had his life ended up so screwed? And why did his eyes suddenly burn? They'd done that too much lately.

His phone chimed, and he fished it out of his pocket, the clouds of gloom lifting somewhat at Bo's message. *"U done good. Get yo ass back here. Miss U."*

Despite the bittersweet view of the only family he had left, Lucky managed a smile as he keyed in *"B there soon."* He paid his tab, and wandered across the street to leave the package containing his gifts on the front porch. Charlotte would think of something to tell the boys, but she'd also know that, no matter what happened, Richie hadn't deserted her.

CHAPTER TWENTY-SIX

Lucky sat in a lounge chair on the Pensacola fishing pier, dangling an unbaited hook in the water. Reeling in a fish took more effort than he wanted to expend. Still, he loved the salty spray of the ocean breeze, the sunlight dancing on the water, and whiling away the day on a hobby meant he didn't have to do anything constructive. Being unemployed might not be a bad deal, until his funds ran out.

He reached down and scratched his foot, the healing scars still itching from time to time. His walking cast lay propped against his tackle box.

The June sun beat down, a far cry from Calgary and Spokane. Vacationing in two different countries had been nice, but he belonged in the southern US. He'd made a life here. He'd met a man here. *"The man of your dreams,"* Charlotte might call Bo. Lucky didn't get mushy, but he certainly hadn't run screaming yet, and neither had Bo, though few would argue that Bo got the raw end of the deal.

He suddenly found himself in man-shaped shade. "You're blocking my sun."

"Then perhaps I should sit down." Walter groaned, popping open a chair of his own and easing into it. "Only, this close to the water, I worry about Greenpeace showing up and trying to push me in, yelling 'Free Willie!'" He laughed at his own joke. Poor bastard laughed at anything.

So Walter had tracked him down—not that he'd been hiding. At least not very well. "How'd you find me?"

"Wasn't hard. If you ever want to disappear for good, you do realize you'll have to dispose of your landlady first, right?"

Lucky reached into his cooler and extracted a beer. "Yeah. The fact that she's still alive might tell you I didn't leave for good." He held the brew out toward Walter, who shook his head.

"That's good to hear, because she says Patches misses you dearly and wants you to come home."

Damned varmint. Ever since Lucky held him the first time, the critter came strolling in every time Lucky left the door open. And the damned thing snored! Cats weren't supposed to snore.

"Why are you here? 'Cause a darned cat wants to use my lap as a bed?" Lucky popped the top on the can and chugged down a few swallows.

"Actually, I've come to update you on your last case."

"Oh really?" Like Lucky hadn't been trolling the Internet for news about Rasmussen's crew and their little enterprise going up in smoke. Or that Bo hadn't been in almost constant contact.

"It seems the Canadian Mounties intercepted a delivery of counterfeit cancer drugs to a hospital in Alberta, Canada. Calgary, I believe." He regarded Lucky, one bushy gray brow reaching for his hairline. How did he do that? Lucky's brows, unlike himself, seemed to work only as a team. "This time the drugs tested pure, but no more legal than the shipment you discovered in the old mill. The DEA traced the goods back to a manufacturer in China, the same one who produced the Rosario shipments. I imagine they're still rounding up suspects and pressing charges."

Lucky pretended ignorance. "What about Grayson?"

"Odd thing that. He suddenly surfaced in Mexico. Seems the local police received an anonymous tip." Walter stared at Lucky, a corner of his mouth twitching. "Even with a precedent, he may be forced to surrender his medical license."

Unless Walter asked directly, Lucky owed him no answers. "Yeah, and the drug shortage rages on." He gazed out over the sparkling water, the stress of the last few months slowly leaking out of him. Overhead gulls scolded each other, swooping and diving. "I don't understand it. Danvers dodges the bullet with a heart full of greed, and a doctor trying to save his patients winds up losing his license."

"Ours is not to judge motives, but uphold laws. On that note, the FDA gained approval to temporarily import medical supplies from the UK. The Rosario situation is much improved now. Not ideal by any means, but much improved."

Lucky said a silent "thank you." No doubt Walter had weighed in on the decision. "Danvers still got off scot-free."

"I wouldn't say that. I'm sure his in-laws aren't happy with him for leading the FDA to their doorstep. Particularly not when their name is being bandied about as ammunition to push through the anti-gray market bill."

The guy still got off too fucking light. "So all's right in the world again?"

"Not exactly. There's been a rash of prescription overdoses in the Atlanta area."

"And you expect me to do something about it?" Lucky peered at his former boss over the top of his Ray-Bans.

"No, I'm merely here to give you your back pay."

"My back pay?"

"Why yes. It seems that in your time with the SNB, you rarely used your vacation days. You'd built up nearly six weeks of time. And if you'd been at the office you'd know about the terrible IT fiasco."

"What IT fiasco?" While Lucky didn't often praise coworkers, the SNB had some of the greatest information technology geeks in the world, if you didn't count Keith.

"It seems a server crashed. I lost an entire day's worth of e-mails. Can you imagine? I think it might have happened around the day you started your vacation." He dropped an envelope on Lucky's lap. "I've done what I came to do. You have your check and I need to inform you that you're nearly out of accrued time. I expect you back in the office on Monday morning."

"Wait, you came clear down to Pensacola to tell me I still have a job?"

"No, I happened to be in the neighborhood. Dropping by makes this a business trip, and therefore tax deductible. Now, if you'll excuse me, my wife is waiting at our hotel and expects me to take her to dinner." Walter hauled his sturdily built body out of the chair. "I must say I'm not the only one who missed you."

Lucky cut Walter a sharp glance. Sooner or later they'd have to talk. He'd rather wait until later.

"Yes. I believe your cube mate misses you too. He's dared anyone to remove so much as a paperclip from your desk, and he asked for the day off today and was most vague when I asked where he was going." He landed a hand on Lucky's shoulder. "I wouldn't doubt a bit that he's determined to track you down again like he did the last time you tried to quit. You make an incredible team."

Before Lucky managed to get any words out Walter added, "Oh, and if you're not at your desk at nine o'clock sharp, I'm giving your case to Keith." He folded his chair and ambled away the way that he'd come.

Like hell will Keith fuck up my case.

Lucky strolled back toward his hotel. Maybe he should take a nap since he had a long night ahead of him. While on a glorified work release program, he'd not enjoyed the freedom to roam clubs, though Walter normally turned a blind eye to the occasional bar visit to pick up a willing partner.

Now he was so far out of practice clubbing that he might have forgotten how. He showered and dressed comfortably, wearing long pants to hide his recent injury. A tight wife-beater shirt displayed his chest and shoulders to full advantage, though with his having to cut back on exercise due to his leg, he'd lost a bit of muscle tone. He studied himself in the mirror, hoping the longer he stared the better he'd look. No such luck. Maybe the darkness of a club would add a point or two to his "On a scale of one to ten." What was he worried about? He'd never really cared about his appearance before.

"Damn man's changing me already," he mumbled to his reflection while sucking in the bit of softness around his middle that hadn't been there a few weeks ago. Blast that waitress in Spokane and her "Have another pancake." Oh well, he'd have to make up for lost time once he was able to. His doctor might have a few choice words to say on the matter, but Lucky left the walking cast in his room.

Pensacola boasted several good gay clubs, but Lucky set his sights on Whisper, a venue with a mix of both music and patrons, where a banker could pick up a truck driver, and vice versa. He reared his shoulders back while in line, hoping for an illusion of height. After passing over ID and cover charge, he sauntered into the flesh market, murmuring, "Daddy's home."

He caught a few eyes among the button-down crowd, probably searching for a night of slumming before returning to their yuppie-dom. They didn't interest Lucky and neither did the twinks. Heh. It'd be fun to flash his badge a bit, flush out the underage ones. *Not your job unless they're holding.* The pounding rhythm of a techno tune reminded Lucky of his former neighbors in Anderson. The fuckers. Not his problem now.

Tonight, the only care he had in the world was finding the right man. He'd begun to get a bit frustrated in his search and approached the bar. A guy stepped into his space. "Buy you a drink?"

Lucky glanced up, staring into chocolate brown eyes so deep he could stay lost in them for days. Pay dirt! He groped around back, finding the impressive swell of a familiar bubble-butt. Damn, but Lucky couldn't resist that gorgeous ass. "Sure. I'll have whatever you're having."

If and when he showed up at the SNB on Monday, he intended to walk with a limp, and not because of his recently broken bones, either.

A beefy bartender gave Lucky a wink. "Two ginger ales, coming right up."

"Ginger ale? You're shitting me, right?" Their first night out together and Bo ordered damn ginger ale?

"That's what I'm having. Be careful what you ask for."

They sipped their drinks, leaning against the bar. Lucky might have dropped his hand a bit low on Bo's ass for being in public. Of course, Bo seemed to be practicing frisking maneuvers. Maybe Lucky should have stashed a vial down his boxers. SNB agent and drug trafficker. That would be some interesting roleplaying. It might also count as job training too.

A twink giggled, shoving his way to the bar. "Why don't you two get a room?" Oh, if Lucky only had his badge...

"Down, boy," his partner said. "I think it's a great idea." Bo flung a handful of bills on the bar and took Lucky's hand, towing him to the front door.

The envious stares made up for the indignity of being dragged bodily from the club—somewhat. They escaped the steamy confines of the overcrowded building, Bo leading Lucky around the corner and down to the beach. He stopped and smashed their mouths together.

Lucky struggled. Fuck! No telling who might see. Oh, right. No one here gave a flying fuck what he did but Walter and his missus, and the Smiths certainly wouldn't be hanging out at gay clubs.

"Relax, that's why we're out of town, remember?"

He returned the kiss with a little more feeling.

"That's more like it," Bo murmured against Lucky's mouth.

With a gleam in his eye Bo pulled away, gripping Lucky's fingers and starting off down the beach. Lights from restaurants and bars shimmered on the water, and waves washed up on shore as high tide crept in. The constant ocean breeze caressed Lucky's face, and he couldn't remember a time he'd been so unencumbered. The world might come crashing down sometime in the near future—he'd deal with the next crisis when it happened.

"I looked up hummingbird totems on the Internet." Bo slid a finger down the chain hanging from his neck to caress the pewter charm.

"That's nice." Never in a million years would Lucky admit to putting thought into the gift. He'd catch enough hell once they got back to their hotel room and Bo discovered the candlelit dinner he'd tipped the manager heavily to arrange—eggplant parmesan, Bo's favorite.

"Yes, it is." More quietly, Bo added, "Thank you." He stopped suddenly, glancing down. "Where's your walking cast?"

Nothing escaped Bo's notice, apparently. "Don't need it."

Bo answered with a scowl that quickly eased. "Walter hunted you down, didn't he?"

"Yup."

"Did he ask you to come back?"

"No."

"No?" Bo's mouth dropped open. "What do you mean 'no'?"

"He didn't ask me to come back, he told me I'd never left. Apparently, I've spent the last few weeks on vacation."

"You going back?"

"Should I?" Lucky asked, merely to goad Bo into righteous indignation. The guy was too easy to provoke sometimes.

"Damn it, Lucky! Are you outta your mind? Of course you should. Where else are you gonna find a job you love?"

"I hate my job."

"Of course you do. That's why you're damned good at it."

"You think I'm good at my job?"

"No, you suck at it. You suck at it so bad that you're willing to leave to finish what you started, you stubborn son of a bitch."

God, but Bo's rants turned Lucky on. "Yeah, yeah. Whatcha wanna do before we go catch bad guys?"

"I want you to take me out to dinner someplace where we can eat without you watching over your shoulder, worried who might spot us. Jeez, man, it's not like we're famous or anything."

Lucky raked his lips over Bo's ear. "They got one hell of a sex shop here. I... picked up a few things."

"Really?" Bo's tone softened. "Maybe we'll get takeout."

Lucky smiled. Damn, he'd won the argument easy.

"You can take me out tomorrow."

Then again, maybe not. He slowed and finally stopped, gazing up at a full moon. If Charlotte were here she'd be spouting nonsense about how romantic it was to be walking on the beach under a full moon. Bo stood at Lucky's side. "Now that's downright pretty, isn't it?"

"Yes, it is." Lucky eyed Bo, who stared upward. Lucky's chest grew tight, the heart within too large to contain. He took a step back, wrapping his arms around Bo and burying his face in the back of the man's T-shirt, breathing in the combination of scents that meant "Bo."

He reached his hand down the front of Bo's shorts, only intending to be playful. Bo groaned when Lucky palmed his rising shaft, pushing into the contact. Lucky rubbed him, slow, even strokes through the cotton of his boxers.

"It's kinda wicked, standing out here on the beach getting stroked off," Bo said.

"Yeah, anyone wearing night goggles is getting a show."

"How many folks around these parts you reckon have them?" Bo didn't sound a bit worried.

At any second a cop could arrive, in which case Lucky would take resisting arrest to whole new levels. "I don't know. WalMart might be having a sale." Who cared who watched at that moment? If they saw something they didn't want to then they shouldn't be hanging around the gay bar district after sundown. He wriggled his hand beneath Bo's boxers, groaning when his rough fingers enclosed smooth skin.

A bit of slickness met him at the tip of Bo's cock, and he smeared the wetness beneath Bo's foreskin for lubrication. His own cock nestled between Bo's ass cheeks, and Lucky humped in time with his stroking. For a split-second he considered grabbing Bo by the hand and hauling ass to their room. The big moon shone down like it had the lonely night he'd spent in the mountains. He hugged Bo tighter.

Say the words, Lucky, say the words. He buried his stiffness in the cleft of Bo's ass. The words wouldn't go away—persistent fuckers. Rhythm never faltering, he ventured, "I've got something to say. I don't want to spend hours discussing it, I don't want to analyze it, and I'm sure as hell not gonna spray paint it on some damned water tower."

Bo stiffened, then relaxed again. His needy whimpers quieted. "And?"

Lucky rose on his toes, ramming himself harder against Bo's body. He opened his mouth but the fickle words ran away, laughing at him all the while. Well damn, just damn.

"Lucky?" Bo's voice came out strangled.

"Yeah?"

"Lucky, I'm gonna..." He stiffened again, every muscle tensing as he gushed across Lucky's fingers.

Oh dear Lord in Heaven. Standing on a beach, in front of God and everybody, and Bo just... Lucky muffled a groan against Bo's shoulder and shouted, "I love you, you son of a bitch!" into a mouthful of shirt. He pulsed, coming in his pants like a horny teen. His knees buckled and he clung to Bo to keep from falling over. Oh fuck, oh fuck, that was... that was... Hotter than fuck!

He sagged against Bo's back. Bo laughed, entire body shaking. "Smile when you call me that," he replied, in a bad impersonation of an old western.

Yeah, the guy had a six-shooter all right. Holding on for dear life, Lucky laughed. His chuckles grew into guffaws, until finally he and Bo overbalanced and flopped onto damp sand.

"Oh my God, Lucky! Are you all right? Your leg!" Bo brushed sand away from Lucky's leg, running his fingers over the newly healed ankle.

"Bo?"

"Yes?"

"I'm okay. Now would you stop fussing and just fucking kiss me?"

Grit scratched between their bodies as Bo lay across Lucky and sealed their mouths together. A shock of cold and the gulf waters joined in, washing over them, sucking sand from beneath them. Sand, ocean breezes, the moon, the stars, and Bo. Perfect.

Lucky ended the kiss. "I gotta ask you something. Why are you with me?"

"What?"

"You heard me. I saw how those guys were checking you out in the bar, how they wanted to rip my head off for being the one you left with. You could have any damn body you wanted. Why me?"

Bo's eyes glittered in the low light, the wind and waves nearly drowning his softly spoken words. "Because you're one hard-assed son of a bitch, cocky little bantam rooster—"

"Hey!"

"And I never have to turn around to see if you're there. I know you got my back." Waves crashing on the beach, fragments of music from the seaside bars, all faded into the background. The night boiled down to Bo. Smiling. Staring at Lucky, and truly seeing him as no one else did.

"Yeah, I got your back. Always will." Lucky shut up before things turned sappy.

The promise in Bo's eyes no longer inspired fear. "I love you too," he said. "T-Rex."

ABOUT THE AUTHOR

You will know Eden Winters by her distinctive white plumage and exuberant cry of "Hey, y'all!" in a Southern US drawl so thick it renders even the simplest of words unrecognizable. Watch out, she hugs!

Driven by insatiable curiosity, she possibly holds the world's record for curriculum changes to the point that she's never quite earned a degree but is a force to be reckoned with at Trivial Pursuit.

She's trudged down hallways with police detectives, learned to disarm knife-wielding bad guys, and witnessed the correct way to blow doors off buildings. Her e-mail contains various snippets of forensic wisdom, such as "What would a dead body left in a Mexican drug tunnel look like after six months?" In the process of her adventures she has written fourteen m/m romance novels, has won several Rainbow Awards, was a Lambda Awards Finalist, and lives in terror of authorities showing up at her door to question her Internet searches.

When not putting characters in dangerous situations she's a mild-mannered business executive, mother, grandmother, vegetarian, and PFLAG activist.

Her natural habitats are airports, coffee shops, and on the backs of motorcycles.

For more information about Eden, please visit her website at www.edenwinters.com.

CORRUPTION

(DIVERSION #3), THE SEQUEL TO COLLUSION

Another night in Hell.

Simon "Lucky" Harrison paid the cover charge at Armageddon, or whatever the fuck they called this gussied-up bar. The pretentious crowd the club catered to made the place close enough to Hell in his book. And nobody even frisked him. He shifted the holstered department-issued gun beneath his jacket. Damn, but he missed his own weapon, and damn the son-of-a-bitching bastards who'd swiped his .38.

The bouncer waved him through. Wasn't much use in finally having an honest-to-goodness Southeastern Narcotics Bureau badge if he didn't get to flash the shiny gold shield once in a while to get his way, but going high profile would blow the whole undercover thing to kingdom come.

Heavy bass pounded against his skull before he'd even gotten properly inside the door. These assholes called this racket music? If he wanted to bust somebody, he'd definitely come to the right place—they had to be taking some weird-assed shit.

Tonight wasn't about taking down the bad guys, though. Tonight merely laid groundwork, Lucky showing himself off as another run-of-the-mill club-goer. The better to lull the sheep in the presence of a wolf. A drink or two, some mingling, then home to bed. Alone, damn the luck.

Fuck this off-duty, keep-your-hands-to-yourself recognizance, he could see half a dozen people who needed a tap on the shoulder from the long arm of the law. Was the guy in the holey jeans reaching for his wallet or a baggie? The mullet-haired asshole should be reaching for the door, 'cause he sure as hell didn't fit in with a crowd where *casual* meant *lose the tie.* What a huge pocketbook on that lady's arm. A whole kilo would fit in there. And one big-assed alligator gave its life to make the thing.

A trip to the bar yielded a club soda with some kind of green vegetable sticking out of the glass. Seemed a man couldn't even drink without finding greens. Bad enough they made their way onto dinner plates. The guy standing two feet too close turned away. Lucky took the opportunity to shove the offending stalk into the man's glass of orange liquid.

To the club's credit, he'd been in the place a full five minutes and hadn't witnessed a fight, and no peanut shells littered the floor. His elbows hadn't stuck to the bar when he'd waited for his drink, either. The bartender'd been hit with a few ugly sticks, but he controlled the booze, giving him an automatic upgrade from a three to an eight. He seemed friendly enough and kept his fingers away from the top of the glass—all Lucky needed in a bartender.

Now to find a vantage point on the second floor, the better to see and be seen. The nooks and crannies near the balcony also provided discreet enough venues for drug dealing. His scouting mission didn't mean he couldn't tag someone dumb enough to mistake him for a buyer.

Lucky sipped his drink, staring down at a writhing mass of humanity, folks who didn't have anything better to do than waste their hard-earned money on watered-down drinks and spine-rattling dance tunes and go home with someone they'd deny knowing the next day. Huh. And to think he'd dressed up for this. He scratched his leg through the unfamiliar stiffness of a pair of dress slacks. Hell, he'd even ironed a shirt for the occasion.

Nothing much seemed to be happening on the main club level, except for one couple hanging on the fringes, pushing the envelope of public decency. A table in the far corner provided entertainment when two women kissed their male dates and disappeared toward the ladies' room. Their dates waited a full thirty seconds before pouncing on each other like starving wolves. They'd better come up for air before the ladies returned.

A woman's scream jerked Lucky's attention away from the two men in need of a room. "Get away from me!"

Lucky grasped the railing, leaning over for a better view of the packed floor below. There, in the red dress. The woman screamed again, "Go away!" She swatted at the air above her head.

Oh hell. Let the crazy begin. Fighting with shit that wasn't there was never a good sign.

"'Scuse me," Lucky muttered, squeezing through the on-lookers. "Get the fuck out of my way" worked better, but the department frowned on the direct approach. They should stick with what worked.

The woman's shouts carried over the throbbing beat from the DJ booth, and Lucky lost sight of her a time or two while struggling to get past a couple who didn't want to move. A hand landed on his ass from behind. "Wanna keep that hand?" he snapped. The hand disappeared, and the couple jumped out of the way. Fuckers.

He caught sight of the screaming woman again a few yards to the left. Her friends stood back, creating some space. "Can't you see them?" she shrieked, staring toward the ceiling.

"Move, dammit!" Lucky pushed against a wall of gawkers four or five inches taller than him. They didn't budge. All hell was about to break loose. "Get the fuck out of my way!" bought Lucky enough space to slither through.

A man grasped the woman's arm about the time Lucky got within grabbing distance. She pulled back for a swing. Lucky jerked back. *Crack!* She bypassed Lucky and slammed her knuckles into the man's jaw. He fell with a thud. *Better him than me.*

Two uniformed security guards approached, middle-aged men who huffed and puffed by the time they reached the ruckus. *Here come Doofus and Dipshit.* 'Bout time the fuckers got here before Lucky blew his cover. Back in his day, clubs employed muscle-bound gym bunnies to work the crowds. They didn't make bouncers like they used to. "Ma'am, you need to settle down," the first one said, standing outside the woman's reach.

Doofus. Was he for real? *Settle down?* Did he have any fucking idea what he was dealing with? She might appear a sweet young thing in a red dress, but whatever she took/snorted/shot up had definitely taken control of the wheel.

"Make them stop!" The woman ducked beneath her arms, batting away invisible attackers.

"There's nothing there, ma'am," Doofus said, while the other guard rolled wary eyes upward.

"Maybe you better come with us." This time Dipshit spoke. He must have gone to the same training program as his partner. Didn't they at least watch some outdated training video on the warning signs of drug use and dealing with folks on their way 'round the bend?

The woman straightened, eyeing the guard. "Ahhh! You're one of them! Get away, get away!" Flinging another woman to the side, she charged toward the exit, screaming and swatting. The guards trotted behind her.

"They better pay me extra for this." Lucky stepped on a couple of toes and bumped a drink or two while zigzagging in pursuit.

He burst through the front door and followed the screams down an alley. The ankle he'd broken during an investigation last summer squealed in protest at being forced into a run.

Doofus and Dipshit had the woman cornered by the time Lucky caught up. Damn fucked-up leg. *Heal, you sumbitch, heal! Six months should be long enough.*

"Stay back! Stay the fuck back!" the woman squawked. She grabbed a hank of her not-found-in-nature-red hair, and jerked the strands out of her head with nary a wince. Holy shit. That had to hurt. Her breath turned to fog before her face, adding another layer of creepy to the moment.

She took a few wobbly steps back, a high-heeled shoe on one foot and the other bare. A sleeve hung from what had likely been an expensive designer dress. Eyes wide, she pressed against the brick wall of the club. Lucky shivered, wrapping his jacket tighter around him. Late October, close to midnight, and the woman didn't appear to feel a lick of cold.

"Easy, ma'am, we don't want to hurt you," Dipshit said, empty hands splayed to show he wasn't armed. With his graying hair and bulging belly, he probably had kids this woman's age.

Wild eyes stared out from an ashen face, heavy with black and red makeup smears. The woman's hair hung in strings over her face. She glanced right and left, then focused on the guard nearest her. "I didn't do anything. Leave me alone."

"We can't do that," Doofus replied, edging closer. "You attacked a man. We need to ask you a few questions."

Stupid assholes. They ought to know better than to say such shit. Tell her whatever lies were necessary to calm her ass down.

Lucky held back, cataloguing symptoms: delusional, paranoid, any number of street drugs produced the same effect. The woman quieted, and the guards held their ground. Fat tears rolled down her cheeks. Torn knuckles oozed blood. Her hand would hurt like hell once she came down. "I didn't mean to, I really didn't mean to."

Crazy lived in her eyes. By day she probably drove a fancy car to a high-rise office complex downtown. Tonight, she lived in a hell created by her own mind. And her demons were more real to her than two security guards trying to talk her down off the proverbial ledge.

The guards exchanged worried glances. Between the two of them, they'd probably never dealt with bad drugs to this degree before. And why the hell were their guns still holstered? Didn't they have a taser? They sure as shit needed one. One hundred and five pounds of unpredictable with superhuman strength, no pain threshold, and no concept of right and wrong made one volatile threat. Little Miss Red Dress might be the most dangerous person they'd ever met.

The guards took a few steps back. Bad move. A split second later, the woman screamed, staring past the first guard's head. "They're back! Oh my God, they're back!" She dove toward Dipshit's sidearm while Doofus grabbed his gun. "Don't let them get me!"

She wrestled with the guard while his partner hesitated a moment too long. Lucky raced across the alley on his uncooperative leg. He slammed into both guard and the attacker, knocking them to the ground. The woman snatched the gun from the guard's holster. Lucky fished his own weapon out from beneath his jacket and took aim.

The tiny assailant gawked at something Lucky couldn't see. "I can't let them get me." She knelt on the pavement, shivering with unknown terrors one minute, and the next she pointed the gun.

Lucky lunged. A shot rang out.

More from Rocky Ridge Books:

Diversion (Diversion #1)

Corruption (Diversion #3)

Manipulation (Diversion #4)

Redemption (Diversion#5)

Summer Boys by Eden Winters

Tinsel and Frost by Eden Winters

The Match Before Christmas by Eden Winters

Fanning the Flames by Eden Winters

Spokes by P.D. Singer

On Call: Dancing by P.D. Singer

On Call: Afternoon by P.D. Singer

On Call: Crossroads by P.D. Singer

Training Cats by P.D. Singer

Donal agus *Jimmy* by P.D. Singer

With Wings (Dark Angels #1) by Z. Allora

Tied Together (Dark Angels #2) by Z. Allora

Finally Fallen (Dark Angels #3) by Z. Allora

Happy Holidays (Dark Angels #4) by Z. Allora

Wanting More by Cari Z.

Lola Dances by Victor J. Banis